BY
PAUL R SOMERVILLE

THE STONE OF
RADNOR

ISBN: 9798414014744

DEDICATION

To Fraser and Isla – both sources of inspiration.
I am incredibly proud of the young adults you are both becoming.
Love Dad x

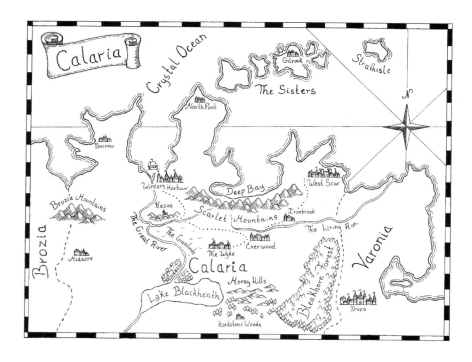

MAPS

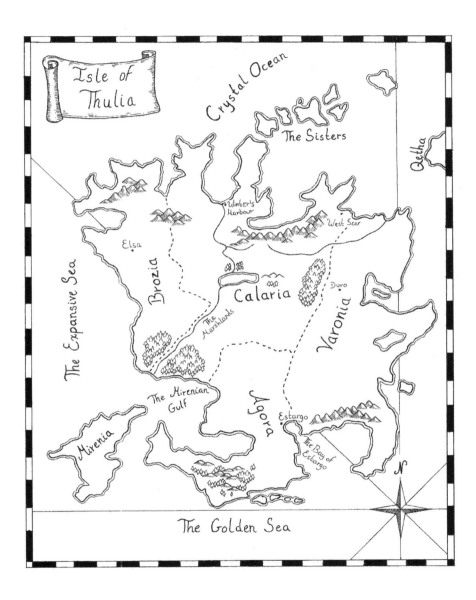

PART ONE

CHAPTER 1
THE RAID

———— •••◆••• ————

Jaydon's eyelids fluttered awake to the sound of scratching. The dog was scrabbling and whining at the door.

Groaning, he lay on his straw mattress a while longer, wrapped beneath his furs and rough blankets, allowing his eyes to adjust to the greyness of early morning before heaving himself from the warmth of his covers with a grunt of annoyance.

'Shush, Magen. Quiet now,' Jaydon whispered between his teeth

Magen, a scruffy hound, with gangly legs and rough brown fur, turned her whiskery face toward him, nose glistening. She looked at him with pleading eyes, then turned to the door once more, paws scraping on the wood, continuing to whine.

Jaydon glanced across the room at his parents. Both slept soundly, still, under their furs. His father, snored quietly, strong arms wrapped around his mother. Jenna, Jaydon's younger sister, beside them breathing gently, blonde hair strewn wide around her head, a few loose strands had strayed across her face.

With another groan, he eased himself off his bed, rubbing his face to wake himself. 'Quiet, Magen. What's the matter with you?' The dog responded with another whimper. 'Do you need to toilet, girl? Come on, I'll let you out. But hush before you wake everyone.'

Jaydon crept to the door, bare feet padding on a floor scattered with the fresh straw his father had laid just yesterday, the sweet smell still filled his nostrils. He opened the door a fraction, a weak shaft of dawn light spread across the floor. Magen prised her head into the gap. Then with her nose, nudged the door wide enough to squeeze her whole body through and sprinted off into the gloomy morning.

'Magen, come back. Stupid dog,' Jaydon hissed, trying to keep his voice quiet, not wanting to disturb his sleeping family. Cursing under his breath he huffed to himself and shook his head. Well, you can wait until we're all up and awake then, he thought, as he closed the door behind him, yearning to get back to the warmth of his furs. Then he heard a distant squeal. The hairs on his arms pricked with alarm. A cry of pain? Magen?

Jaydon, grabbed his boots from beside the door, thrusting them onto his feet, taking his spear and hunting knife he lifted the wooden latch as quietly as he could. Squinting through the tiny crack of the door, Jaydon cocked his head and listened. Nothing stirred except the fingers of early morning mist creeping along the ground.

'Magen?' he hissed as silently as he could. 'Magen? What's up, girl? Where are you?'

Silence.

Jaydon glanced behind at his parents, still asleep. Perhaps he should wake his father? No, he would only get cross for troubling him over nothing. He could deal with Magen himself.

Jaydon's heart pounded like a galloping horse as he steadied himself.

Sliding the door open he heard a shuffling behind him. 'Hey, you said you'd take me hunting with you.' Jenna sat up in her bed, rubbing away the sleep with the palm of her hands, a strand of straw from the mattress stuck to her cheek.

'Shush! I'm not going hunting,' Jaydon put a finger to his lips. 'You stay here.'

'Why? What's up? You have your hunting spear.'

'Quiet, Jen. I don't know. I'm going to check. It's probably nothing, but stay here… go back to sleep.'

'You should wake father,' Jenna scolded, screwing her eyebrows, a familiar frown she wore as a warning to Jaydon.

'Be quiet. I've told you, it's probably nothing. Magen just ran off and I can't see her. I won't be a moment, she's probably chasing after old Odric's chickens again. If there's anything wrong I'll come back and waken father.'

The frown on her face grew to one of concern. 'Magen? What's happened? Where is she?' Jaydon felt a pang of guilt. Magen was Jenna's dog, although a working hound, she treated her more like a pet. They were always out in the meadows dashing through the long grasses, careering after each other, or Jenna would often throw her sticks to chase, which Magen would bound after with her gangling legs, tongue lolling wildly.

'Nothing. Look, I won't be a moment. Now go back to sleep.'

'I'm coming with you,' she said, pulling back her furs.

'No. Stay here Jen. I mean it. If I'm not back within a few minutes wake father. Now be quiet, will you?'

Jenna huffed and pulled the furs around herself again, turning her back on Jaydon. 'Magen had better be okay,' she mumbled sulkily. 'And you'd better not be hunting without me.'

Strapping on his belt and sliding his knife into the sheath, Jaydon squeezed through the door, closing it softly behind him and slunk out into the village. Making his way around the low wooden fencing that surrounded the small pig pen, he crept towards the other village huts, his spear gripped firmly in his hand.

He crossed a muddy path and waited against the wall of Ober's hut. Like all the other huts in the village of Hardstone Woods, Ober's had wooden walls with a great thatched roof. Jaydon had heard stories of towns in the north of Calaria, made of stone and rock. Castles with great towers that reached to the heavens. His mind struggled to picture such buildings.

He peeked around the corner. Still no movement—Where is that damn dog? Senses alert he moved stealthily around the corner, crossing the horse paddock.

'Magen. Magen. Where are you girl? Come now.' He called, letting out a low whistle.

Still nothing, just silence and the distant sound of dawn birdsong from the surrounding woodland.

Jaydon kept low; feet silent on the dewy ground. He paused at the far-side of the paddock, crouching by the fence. From within the paddock, a horse snorted. Ahead on the ground something caught his eye, partly hidden from the mist, a lumpy shape. Oh no, he thought. Please, don't let it be.

Jaydon crept towards it; slowly the mist cleared, revealing the shape—Magen. Her limp body lying lifeless on the damp ground. An arrow buried deep between her ribs, its greying feathers spattered with droplets of red blood.

Kneeling next to her, Jaydon stroked Magen's head, her tongue drooped out from her gaping mouth. Jaydon dipped his forehead to her nose, which still felt cold and wet on his skin. How would he tell Jenna? It had been him who had let her out, surely, she would blame him?

'Silly, girl,' he said to her lifeless form. 'What happened?' He scanned the ground behind Magen, spotting a trail of dark blood, which ended where she had fallen. Jaydon pulled at his ear as he thought.

In the distance, a sudden commotion as a flock of crows erupted from the trees in the surrounding woodland, squawking in alarm. Jaydon glanced up. Blood curdling screams ripped the silence apart, making the hairs on Jaydon's arms stand erect. Armed men, some running, others on horseback emerged from the treeline of the woodland; roaring and whooping.

Others carried bows and lifted them, releasing flaming arrows that arced through the dawn sky, falling into the village, thumping into the ground and landing onto the straw roofs of the wooden huts. The thatch caught easily, a few embers burned then within moments the fires took hold and blazed furiously. From within the homes screams of surprise and terror emitted as the villagers awoke to the attack.

Heart pounding, throat dry, Jaydon grabbed his spear, which slipped in his sweating hand. The attackers coursed through the village, from around the scattered buildings a group of them appeared, armed with swords and spears, dark shadows in the drab morning.

Instinctively, Jaydon dived over the low fencing of the pig pen. Slithering on his stomach through the stinking mud he could feel the heat on his face from the surrounding buildings getting stronger as the fires raged.

Worried that the glow from the fires would give away his presence he slid on elbows and knees through the sticky mud, he turned his head wildly to the chaos surrounding him, trying to conceal himself within a dip in the ground. Screams of the villagers penetrated through the roar of the flaming buildings. His whole world exploded into chaos.

Warriors rampaged in all directions, cutting down anyone trying to escape from their homes. Jaydon saw his friend, Ober, sprinting from his hut.

'Run!' Jaydon screamed.

Ober's eyes searched for Jaydon, who waved frantically from the dip, beckoning Ober toward him. A look of recognition came to Ober's face as he saw Jaydon, a face drawn with lines of fear. They had lived peacefully in this village their whole lives. Fierce warriors and battles were stories told around open fires, it did not happen to them, not here in Hardstone Woods.

Ober began to move toward Jaydon, but as he stepped forward he stumbled, with widened eyes and fell to the ground. Through the narrow gaps in the fence, Jaydon stared at Ober in silent horror as he lay face down, still and lifeless. His life-long friend's body lay half-hidden in the wispy mist, a spear lodged deep between his shoulder blades, shaft pointing to the sky above. Helplessness washed over Jaydon, move, he told himself. Summoning inner strength, he crawled further into the shadows. Sliding on his stomach through the sticky mud, using the misty ground as cover, trying not to glance back at Ober.

The pigs in the pen squealed in fright, heavy bodies pushing against each other in panic. Jaydon had to fend them off to stop them from trampling him, shoving and prodding them away with his spear. Batting them back as they sought an escape from the chaos. Still on his stomach and caked in mud and pig dung, Jaydon forced himself further into the wooden-slatted pigsty, squeezing in tight and wriggling his body around to peer outside, his spear still clutched tightly in trembling hands. His heart turned to ice as he heard the shrieks from his family trapped within. His family home, violently ablaze, with thick black smoke rising upwards, changing the dawn sky back to night. Tears streamed down his face.

Jaydon's heart thumped wildly. He should run and help, but it was just him with his spear. One fourteen-year-old boy against dozens of seasoned warriors. He'd be powerless against them. He shrank back into the protection of the pigsty, as yet it still remained unscorched.

Jaydon's hands shook. He tried to summon some courage. Come on Jaydon, come on. He imagined himself dashing forwards, screaming out his rage, plunging his spear again and again into the flesh of the warriors, avenging Ober. But his legs wouldn't move. His whole body shook like old man Odric.

A large human frame erupted from the door of his home, roaring loudly, broad sword in hand, swinging wildly, flames streaming from his clothing. 'Father, Father!' Jaydon screamed.

The waiting warriors surrounded the flaming figure of his father. Despite the flames blazing from his clothing, he cut down the nearest of them with a wild swing of his sword, taking his head clean off his shoulders. A second lunged toward him, but he feinted to his right, swung back and drove the sword through his stomach, the man wailed. His father, now screaming, as the fire began to overwhelm him. Yet somehow, he kept going, fighting on, Jaydon knew not how, as he watched his father withdraw his sword from the kill to run at a third warrior with an ear-splitting roar, his sword held aloft.

A giant, broad-shouldered man atop a black horse surged forward, slashing his sword across his father's face, who crumpled onto his knees as fire consumed him. From the melee, another warrior stepped forward, hefted a war-axe over his head with both hands and brought it crashing down onto his father's skull, splitting it in two. Jaydon's father slumped forwards, crashing face down into the muddy ground, the flames had now reached his hair, engulfing his corpse.

'Noooo!' Jaydon screamed, sobbing. 'Nooo, no, no, no.'

The man on the dark horse laughed, hawked and spat at the burning body, hissing curses. Then he turned his horse around and scanned the village. Jaydon heard him issuing orders to one of the men, gesticulating with his arms and sword.

'You, Kitto. Gather a band of men and stay guard over this house – no-one flees it alive. When the flames have died down search it inside and out. I am looking for a red stone. No bigger than a child's fist. It must be here somewhere. Search the whole village, leave none alive.'

Kitto nodded. 'Yes, lord. Is the stone precious?'

'It is to me, and it must be found. Check for any trunks or hidden places – don't let me down, Kitto. Oh, one more thing. Make sure all of Riler's family are dead. I'm led to believe he had two children…a boy and girl. They should be in there,' He pointed his sword to the burning hut. 'I want none of his blood-line to survive – do you understand?'

The warrior turned his horse, leaving the men to carry out his orders. Kitto spat on the ground in front of him. 'I ain't murdering no kids.' He said to one of the men to his right. 'They'll burn in there anyway. We wait as the lord said. If this stone is not there, then it can't be found. I would rather have silver and gold than a stone.'

The men around him nodded their agreement.

The words hit Jaydon as he remained hidden in the shadows. They came for his father? And wanted him dead too? He felt bile push at his throat. Then a realisation; he knew of the warrior on horseback. That scar running down the left-hand side of his face, a pale line running from below his eye and through his heavy beard. The dark winged eagle tattooed on his forehead. Landis Thornheart, an enemy of his father from the old wars. Wars that had raged across Calaria for generations. Jaydon had been told the stories, and there was no mistaking the murderer of Stefan Riler.

Then his mind turned to his mother and sister, still trapped inside the hut. Jaydon spun his head back toward the family home, the screaming had ceased, the building engulfed in flame, then a crack and dull thud as the beams of the roof collapsed inwards. Jaydon clasped his hands over ears, his eyes squeezed tightly shut. Shielding himself from the horror. His heart pounded, blood pulsed in his ears as he trembled, muttering silently to himself.

CHAPTER 2
THE PRICE OF FAILURE

Thornheart dismounted his stallion, the air around him hung heavy with smoke from the burning village. Mutilated bodies, men, women and children, lay strewn as his men had rampaged in a thirst for blood. A few of them now meandered back to the edge of the woodlands where he waited.

He took in the sight before him, satisfied, the stone would be in his grasp this day. It had taken him years to track down Riler. Thornheart fingered the scar on his cheek, and spat on the ground before him. Now Riler was dead, vengeance was his and he was a step closer to immortality.

Two riders approached, Thornheart greeted them. 'Ah, Nyla. Any news yet. Has Kitto found the stone?'

Nyla Mar, his long-serving second-in-command and trusted advisor, slid her slender frame from the saddle. Thornheart looked upon her olive-coloured face and oddly shaped eyes, recalling how he had raised her from a slave to his lieutenant. He relied upon her as the brains, the guile to the brawn of his other warriors. But Nyla could fight too, a fierce combatant. Quick, agile and cunning. A woman who had deserved to rise up at his side.

'He was still searching the ruins with a couple of men when we left,' she replied, brushing away an insect from the sleeve of her tunic. 'None survived.'

'Good,' Thornheart glanced to the second rider, Kartis, a man who served Nyla directly, then said quietly under his breath so only Nyla could hear. 'I will have the stone soon enough. Tonight, we will celebrate and drink enough wine and ale for all the gods. Elokar will reward us soon enough.'

Nyla raised an eyebrow. 'I hope you're right, Lord. The men's patience has been tested of late, but at least their blood lust has been sated this morning.'

'Indeed, and they will soon have more riches than they could ever imagine.' Thornheart nodded his head back toward the village. 'Ah, look, some of the men approach. We shall discus this later, Nyla. Let's see if Kitto has what we seek.'

The group of men drew closer, warriors with bloodied swords slung over shoulders as they strolled back relaxed, full of banter on how many they had killed and laughing at the devastation around them. Uther Kitto walked to the rear of them, head bowed trying to blend in, but Thornheart had seen him.

'Kitto, did you find what I seek?' Thornheart commanded.

The men parted, leaving Kitto exposed to Thornheart's glare. Kitto's eyes fixed to a point on the ground before him. 'No, lord. We searched everywhere. This red stone wasn't there, nor anything that looked like such a treasure.'

'He's right, lord,' one of the other men cut in. 'We turned over every bit of timber, checked any chest and dug around the rubble of the home, and some of the others too…nothing.'

Thornheart's gaze turned on the one who had spoken. 'Silence. I was not speaking with you, Baldock.' Thornheart felt the heat in his blood begin to rise. Then turning back to Kitto. 'Tell me you checked everything. You left nothing unturned.'

'Y…Yes, lord. I swear, we tried all we could. There was no stone.'

Thornheart cursed, kicking a stone across the ground in his frustration, which bounced off a lump of turf, spinning off to one side.

'And Riler's family? At least tell me all his bloodline are dead.'

The men remained silent, heads swivelled back to Uther Kitto. He hesitated a moment before responding. 'We found only two bodies in the rubble, lord. The wife and a small girl.' In three great strides Thornheart was on top of Kitto, grabbing him by the front of his jerkin. Then screamed into his face, spraying spittle into Kitto's beard. 'What! You have failed me you useless fool.'

Thornheart flung Kitto to the muddy ground, the gathering men spread themselves wide, distancing themselves from Thornheart's wrath. Only Nyla stepped forward. 'Lord,' she called out but stopped abruptly as he withdrew his broadsword from its sheath, holding it aloft as a sliver of morning light reflected on the steel blade, still dripping with crimson blood. He ran a finger across the edge, feeling its sharpness, before looking around at the assembling crowd. Good, he thought, he needed the audience to witness how he rewarded failure. To send them a message.

'Kitto, you were instructed to oversee the search, yet you did not find the stone and you say there were no signs of Riler's son's body in the ruins. Do I have that right?'

Kitto dragged himself to his knees. 'Lord, I…I… Yes lord. I have failed you.' He pleaded, clasping his hands together as though in prayer. 'Sorry, lord, it will not happen again. I have never let you down before. I have always stood by you. Please, lord. I have a family. You know my wife. It was through you we met. I will make this up to you. I promise.'

Thornheart curled his upper lip, the eagle on his forehead creased into the lines. He patted Kitto on the shoulder and sighed. 'Indeed, I do remember her,' he lightened his tone. 'A good woman.'

He moved slowly behind Kitto, and continued. 'Yet, you still failed me, Kitto. Failure only has one consequence, one outcome.' He raised his voice, so that the crowd could hear. 'I will not tolerate failure. You all know the price. Our need is for a greater power, for a wider goal. At the end of our journey your rewards will see you, your families and your ancestors well for years to come. We will run these lands. Songs will be sung of the deeds we do. We will be remembered in the histories.'

Thornheart paused, looking at the throng of men now surrounding them, making eye contact with one or two of them, holding their gaze for a few seconds each. Then he continued 'Yet, weakness and failure I will not endure, no matter who you are. This man, Uther Kitto, has failed you all. Today we should have been basking in the glory of a victory, with a great treasure in our hands. But alas, he let a boy, a child, slip through his incompetent fingers. And, for that, the price is his life.'

With one quick movement, Thornheart swung his sword, the silver of the blade flashed as it struck clean through Kitto's neck. The watching crowd remained silent, not even a gasp as Kitto's body slumped to the floor, turning the muddy grass a deep crimson.

Thornheart wiped the blood from the blade on Kitto's jerkin, sheathed it and turned to Nyla. 'We return to camp, gather the men. I need to speak with Elokar.' He said grimly.

CHAPTER 3
THE SHRINE

————◆————

Minutes, maybe hours, passed. Jaydon was unsure exactly how many before he summoned the courage to peer out from the pigsty. The sun had risen high in the sky. He crawled out from his hiding place, the stench from the pigsty lingered in his nostrils. His face streaked with mud and tears. Smoke still rose from the smouldering buildings.

Death hung in the air still heavy with the bitter smell of the scorched remains of all he had known his entire life. His heart felt like a dense weight, his legs quivered, reluctant to move, yet somehow he propelled himself forwards. Clambering over the fence, he staggered toward his father's corpse and knelt sobbing by his charred remains; the once hulk of a man, gone. Jaydon's father lay face down, his head a grotesque mess, blood seeping into the muddy ground around him.

Jaydon wiped away the tears and the streaming snot from his face with the sleeve of his under shirt and slowly dragged himself to his destroyed home.

The air reeked from the smell of smoke that rose from the fire-blackened timbers of the ruins within. In the centre, buried beneath them,

Jaydon saw what he didn't want to find, yet he couldn't tear himself away from. Arm in arm were the charred remains of his mother and sister—poor, innocent Jenna. He stared upwards and wailed at the sky before sinking to his knees, howling, weeping, cursing the gods.

When there were no more tears left, Jaydon gathered himself. He knew he had to act, but he couldn't leave his family like this either. What would his father do? Had anyone else survived the attack? Was he alone?

He began searching through the rubble, discovering his father's old shield, buried beneath timber and rubble – thankfully it had little damage from the fire. He put it to one side. Barely registering the faded symbol on the front, where once a bright red painted sword emblazoned the face of the shield.

The village was desolate, burnt and mutilated bodies—people he had called his friends—were scattered, lifeless, as though their lives were nothing. No-one else remained alive. Jaydon moved trancelike as he worked his way through ruins. Scavenging for anything of use that could be salvaged; mouldy cheese, stale bread, some old rope and charred blankets and furs.

Finally, packing his meagre findings into a saddle bag, he returned to the wreckage of the family home. He found a shovel, buried beneath a fallen wall, and started digging in the damp ground. A grave, the last act for his family. Despite all his weariness, Jaydon kept going, shovel full after shovel full. Only stopping to drink mouthfuls of water before carrying on with back-breaking effort. Sweat poured from his forehead, dripping from the end of his nose.

Enough, he thought, throwing the shovel to one side. That's deep enough. He stared down at dark hole in front before him, taking a moment to gather his composure. That was the easy bit, he told himself.

Jaydon, summoned all his courage for what he must do next. Slowly, he dragged the remains of his family to the grave. First his mother and sister. His stomach heaved from the smell of their burnt flesh, like roasted pork, as he pulled them across the earth on a scorched fur. Acid rose in his throat, bending to the side he vomited, retching a stream of vile liquid onto the ground, before composing himself once more and continuing the wretched task.

Next, his father, with immense difficulty and using as much strength as he could muster, Jaydon rolled him over onto his back. As he did something caught his eye—a gleam of red and silver in the mud, beneath the corpse...his father's sword. Jaydon took it from the ground and wiped it with the sleeve of his shirt. cleaning the dirt from the blade. Then, setting it aside, with the saddlebag, he continued, eventually managing to place his parents and sister side by side in the grave.

He wrapped his mother's blackened arms around Jenna—laying them together for an eternity. Next, he took his father's war axe, which he had found hidden within the remains of their home, placing it across his barrelled chest.

He waited a moment, looking upon them one final time, before picking up the shovel. Jaydon started to cover the bodies with the loose earth, trying not to watch as the dirt covered their faces.

Gathering rocks, Jaydon placed them on top of the grave, marking the shrine; the final resting place of his family. Once done he slumped to the ground, exhausted. He lay with his face down on top of the mound, tasting the earth and grit on his tongue.

Blame surged through him. Why did he not get back in time to warn them? He just panicked, remaining in the pigsty like a coward. Images of his father's death rattled through his mind—and all he did was watch and cry. Why did he leave them? He could have taken Jenna with him when she woke, if he had would she still be alive now? What if Magen had not run out of the home? Would Jaydon be dead too? Buried beneath timbers and left to rot with the rest of the village. Guilt, anger and grief tore through him.

Dusk came, the skies darkened. Sighing, Jaydon realised he should move. But where? He no longer had a home. The silence was broken with the cawing of the crows that descended into the village from the surrounding woodlands, fighting and feasting and over the bodies of the dead. Jaydon retched once more at the grim sight.

Hastily gathering what he'd salvaged, slinging the shield and the saddle bag over his shoulder. He picked up his fathers' sword, the leather wrapped hilt, well-worn, the dark blood-red stone at the pommel. Jaydon briefly gazed at the stone, watching his reflection in the its surface. He recalled the words from Thornheart earlier, *I am looking for a red stone. No bigger than a child's fist. It must be here somewhere.* Was this that stone? If so, why was it so special? It was just a decorative jewel on a sword – could it be a rare treasure?

Jaydon cast the thought to one side, that was something he need not worry about at the moment. He slid the sword into a sheath he had strapped to his belt. The heavy blade trailed behind him— his father's sword, it had also been his grandfathers before that and even his father's grandfather's sword—passed down through the generations, *Devil's Bane*, and now it belonged to Jaydon.

Wrapping a pelt tightly around his shoulders, Jaydon turned his back on Hardstone Woods as dark clouds formed in the twilight sky overhead. He walked into the surrounding woodland, from which hours earlier the warriors had emerged, just as the rain started to fall, dampening the last of the smoking village behind him. Entering the woods, he vowed to himself, and to his murdered family, that he would seek revenge. He would hunt down Landis Thornheart, and he would kill him, with *Devil's Bane*. At fourteen Jaydon knew his destiny would be to follow into his father's footsteps and become a warrior.

CHAPTER 4

LAKE BLACKHEATH

——— ◆••◆••◆ ———

Jaydon sat on an outcrop overlooking the rocky southern shores of Lake Blackheath. A vast water positioned between the Moray Hills, the Great Grasslands and the distant northern ranges of the Scarlet Mountains—named for the way their granite surfaces radiated the sun in the evening twilight.

After Jaydon had left Hardstone Woods he had travelled north-wards, using the cover of the night to travel to the lake, whose familiar dark and still waters made him feel safe. Jaydon had camped here many times with his father. He'd learned to fish on the shores, trap rabbits, squirrels and other game in the surrounding hills. For many an hour he had practised his sword craft with his father here, which always left him bruised, aching and sore.

He could hear his father's voice now; *One day you may need these skills* he had said, when Jaydon had wanted to give up. But he never did yield to the soreness within his muscles. Always pushing himself to exhaustion, eager to make his father proud. Stefan Riler, had once been a famous warlord of Calaria, and had commanded armies in the old wars.

Perched on the edge of the outcrop, Jaydon watched a heron stalking its prey in the waters below, poised to strike at an unsuspecting fish, waiting patiently for that perfect moment to attack. As Jaydon observed the bird, his stomach growled with hunger. He had hardly eaten since leaving his village, just the stale bread and mouldy cheese he scavenged from the ruins. He needed to eat something more substantial. To hunt, and soon, he told himself.

'Hey, save some fish for me, heron,' he called out, his voice echoing off the rocks and boulders around him.

As visions of his burnt and blackened sister flashed through his mind, Jaydon's heart felt as though it would burst with grief – a grief that overwhelmed him as the tears streamed down his face leaving streaks of pale skin. Yet he knew he must put it to one side if he was to survive.

His mind whirred between sorrow, anger and revenge. He glanced down at this father's sword, *Devil's Bane*, which lay flat on the ground beside him, his eyes once more drawn to the red stone at the pommel – he felt as though it scrutinised him, a great red eye judging what he did next, as though his father was watching him.

Jaydon imagined himself thrusting the blade through Thornheart's guts. But, what could he do on his own? He needed help. Maybe he could prise the stone from the pommel, if it was indeed a rare jewel he could get silver for it, surely? Buy food and shelter. But what was so important that Thornheart had massacred his village for it?

Thinking this over Jaydon walked idly into the cave, scratching at his itchy scalp; fingers scrabbling beneath his thick dark hair, matted with grime, sweat and dust. The air within the gloomy interior of the cave stank musty and damp. Jaydon waited as his eyes adjusted. In the corner lay a pile of old furs and blankets left from the last trip he and his father had made there. Next to them a circle of stones, surrounding the greying ashes of an old campfire. Glad he had brought a flint stone in the saddle bag; Jaydon knew he would at least have warmth. He could cook meat once he had caught something, he told himself as another pang of hunger rumbled.

He sat on the furs and blankets, resting his back against the damp cave walls, his mind stewing with hatred and revenge. Closing his eyes, Jaydon's thoughts turned to the times he had spent here with his father. Nights in the cave, wrapped up in their blankets, his father would often regale Jaydon with stories of his younger years. Battles won and lost, the women he knew, the men he'd fought with, the enemies he'd killed. Every story told with animated movements of his powerful arms, casting vast shadows on the walls of the cave. The glow of the camp fire adding to the excitement, transporting Jaydon to a world full of heroes as he would sit in awe of the man his father had been.

Landis Thornheart would sometimes feature in these stories. A foe his father had encountered in the battlefield, with whom he had locked swords, beating him, only for Thornheart to escape wounded. Jaydon's father had given Thornheart the scar on his face. It was in the battle of Winter's Harbour, in the final throes of the old wars. They were sitting in this very cave when his father told the tale. It was a mild autumn evening, just like now.

Jaydon and his father had sat by the fire, the cave coloured a deep orange, dark shadows danced across his father's face. 'Did I ever tell you about the Battle of Winter's Harbour, Jay?' his father asked.

'No, Father, but I have heard that it was a great battle.' Ober had told him about the battle that had swung the old wars and, until now, his father had never spoken of it to him. Jaydon had readied himself with anticipation.

'Well son, it was the first time I fought Landis Thornheart. You've heard of him?' Jaydon nodded slowly, Thornheart was a mercenary, fighting for whoever paid the highest price. Feared across kingdoms, never showing mercy to his enemies, nor those foolish to believe him a friend. Jaydon's heart thumped, always enthralled by his father's stories of his battles and this, one of the most famous. Ober had told him his father had single-handedly beaten the Voranian forces.

His father had paused, taking a swig of ale from his skin and then commenced. 'The armies of Vorania had invaded inland, led by Thornheart. They advanced deeper into central Calaria, raiding towns, villages, killing innocents—farmers, women, children. Sometimes, Jaydon, when men are in packs, they become savages when their blood lust is up. They're consumed when violence is all they know. Good men lose themselves.

'Villages were massacred, raised to the ground, just smoking hovels left behind, bodies were left for the crows and wolves. Winter's Harbour is an outpost on the Great River. By the gods, it was a cold place, the chill penetrated deep into our bones. A key trade port and strategically, if the Voranians took control of the port, they had control of northern Calaria.

Stefan Riler shook his head slowly and took another slug of ale. 'We were outnumbered, three to one. We only had five hundred men, a mixture of battle-hardened soldiers and inexperienced farmers and tradesmen raised from the burghs. Young men joined us, barely older than you, wanting to earn themselves a reputation amongst their friends.'

He dragged the back of his fist across his mouth and grinned down at Jaydon who was lost in his father's story. 'We never gave up though. We had gathered in a last stand on the rocky plains on the western boundaries of the town. I commanded the main force, having the honour of leading the charge. It was bloody, the battle raged throughout the day. The rain teemed down on us, the battlefield turning it to a quagmire of mud, blood and guts beneath our feet.'

Jaydon held his breath as his father continued, 'We held firm though Jaydon, we stayed strong, withstanding wave after wave, slowly beating back the Voranian forces. Eventually their lines broke. I have no idea what swung it—it could have been the sheer will of our men, buoyed by vengeance and retribution for the destruction the enemy had brought to our lands when they had infested across the borders. It could have been pure luck or just the will of the gods. Whatever it was they finally broke.

'The battlefield was littered with the bodies of men and horses, strewn across the plains. The air filled with the screams from those still fighting or lying maimed and injured, men crying for their mothers, their bodies mutilated. The stench of death lingered across the fields. In a rare moment of stillness, I remember staring up at the crows, hundreds of them, son, circling high above. Knowing what they were there for, and praying to the gods, not for me. Not for me. They aren't going to feast on my eyes tonight.'

Again, his father paused to take another swig of his ale, unconsciously wiping some of the spilled droplets from his greying beard. Jaydon hardly dared to breathe as his father continued.

'The battle had moved to its final throes, most of the enemy scattered, then from the centre of a band of Voranians came Thornheart. He seemed like a giant striding towards me. A broadsword in one hand. A massive oak shield, with this dark eagle etched across it, black as coal, in the other. He had the same eagle tattooed across his forehead. I had never seen anyone like him before Jaydon. I'd heard the stories. I won't lie, I was scared, as he planted his feet, like two vast tree trunks and staring directly at me he raised his sword, pointing it toward me. A challenge. His face carrying a smirk as wide as the Great River itself.'

Stefan paused again, his eyes closed as he remembered. 'We came face to face, he spat on the ground in front of me. The battle still raged around us, my men hell bent on chasing after an enemy who had turned tail and were running like scared rabbits. But all I could focus on was Thornheart. Me and him, in a pocket of silence. The downpour from the heavy skies above never relented. My furs and leather jacket heavy, soaking me to skin and bone. How I kept going I'll never know, son. I was so tired I could hardly move my limbs, but when the blood lust takes hold, the adrenalin drives you, rushing through your veins like fire. Makes you feel invincible. Only problem is, it's the same for your enemy. So, you have to harness that rage, not let it control you, you have to fight with your head too Jaydon, always remember that.'

Jaydon nodded slowly to himself, hanging on every word his father said.

'Thornheart and I traded heavy blows one after the other, neither of us giving an inch. Eventually I landed a lucky blow, it glanced off the rim of his shield, catching his upper shoulder, throwing him off balance. He toppled, feet sliding out from beneath him in the mud. That's when I drove forward, as he went down on one knee. I was on him in a mere second.

'This was it, my one chance to fell this giant, this oak of a man. I held *Devil's Bane* high over my head and I swung it down, hard, to crack that vast skull in half. But he knew death was coming and was quicker than me. Or, maybe the gods were on his side that day instead. He jerked his head backwards, and the killer blow fell short as it scythed through his face, slicing through to bone. I could see the white through his splitting flesh. But before I could go again, they were on us, a swarm of panicked, retreating Voranian soldiers engulfed where we fought. Suddenly the world erupted into chaos, screaming, shouting, men running wildly. In the confusion Thornheart escaped into the throngs of those retreating.'

The meagre light in the cave dimmed, as outside a cloud shrouded the early morning sun for a moment. Jaydon shivered as he shook away the memories, he needed to focus, to move on and push the grief aside.

He needed a plan. Surviving the attack on his village would be in vain if he starved to death, and the scraps he had found were soon to run out. Jaydon thought through his steps: he had shelter in the cave and comfort, and would soon have a fire lit, to keep chill off him during the night. A pile of old branches and twigs were stacked in one corner, Jaydon would need more, but he felt safe—for the time being. However, he could not stay here forever.

Jaydon trekked down to a nearby stream. Whilst he refilled his skins, his thoughts shifted back to food, he felt his stomach groan again with pangs of hunger. His hands shook with fatigue as he lowered the skins into the cold water. A small fish caught his eye as it dashed away from him. He knew how to fish, his father had taught him and the lake had a plentiful bounty of them. Plus, he knew how to set traps for rabbits too. But for those he needed to make spears and snares.

Jaydon put into practice all his father his had taught him. Using saplings that he cut down and twine he had scavenged from the village, he set the snares in the woods, along small animal trails that he had spotted in the undergrowth. He made fishing spears from the branches of a strong ash tree, whittling the ends into sharpened points. Then taking the spears, Jaydon stripped off his clothing and slipped into the lake, naked.

The sun now hung high above the lake, Jaydon breathed in sharply as the shock of the water hit his midriff, despite the sun-rays, the lake was still cool. Steadying himself he waded carefully around the shoreline to a shallower area a few metres away.

Now the wait.

He stood silently, thigh deep in the cold water, enough of the sun on his body to keep a fragment of warmth on his skin. He could still hear his father's level voice. *Patience Jaydon, strike hard, strike fast. Not too early, timing is key.*

He spied two catfish swimming nearby, he struck too hastily and the fish escaped, much to his exasperation. Cursing his impatience, Jaydon waited further.

The sun shifted in the sky as the day moved onward, Jaydon started to weary and frustration began to nag at him, when at last, he struck hard and true, a young sturgeon.-

The fish thrashed violently, fighting against him, heavy foaming water splashing into his face, blurring his vision. The fish's body thrashed as it whipped its tail to and fro and Jaydon had to push down on the spear as hard as he could, using all his body weight to pin it to the lake bed. He couldn't let the opportunity go to waste. Taking one hand off his spear, he reached down and grabbed his knife from his belt with one swift movement, spinning it quickly in his hand, he brought the hilt down hard once, twice onto the head of the fish.

The waters around him turned dark with its blood, the thrashing slowly subsided, the fish limp and lifeless in the waters.

Breathing hard, knife in hand Jaydon whooped in delight to the gods. 'Thank you, Onir, thank you blessed, Mieses. See, Father, I can do it.' Water dripped down from hair and face, he held his arms high above his head, as though offering the fish to the gods. He may have been tired, but he wouldn't starve, not that day at least.

CHAPTER 5

DREAMS AND DECISIONS

———•••◆•••———

He woke screaming. His body slick with sweat and his heart battering in his chest. Taking sharp intakes of air Jaydon shoved away the furs. The morning sun threw shafts of light into the entrance of the cave, just a few smouldering embers remained of the fire he had stoked during the night.

He lay mulling over the last traces of the nightmare, struggling to make sense of it as it had felt so real. Flames and faces flashed and morphed. Faces of death with melting skin. He remembered searching and calling out; for who? His family? One of the burning faces, a woman, did speak, at least Jaydon thought she did? But what did she say? She had called out names to him – *Arthek. Everwood.* Names he knew were important, yet Jaydon could not explain why. He had heard them before, but from where in his memory he could not recall.

Brushing his palm across his eyes Jaydon wiped away the sleep and sighed, the loss of his family slapping him once more. No more stories from his father, no more loving embraces from his mother, no more teasing Jenna. He took some solace from the thought that they were to-gether in the shallow grave and prayed that Onir would welcome them into the heavens with his ancestors.

Grabbing his tunic Jaydon climbed back up onto the outcrop and into the woods, checking the traps and snares he'd set the evening be-fore. But the names from the dream kept coming back to him repeated-ly; *Arthek. Everwood. Arthek. Everwood.*

His snares had worked. Jaydon sighed in relief as he spotted the limp bodies of two rabbits, eyes bulging from their sockets from the twine wrapped tightly around their throats, hanging lifeless in the un-dergrowth. Unfastening the cords from their neck, Jaydon trudged back to the cave, the two carcasses slung over one shoulder. As he walked, he tried to remember other stories from his father, hoping to jog some memory that might help. Slowly he recalled that his father had a good friend back in the old wars. Jaydon believed his name was Arthek. He was sure of it. Arthek Mulliner. It came to him now. Arthek, had fought with his father. *We were like brothers* his father used to say. Jaydon thought hard. But where had his father said he'd gone after the wars had finished? Jaydon's father had gone home to Hardstone Woods, the village of his birth. But Arthek?

Jaydon creased his brow, his eyes closed. Thinking over the other word from the nightmare? *Everwood?* Had it been mentioned by travel-lers who passed through his village? Yes, it had. A market town in north-ern Calaria – he was certain. His father's voice returned to him clearly, as though he was stood by Jaydon's side: *We parted, vowing to stay friends. To be there for each other. But I haven't seen him for over twenty years now, Jaydon. He went back to Everwood, back to his family trade, a blacksmith. And I came back here to be with your mother.*

The thoughts rattled around Jaydon's skull. Unsure of where that memory had come from, but he didn't care, for now it gave him some-thing to hope for. Somewhere he could go.

He breakfasted on the remains of the sturgeon along with the last of his stale bread, washing them down with mouthfuls of water. He skinned and gutted the rabbits before roasting them over the fire, then went to sit back out onto the rocky outcrop, feet dangling over the lake's edge, taking pleasure in a full stomach.

The sun rose over the hills on the eastern shore of the lake, turning the dark waters a lighter grey, silver ripples cast over the dark surface. The mountains to the distant north radiated as the sun's rays brought them to life.

As the sun hit his feet and the warmth began to fill his body Jaydon made up his mind. He would set out for Everwood. He had no idea where in Calaria it was, but if he followed the Great River downstream he would reach a village or farming community. Someone there would point him in the right direction and then he could seek his father's friend. Without question he would help him seek retribution, hunt down Thornheart and kill him.

Later that morning, his few supplies packed, Jaydon was ready to leave Lake Blackheath. The beginning of his journey had him trekking around the shore of lake towards the Great River. His father had told him the river began on the northern shore, gushing down between rocks and forming the vast river. From there he would follow it north and, with the Gods' luck, make his way to Everwood in just a few days.

The terrain around the lake was rocky at first, peppered with large boulders that Jaydon had to clamber over and around. Finally reaching the far corner of the lake, where the ground changed to wet marshland. Doggedly, he struggled onwards, slipping and sliding ankle deep in cold thick mud, which clogged the soles of his boots. But he spurred himself onwards with thoughts of vengeance and hope, gritting his teeth in determination and relieved to have a sense of direction and purpose.

Despite the continued difficulty of the terrain and the weariness within his body Jaydon trudged onwards, smiling inwardly at his father's voice: *You were always a stubborn child, Jaydon*, he would chide him, with laughter in his voice. Jaydon recalled the hours of practice with his bow. Hidden in the woods so others would not see him. Arrow after arrow he would let fly at his makeshift target, perfecting his grip, his stance and his sight. All so he could beat Ober. Too pig-headed to allow Ober to kill more game than him when they hunted together.

Ober was a marksman and the fastest runner of the all the boys in Hardstone Woods. Jaydon and Ober had been born a month apart, they had grown up together, competing against each other in village games and sports. Only last month they had tied in a horse race, out to the far boundaries of the farmlands and back. Neither giving each other a yard. But despite their competitive natures, they were good friends, and only two months ago they celebrated their fourteenth birthdays—their last year before entering manhood.

After hours of arduous trekking around the lake, Jaydon stood on the northern shore and spun his head around to check his progress. It appeared as though he had covered no distance, yet it had taken him most of the day so far. But still, he remained pleased with himself, he had not faltered, and when he felt as though he would, he brought Thornheart's face to his mind. Picturing the satisfaction as he thrust *Devil's Bane* through his throat.

At long last and by late afternoon Jaydon reached the point where the Great River began. He heard it before it came into view, a low rumble that slowly turned into a deafening roar. By the gods, what a monster of a river. The water churned and foamed as it flowed beneath him, crashing over rocks and boulders down a steep decline from the lake and into a valley.

Jaydon's body was sticky with sweat, his shirt clinging to his back. Exhausted, he drained the last of the water from his skins, refilling them at the edge of the lake, dipping the skins into water that chilled his hands to the bone. He stuck his hands beneath his armpits to warm them, before clambering down the slope and into the forest which the Great River disappeared into.

As the sun began to dip in the sky Jaydon emerged into a vast meadow of long grasses, which stretched ahead as far as he could see. The land was flatter, the Great River now a gentle flow, rather than the torrents further upstream as it meandered through the grasslands. Far in the distance the peaks from the Scarlet Mountains were painted red as the sun began to set.

Jaydon ached. Every part of his body screamed for him to stop and rest. The leather straps of the saddle bag cut into his shoulder. His feet, unaccustomed to walking the distance were starting to blister, hot spots burning his soles. He flung himself onto the ground, enough was enough, this was as good as spot as any to rest for the night. He made a rough shelter against the roots of a fallen tree, set a fire and readied himself for sleep, which washed over in an instant as the last remnants of twilight disappeared and the darkness took hold.

CHAPTER 6
THE CAPTIVE

———◆———

Shafts of light shone through the trees and onto Jaydon's face, he slowly opened his eyes, squinting from the rays that dappled through the tree canopy above him, the sky a smattering of grey clouds breaking up the blue. The air within the woods filled with the chattering of birds, calling their morning chorus, singing to each other, and another sound, closer by. Jaydon's senses alerted...a snuffling noise. Within the fog of his mind Jaydon thought Magen was waking him, then realty dawned on everything that had happened.

Turning towards the sound Jaydon caught a fox sniffing amongst his belongings. He yelped in surprise, scrabbling himself backwards. As he did, his hand brushed against a small rock, without any hesitation Jaydon grabbed the rock and threw it towards the animal. The fox scarpered back a few yards, turned and stared back with yellow feral eyes. Grabbing *Devil's Bane* Jaydon shrugged off his furs, jumped up and rushed at the fox, screaming, yelling to frighten it away. The fox turned on its heels and sped deeper into the woodland, disappearing into the shadows.

Snatching up the rest of his belongings, Jaydon hurried into the long grass of the meadow. But within moments he stopped and burst into a bout of uncontrollable laughter. It felt alien to laugh after the all that had happened, yet he couldn't stop – a pouring of emotion erupted from within. The more he heard himself laughing, the more he couldn't stop.

He collapsed into the long grasses, still damp from the morning dew, before eventually calming himself, shaking his head at his own stupidity. Come on Jaydon, he scolded, that's not a warrior's way to re-act - running off like a frightened child. You need to be a man now. He smirked once more as he sat up, brushing off the lengths of grass from his trousers and shirt.

He sat in the grass deep in thought, sucking on some of the rabbit meat that he pulled from his bag, picturing Ober laughing at him for getting so spooked over a fox. A laugh he would never hear again – he missed Ober.

Finishing his breakfast, Jaydon continued his journey. The hours passed idly by, gone were the meadows of the grasslands and instead open flat fields lay before him with rolling hills and scattered wood-lands. Jaydon ached, his feet were sore, sweat drenched his back. He needed to rest a short while. Finding a perfect spot he sat, resting against a boulder, feeling the coolness of the stone against his sweaty back, tak-ing the pressure off his blistered feet.

Tearing a strip of some of the remaining rabbit meat from the bone with his teeth he absentmindedly gazed at a pair of hares racing each other through the grass. Was this a sign from the gods that he was on the right path? A sense of peace washed over him as he basked in the tranquillity and silence of the open lands around him – his mind calm.

In the distance, the fluting sound of songbirds could be heard over the rushing waters of the Great River. A gentle breeze blew across his face, Jaydon began to relax for the first time since he had left the remains of his village, closing his eyes with the warmth of the sun on his face.

The sun disappeared behind a band of dark clouds, Jaydon opened one eye and looked up. With a resigned exhalation of breath, he readied himself to move onward. The hares were still running through the grasses, darting in jagged lines. He realised he would need to hunt again. Maybe he would happen across a village or farmstead? He could beg for food, or maybe offer to work. Plus, he needed directions for Everwood, he could not follow the Great River forever. He would end up at the Crystal Ocean for sure if he did that.

Jaydon took another glug of water from his skin, the nickering of a horse diverted his attention as he raised the skin to his mouth. He glanced upwards and saw, silhouetted on a low hill, five horsemen approaching. He took in a sharp breath of air, realising he was exposed in open ground. Then, a distant shout as the horsemen began cantering down the hillside towards him.

Jaydon gathered his belongings quickly, turned and bounded towards the river. In a frenzy of splashing and spray he lunged into the cool water, losing his footing as he slipped on the wet rocks and fell head first. Jaydon chaffed his hands and knees on the stones beneath the water's surface. The shield on his back slipped forward, thumping him hard on the back of his head. He tried to scramble forward on his hands and knees, but it was too late, the horsemen now surrounded him as he sat in the river, water dripping from his hair and face. Dazed from the blow of the shield, he cursed his stupidity, shakily getting to his feet. Instinctively, he pulled *Devil's Bane* from its sheath.

'Get back!' he shouted, holding the sword in front of him, willing his hands not to tremble. 'Get back. Leave me be.'

The horsemen circled him. laughing. Rough men, scarred, tattooed, long unwashed hair, shaggy beards, all wearing thick leather and furs. Each man was armed. One of them called back, his voice calm, but firm. 'Put it down boy, it's not a toy.'

'I warn you, get back. I'll run you through.' Jaydon stood, thrusting *Devil's Bane* in the air at the nearest of the horseman.

'Don't get me cross boy, now I won't ask again. Put the sword down before you get hurt.'

Jaydon raised *Devil's Bane* high and ran toward the closest of the horsemen, screaming. As he did so he flung himself upwards, swiping down with his sword in one fluid motion. The man hardly had time to react as Jaydon struck him on the hilt of his sword with *Devil's Bane*. With his other hand Jaydon grabbed the collar of the man's tunic, tugging downwards. The weight and momentum of Jaydon unbalanced the rider and the man teetered then fell sideways from his saddle with a heavy splash into the river.

Breathing hard, Jaydon spun with *Devil's Bane* held in front of him. 'Now get back,' he screamed at the other horsemen.

A flash of movement came from Jaydon's side, but before he could react he felt a sharp blow to his temple, knocking his head sideways. The world around him spun then faded away, as he fell face down into the river before darkness swamped him.

•••◆•••

Jaydon opened his eyes slowly, the shock of water hit his face. Shaking his head, he spluttered, shouting out, he tried to wipe away the water from his face. But both hands were bound tightly at the wrists. He blinked to clear his vision, above him stood a blurry shape.

'Wake up you little mongrel. We need to move,' the shape growled before aiming a boot toward him, striking Jaydon in the guts. 'Come on shift. Now.' Again, the man kicked his midriff. Jaydon yelped.

He struggled to his knees, using his elbows to push his body upwards. Still dazed, Jaydon had no idea of his whereabouts or what had happened. Who was this man? Although his hands were bound, his feet weren't. Momentarily, he considered making a dash for it, but he knew it would be futile. The right-hand side of his head throbbed, he tentatively touched his temple with his fingers, only to feel a blood encrusted lump.

Wincing, he looked around, gathering his bearings. He counted five men, packing up horses, decamping from where they had rested. One of the men was urinating on a fire, which hissed as steam rose from the embers. The fog in Jaydon's mind slowly began to clear. He recalled the river, then the chase as the men surrounded him. He could even remember unseating one of them from his horse. Then nothing. Everything ached; his head, his wrists, his knees, the blisters on his feet.

'Come on. Stand up, lad,' his captor grunted once more. His long and dirty hair was tied behind into a ponytail, speckled with streaks of grey, revealing a dirt smeared face, hidden behind a heavy salt and pepper beard that was tied with red twine beneath his chin. His arms were heavily tattooed; runes and strange symbols covering thick scars.

'Come on, on yer feet. You've been out of it all night and we need to move,' he said again, lifting Jaydon up by the crook of an elbow.

The man held a long coil of rope in his left hand, tying it around the bindings at Jaydon's wrists, then he walked back towards one of the horses, jerking hard on the rope. Jaydon staggered forwards, tripping on a tree root, and watched as the man tied the free end of the rope to the saddle of one of the horses. 'Right, wait here—you say anything and I'll slap you—hard, d'you understand, boy?' he said harshly.

'Where's my belongings? I had a sword,' Jaydon asked shakily. 'And my shield?'

The man, chuckled and shook his head, his pony tail swaying behind him. 'They belong to me now. Listen, I asked you to shut up and be quiet, I won't ask so nicely next time. I'm the kind one. If it was him,' the bandit thumbed in the direction of one of the other men who had his back turned to them. 'Well, he would slit you from ear to ear.'

But Jaydon couldn't help himself. 'Give me my sword!' He shouted back defiantly, standing upright, trying to make himself as tall as he could, oozing confidence he did not feel.

In a flash the man lashed out, slapping him smartly across his cheek. Jaydon's head rocked from the blow then he collapsed onto his backside. The world around him swam, lights dancing in front of his eyes. The lump on his head ached and his cheek burned from the blow. Tears welled, but Jaydon clenched his eyes tightly, fighting them back. He must not show any emotion. He breathed slowly through his nose, telling himself to curb his anger and to stop saying foolish things that would make it worse for him.

'What did I just say?' the man barked, then smiling wryly, he shook his head, his voice a touch softer 'You're a brave one, I'll give you that. Stupid, but brave. Now just do as I ask and you won't get hurt. We have a long journey ahead, and you've slowed us down enough already.' His captor shook his head once more, before walking to where the others were finishing their packing.

•◆•

For the rest of the day they trekked, the men on horseback, Jaydon dragged behind on foot, shuffling as quickly as he could to try keep up with the riders. Finally, early evening came and to Jaydon's enormous relief they decided to rest for the night.

One of the bandits led Jaydon to a lone tree, dumping him onto the hard stony ground and tethered him to the trunk. The men mainly ignored him, unless they were hurling abuse. He felt utterly hopeless as he lay against the rough bark, dropping his chin onto his chest.

The only one of the bandits who had shown any signs of civility was the one who had tied him to the horse earlier. He had given Jaydon a few meagre scraps of meat to eat and droplets of water for his parched lips. This man seemed to be the one in charge, or at least he made the final decisions.

As darkness fell, the men sat around a campfire, a stew bubbled away in a battered pot over the flames, Jaydon could smell the aroma from where he sat, his mouth watered for just a spoonful, yet none came.

He managed to shuffle his body around, to make himself as comfortable as possible, and lay down on the hard ground feigning sleep as he listened to their conversations, hoping to learn more about them, who they were and what of their plans for him as their captive.

'So where are we headed now, Bren? Do we take the boy with us?' The shorter of the five asked. His head shaven but he sported a thick grizzly black beard.

'I reckon to The Wyke. Malin will take him in.'

'Malin? That old dog will drive a hard bargain. Bit out of our way too, ain't it?'

'Nevertheless Morgen, we take him to Malin. We need the silver.'

Two of the bandits were twins, tall, strong, with long dirty blond hair and trimmed beards. Both nodded in unison. 'I agree with Bren, sell the boy. We can get some lodgings and food.' Then added with a wry smile, 'Maybe a couple of women, too.'

'You're always wanting women, Gordar. Of course, you agree with him too, Korban, I suppose?'

Korban, the second twin, laughed and nodded. 'What's not to agree with? Ale, food and women. That's all a man needs, that and a good horse.'

'Not sure your wife would approve, Korban.' Replied Brennand, the men erupted into laughter.

'We should be thankful,' One of twins said. 'The gods have seen fit to bring this lad to us, Bren. The silver will be welcome.'

'You know I don't believe in god's luck, Gordar. No. Things just happen, it's as simple as that. But, I agree. The silver will definitely be welcome.' Their tones were light, finding amusement with each other in their conversation.

The final member of the group remained silent, scowling at Jaydon from across the fire. A tall, wiry man, who walked with a stoop, his shoulders hunched. His grey hair greasy and thinning, revealing a scalp with scabs and scars. But if he acted mean, it was his face that made him meaner, a scar ran across the bridge of his nose, his right nostril missing and instead it was a black and red mush of tissue.

'Wilfrec? What are your thoughts?' Morgen asked.

Wilfrec turned his head from Jaydon, to address the group. His voice like the hiss of a viper. 'Kill the boy. I can do it now if you like?' he replied as he fingered the blade of the knife he held in his right hand.

'No,' Brennand called back. 'We need the silver. Leave the lad be, Wilfrec. I want no harm done to him. Are you still smarting that he got the better of you in the river before Gordar took him down?' Again, the other men burst into bouts of laughter. 'Bested by a child?'

'Maybe more practice with that battered sword of yours is needed.' Gordar teased. 'If you want to run with us, you need to learn how to fight. Come, we can spar now if you like?'

'I only need my knife, it has served me well enough in the past,' then stealing a sly glance back at Jaydon. 'You'll feel the steel of my blade, boy.'

Jaydon's heart quickened, as the goosebumps rose on his arms, sending a cold shiver down his spine. He'd got himself into a mess here, he thought, as hopelessness overwhelmed him once more.

CHAPTER 7

A FLAMING APPARITION

————————◆•••◆•••◆————————

The fires in the camp burned, columns of charcoal coloured smoke lifted into the evening sky. The setting sun, a deep orange over the distant hills, as night began to shroud the remains of the day. A band of horsemen meandered through the tents towards the centre of the encampment, the imposing shadows of Bleakhorn Forest stretched across the fields, engulfing the camp and increasing the gloom that already hung in the air.

Raising a solitary arm Landis Thornheart brought his men to a halt before lowering his giant frame from his black stallion. Turning to his men he barked out orders, handing the reins of his horse to a red-haired slave girl who waited by the larger tent.

A central fire lit the inside of Thornheart's tent, embers burned in the semi-darkness. Thornheart removed his sword, belt, cloak and leather tunic, handing them over to another slave girl who took them to a table in the corner, placing them carefully, like old relics on display.

'Petari, fetch me some ale,' Thornheart demanded as he sat on a grand oakwood chair, carved into an eagle with wide-spread wings, just like the tattoo that he sported on his forehead. Then his voice quavered slightly. 'And fetch me the stone.'

The girl disappeared into the shadows, and returned with a tankard of ale. Thornheart's hand quivered slightly, before he took an enormous gulp of the murky liquid and placed the tankard down half-empty on a bench beside him. Petari returned, bringing with her a wooden casket, which she momentarily held close to her chest before offering it ceremoniously to Thornheart with open palms. He held the casket as carefully as he could within his enormous hands that trembled with the anticipation of what was to come. He noted the way Petari protected the box before passing it to him. It irked him, he didn't like anyone being near the casket when he wasn't around, he should keep it with him. However, he let it go, for now, instead thinking ahead to what he would say to Elokar.

The smell of beeswax wafted into his nostrils. The casket was engraved intricately with runes and symbols on its surfaces – four symbols, three for the gods, and one for Elokar. A symbol showed the sun for Onir the God of the skies, father of them all. A chalice representing Mieses, goddess of hope and fertility. A sword for Radnor, brother of Onir and God of war. Finally, on the lid of the casket, a winged eagle for Elokar, banished God of the underworld.

Thornheart apprehensively brushed his forefinger over the casket's surface; working his way over the symbols, lingering over the eagle. Holding his breath, he slowly opened the lid. Within the centre, a dark green rounded stone, the size of an owl egg, rested within a deep red silk protective lining.

Across the smooth glass-like surface of the stone, crimson flecks seemed to shimmer and swim as they caught the reflections from the fire. Thornheart hesitated a moment, then picked out the stone between forefinger and thumb, the surface strangely warm to his touch. He held it within his calloused palm, his thick fingers clasping it tight.

He could feel the heat from the stone as it pulsated like a beating heart, alive in his firm grip. 'Leave me Petari,' he called, almost a whisper. 'That will be all for the evening.'

She left silently, closing the tent awning behind her as she disappeared into the twilight.

Still holding the pulsating stone, and breathing in the smoke from the fire, Thornheart brought it to his mouth, enclosed within his heavy fist and whispered into the gap between his curled forefinger and thumb. 'Great Elokar, I am returned. It's done. Riler is dead along with all his family. None survived.'

The room dimmed to an unnatural blackness. A putrid smell of decay hung in the air. From within the flames a swirling image appeared, a dark shadow with deep red flaming eyes, taking human form, cloaked and hooded. Within Thornheart's mind it spoke, a low voice, like a sigh on the breath of a tiny wind.

Thornheart, all of them you say? Can you be certain?

'Aye. My men left none alive. We butchered them all, women and children, leaving nothing to chance.'

And the stone, you did retrieve the stone from Riler did you not?

Thornheart hesitated, his heart thumped hard against his ribs. 'No…your greatness. It was not there. My men searched but in vain. Riler did not have it. It was gone, or at least not in the village. The man responsible for this failure has paid with his life.'

The heat from the fire that surrounded the image of Elokar intensified, Thornheart could feel the raw power of Elokar's rage burning inside his brain, red-hot, searing pain. His face screwed in agony. It lasted for mere seconds, but felt like it would scorch his mind forever.

Gone? Gone? You fool, it is not gone. I can feel it's presence, out there like a burning beacon. Maybe I was wrong to trust you, to give this task to you? I thought you were a warlord of stature, with ambition to rise above the self-pitying mere mortals of this world. A destructive force to sit by my right hand as we bring the world to my mercy, but yet you are just another disappointment. I thought I could trust you with this task, but here you sit, another weak fool, incapable of carrying out a simple order. You have failed me before Thornheart; you will not fail me again.

'I swear to you. The stone was not there, my men searched. He must have hidden it somewhere, with someone. You can still rely upon me, Great Elokar. I called upon you this evening to inform you of my plans. There is one Riler trusted more than all others, his lieutenant, a man named Arthek Mulliner. I will send men at out at dawn and seek him out. I will get the truth from him…one way or another.'

The stone throbbed harder in his palm, the heat almost unbearable, scalding his skin, yet Thornheart gripped it harder still, waiting for his fate. Moments passed before Elokar responded.

Very well Thornheart, however, fail me again and I will take your soul to the darkest depths of the underworld and gorge forever on your torturous anguish. Bring me the Stone of Radnor. We must unite the four God stones so I can rise once more, then the whole world will tremble in my glory—and you, Thornheart, you will be rewarded with riches far greater than you would ever imagine. Now go before I change my mind.

The swirling figure within the flames disappeared as the eerie darkness evaporated. The pulsating of the stone subsided, the searing heat slowly cooling to a warm glow. Thornheart breathed heavily, heart pounding. Then sighed in relief, placing the stone back into the casket and closing it.

Taking the tankard, Thornheart let out a sigh of relief and clasped it with both hands. He drained the remains in deep gulps, the ale dribbling down his thick beard. He swiped them away with the heel of his hands and stood for a refill.

••◆••

The next morning Thornheart woke in a stupor, his head heavy from the drink. He summoned Nyla to his tent.

'Ah, Nyla. Instruct the men to decamp, we travel light, leave the main base here. Just the soldiers and essentials only. We move as soon as we're ready.'

Nyla stood within the entrance to the tent and raised her chin. 'Where do we move to, lord?'

'Tell the men we will travel deeper inland into Calaria. There'll be plunder and silver to be won. I know they are restless, and I know their concerns. I keep my promises to those loyal to me. I hear there is unrest?'

'Indeed. Landis, if I may?' Nyla hesitated. 'The men do wonder if they are being misled. Most are loyal, but some question where and when they will be rewarded. If they understood the importance of this stone, surely that would sway them? Ease any concerns on payment for their loyalty.'

'No, this information is for you and you only, Nyla. If we can retrieve all the god- stones, then yes, then it will all become clear. What about you, Nyla, you don't doubt me do you?'

Nyla shook her head, her long pony-tail swung down her back, her eyes widened. 'Lord, Landis—no, how could you say such a thing after all I have done. All these years I have stood by you.'

Thornheart nodded. 'Of course, my apologies old friend,' he replied, clapping a hand on her shoulder, then a dark shadow crossed his face. 'Forgive me. I spoke with Elokar last night. I am not myself.'

'Did you tell him? Tell him everything?' Nyla asked with a raised eyebrow, the question quavering in her voice. 'Does he know that we could not find the stone nor the body of Riler's son?'

'The stone, yes—I felt his wrath for sure. But the boy? No, of course not. I doubt I would be here now if I'd told him everything. His fury on not finding the stone was enough. I can still feel that rage in my head. No, that was something I could not bring myself to reveal. Not yet at least.' Thornheart fingered the scar down his left cheek. 'We made an example of Kitto already for the failure. Start asking the men about this Mulliner who served under Riler. Do any know where he may be?'

'I have been asking already, lord. The general consensus is that he could be at Everwood.'

'Good, you know me well. You always have. Even when you were just a mere slave. I saw that cunning in you back then.'

Nyla dipped her head in acknowledgement. 'Thank you, Lord. And you had the sight to see that and give me my freedom.'

'I did, and you have been loyal ever since. And here you stand, my lieutenant. Few rise so far. It was your ruthlessness. Killing those two traitors, and stopping me from stepping into that trap. You have earned my trust, Nyla, and your place by my side. When this is over you will be justly rewarded. Now ready the men, we must leave.'

His eyes followed her out of the doorway, watching her before he readied himself, grabbing his sword and pulling on a fur cloak.

A good leader, he thought, rewarded loyalty, just as much as punishing failure. Just has he had rewarded Nyla, he had punished Kitto. Thornheart turned to his slave girl. 'Petari, start packing my things, I am in no mood for food this morning.'

Later that morning Thornheart's army were gathered, he sat atop his black stallion, an old battle-hardened warhorse. Nyla mounted to his right. 'I want you to take a band of trusted men and travel on ahead,' he ordered her. 'Make your way to Everwood and search for Mulliner. Find him, then return with haste back to me. I will be found at The Wyke.'

CHAPTER 8
THE WYKE

———— •••◆••• ————

'Come on you piece of filth, keep up,' Wilfrec snarled, as Jaydon shuffled behind Brennand's horse. Wilfrec rode up beside him swinging out his right leg, striking him between his shoulder blades.

Jaydon stumbled forward, spitting out a piece of the dried bread he'd been chewing. He tried to jog on again, his legs weary, feet blistered.

'If you don't get a move on, I'll carve out a piece of your behind for my supper.'

'Leave him be, Wilfrec, the lad's doing okay. We'll be rid of him soon enough. Look, we're nearly there.' Brennand pointed ahead where a town emerged from the mist in the valley below.

The past couple of days Jaydon had been dragged along by his captors, his wrists were raw from where the rope had chafed at his skin. He thought he would die – in fact he prayed to the gods he would drop dead and end this suffering.

A blanket of clammy, clogging mist had surrounded them. Jaydon's damp and cold clothing clung to him. His legs barely moved as he shuffled along, head lolling from side to side.

The Wyke slowly came into view, grey shapes forming in the mist, slowly deepening in colour as the band of men approached. A wooden palisade surrounded the town, the thatched and red-tiled roofs emerging ahead of them. Charcoal coloured smoke could be seen rising from their chimneys. The closer they got, the more the reality dawned on Jaydon as he recalled the conversation from Brennand and his men and their talk of selling him for silver.

What fate had been decided for him here? What happens to boys who are sold? Jaydon imagined he would be put to work with some cruel master, the best he hoped would be to a farmer, where he had some experience at least.

Despair punched, only days ago he had been safely at home with his family, fixing a fence with his father, teaching Jenna how to shoot a bow and arrow, laughing at her when she missed the target and then howling in pain when she would kick out at his shins in frustration, chasing him as he ran off in mock fright. Magen barking in delight and running after them. Now all that he loved and knew was dead and destroyed. Downtrodden, his hopes of vengeance vanished, Jaydon felt distraught as they made their way to the town ahead, cursing the useless gods for abandoning him.

'One for luck.' Wilfrec sniggered, as he lashed out at Jaydon, with his boot, causing him to yelp aloud, before riding on.

Jaydon tried to raise his weary head as the men dragged him into the town. Every muscle in his body sapped of strength. Yet look up he did, forcing himself to stand tall, to show no weakness. He forced back tears – he would not let them come.

The Wyke looked so different from his own village. The buildings were taller and made of strong dark wooden beams, with grimy wattle and daub walls. The streets were cobbled or laid with stones and pebbles.

Jaydon thought back to the homes in Hardstone Woods, which all had thatched roofs atop triangular shaped huts with thin wooden walls.

In the winter months they had to pile straw and hay bales outside to keep in the heat. None were as big as the buildings surrounding him in The Wyke.

The noise and smells were familiar though, animals bayed from small pens. The sooty smell of fires, mingling with the aroma of roasting meat – Jaydon's stomach yearned for good meat. His dry mouth salivated with hunger.

From their left Jaydon could hear the shouts of market traders, their calls drowned by barking dogs, and the laughter of children; giggling as they ran through the cobbled and muddy streets, chasing each other.

As they wound their way through the town a crowd started to form and some of the onlookers followed them. They think I am a petty thief, being dragged to the law makers, thought Jaydon. Two young boys ran up to him, laughing, screaming obscenities in his direction. One threw a stone, which struck Jaydon square on the shoulder. He grunted as its sharp edge struck him on the bone, then he cursed himself for showing weakness.

Brennand turned and growled at the young boys, his hand on the hilt of his sword as a warning. 'Get out of here, you turds,' he called.

The boys, no more than seven or eight, turned and sped off in mock screams, then burst into laughter as they hid around the corner of the next street.

Brennand finally called his men to a halt in front of an imposing timber framed building. It looked similar to the others in the town, but longer and taller. Larger than any building Jaydon had ever seen, at least the height of four, maybe five men. To Jaydon it brought memories of the great halls described to him by his father in stories of old.

Brennand dismounted. 'Korban, Gordar, come with me, Morgen, get the horses sheltered and fed, then find us a couple of rooms at *The Black Stag*. Tell Wendell I'll pay for them after I've attended to business here. Wilfrec, you stay with the boy whilst we go and speak to Malin—if the old dog's around.'

The men followed their orders, going their separate ways. The crowd had now dwindled, people going back to their daily business, dispersing back to the dark, filthy streets that spoked away from the hall in front of them. Morgen followed them, leading the horses by their reins down a narrow street to their left.

The twins followed Brennand into the hall, again Jaydon awed at its size compared to the straw roofed shacks from Hardstone Woods. A couple of younger boys, covered in dirt and dressed in rags, ankles bound in chains, were outside chopping firewood—their eyes focussed on their chores, not giving the men a second glance as they strode past them. Exhausted, but grateful for any small respite, Jaydon sagged against the wooden fence that surrounded the hall, his dark greasy hair hanging over his face.

'Stand up you snivelling dog,' Wilfrec loomed over Jaydon, sneering. 'You won't get any soft touches here runt, Malin is a tough old goat, a pathetic worm like you won't last the winter.'

Wifrec stepped forward, his scarred face broke into a foul grin. He unsheathed his hunting knife from his belt, raising it towards Jaydon's face, placing the tip of the blade beneath his right eye. Jaydon's heart quickened. He flinched and tried to move his head away. Grabbing tufts of his hair, Wilfrec yanked Jaydon's head back and pressed the knife harder, breaking the skin. A trickle of Jaydon's blood wound its way down the silver blade.

'I ought to kill you now for what you did to me in the river, boy. No-one makes a fool of me. D'you understand?'

'I'm not scared of you.' Jaydon hissed through gritted teeth, trying to exert a confidence he did not feel, his heart thumping wildly.

'You ought to be, you little mongrel.'

'Wilfrec!' Brennand and the twins were striding purposely from the hall, accompanied by a shorter but stockier man, 'Wilfrec, what in the gods are you doing? Release him, now!' he bellowed.

Wilfrec pulled back the knife and sidled backwards, releasing Jaydon, who sank to the ground.

'What the hell are you playing at? We can get good silver for that boy.'

'Sorry, Bren, he...he tried to escape, I...I was just keeping him from running off, honest I was.' Wilfrec shot Jaydon a warning.

'No, you wasn't,' Jaydon called back defiantly before he could stop himself. 'He threatened to kill me.' He wiped away the blood from his face with the sleeve of his right arm.

'Shut up boy, now stand up and stop snivelling, let Malin have a look at you.' Ignoring Jaydon's claims Brennand turned back to Wilfrec. 'Go and find Morgen at *The Black Stag*, and help sort out the horses.'

Wilfrec sloped off, firing a last look of scorn at Jaydon.

'Right, Malin, this is the lad...we caught him out near the Grasslands. He has a bit of spirit about him, that's for sure. Wanted to fight the five of us, he did.'

Malin had broad shoulders with arms as wide as stout branches of an ancient oak. He sported a shaven head and below a heavy brow, a crooked nose. Grunting he squeezed Jaydon's shoulders and arms with thick, heavy fingers, feeling the muscles beneath his clothing.

Despite the strength of Malin's grip Jaydon stood firm – standing tall, remembering words from his father; *never show fear, Jaydon. Never let your enemies see your inner feelings. Your face is as much a shield as one made of iron and oak.*

Malin grunted again as he roughly spun Jaydon around. Eventually, he spoke, his voice like the bark of an old wolfhound. 'One hundred pieces, he's a bit gangly, nothing a bit a food can't sort out. But, yer right

Brennand, I can see something in him. There's a bit of spirit in those green eyes of his. A fighter fer sure.'

'One hundred? Come on Malin, he's worth one-fifty at least—you bought that weed over there for nearly that price.' Brennand pointed at one of the boys who worked in the yard, chopping wood.

Malin grunted, rubbing his shaven head as he pondered the deal 'Hmm…one-twenty, then.'

'One-thirty and I'll shake on it.'

'Bren, I have mouths to feed. A place like this don't run itself y'know?' Malin paused, in thought. 'But, okay. I think I can make some silver out of the lad…done, One-thirty.' Both men spat into dirty palms and shook firmly.

Jaydon stood dumb-struck. He could not believe he had been bartered like a market trader would do with cattle, as though he was just a worthless piece of meat. His insides became numb but he stood doggedly, unmoved, determined not to show the horror he felt to these men stood before him; just as his father had taught him.

Malin turned back to Jaydon. 'Right, what's yer name, boy?' Jaydon didn't respond quick enough. In a flash Malin punched him in the stomach. Letting out a gasp of air, Jaydon sank to his knees, winded, crying out, the acrid taste of bile rising in his throat.

Malin bent down and growled quietly into his ear, 'I don't like to ask for anything more than once, you understand? Now, again, what's yer name?'

Jaydon swallowed back the bile, before spluttering a response. 'Jaydon, Jaydon R…erm, I… I'm from Hardstone Woods.' He stopped short from revealing his full name. His father's name. It would be known, and for now Jaydon couldn't be certain if it would be known for good or bad?

Shakily, he brought himself to his feet, using as much inner strength as he could muster.

Malin nodded. 'Good, let that be a lesson to you, Jaydon. I don't give a toss where yer from either. Now, yer mine, I own you and yer miserable sodding life. My name is Malin Taler… you call me Master, got that? And I am a right son of a bitch. And you…' He poked a hard, stiff finger into Jaydon's chest. '…you will be trained for fighting in the arena. You will feel pain, you will wish you were dead, but you will fight and you will make me silver and if yer any good you may even survive long enough to win yer freedom. Do you understand?'

Jaydon nodded. 'Yes.'

Malin struck him once more hard across his face, Jaydon staggered back a step or two, his head rocked sideways, as his lower lip popped.

'Yes, what?' Malin barked.

'Yes, Master.' Jaydon responded, spitting blood onto the grass beneath his feet.

'Right…Ridley. Ridley, get yer lazy backside over here,' Malin shouted toward the boys in the yard, one dropped his axe and shuffled over, the shackles at his feet jangling.

'Yes, Master?' he said, still staring down at his feet.

'Take this worthless rodent to the cells. Make sure he gets a straw mattress. And get him cleaned up too.' Then turning back to Jaydon, he said, 'Supper is at sun-down. Rest tonight, but tomorrow you'll join the others in the training yard. We can see what you're made of then. Ridley here will ensure you know what's what and show you the ropes.'

Jaydon hesitated. 'What about my sword, Master?' he asked, glancing sideways at Brennand, who had *Devil's Bane* slung over his back, wrapped in cloth, the glassy red stone sticking out the top.

Malin gawked back at him. 'What? Are you taking the urine out of me, son?'

'No, Master. I…I just want my sword…you said I had to fight.'

Malin turned to Brennand, 'Do you have the boy's sword?'

'It's mine now, Malin, you only bought the boy.'

'You never said he came with a sword, show it to me, I may make you a fair offer for it. I can always do with good weapons. A good sword can have the edge when the lads fight in the arena.'

Brennand arced his eyes upward and unslung *Devil's Bane*, rolling it out on the ground in front of them all, a broad sword, a warrior's weapon. The hilt, tightly bound in worn leather, with a blade forged of good steel, strong and weighted for balance. The cross-guard covered with intricate swirling patterns and the blade itself engraved with runes and symbols of real craftsmanship. The glassy red stone on the pommel gleamed brightly despite the overcast day. No ordinary blacksmith had created this weapon, the intricate patterns were the work of an artist. Jaydon's heart lurched with desire and longing.

'That's a fine blade. And the boy had it?' Malin asked, scratching the bristles on his head. 'I'll give you fifty pieces for the sword,' he said greedily.

'Seventy.'

'Seventy? You'll see me left destitute, Bren, if you keep bartering with me like this. Seventy and that's it.' Again, the two men shook on the deal.

Jaydon sighed with relief. He may not have *Devil's Bane* in his hands yet. But he vowed he would soon. Once he found a way to escape from here. For now, he was just pleased that the sword would remain close by. He made a further promise to himself, other names to add to Thorn-heart on his list, to avenge all his captors, Brennand, Malin, but especially Wilfrec. He would see *Devil's Bane* deep in that foul animal's guts one day.

Malin cut away the bonds tied around Jaydon's wrists and waved Ridley away, who walked around the back of the hall. Jaydon followed, trying to stand tall, and walk proud despite the weariness of his body and the blisters on his feet.

•••◆•••

The cells were located in an out-house at the back of the grounds. The walls, though, were stronger, built of flint stone beneath a red-tiled roof. A group of boys aged between seven to around twelve were working within the grounds – some were mending broken fencing, others raked autumn leaves into piles. But all were bound at the ankles with rusty chains. Jaydon had never seen boys chained before, slaves surely? Why else would they be shackled like that? And he would be one too.

A couple of adults stood guard over them, barking out orders, swords at their hips, one hand always resting on their hilts as they strode around.

It took a moment for Jaydon to adjust to the dimness in the cell block that Ridley guided him to. He dragged in a weary breath and inhaled the damp aroma of dung and piss from the stale air within. His eyes watered from the sting of the stench of the place.

Jaydon followed Ridley down a narrow corridor and to the last cell on the left. The room was bare, with the exception of three straw mattresses that lay on the floor and a dirty wooden pail that sat in one corner. Ridley took a small flint from his pocket, striking it until the sparks lit the candle, then placed it in the middle of the floor, giving some light to the dark room.

'You take the one over there,' Ridley poked a finger toward one mattress in the far corner. 'The others will be in soon, we're allowed some rest before supper. Rodrick will probably be here before then, with your chains.'

Ridley hesitated, his fingers nervously weaving through his grubby, shoulder length blond hair. He regarded Jaydon nervously. Jaydon considered him, he looked a similar age to Jenna – nine, maybe ten. How did such a young boy end up in a place like this?

Lowering his voice to a whisper, Ridley said, 'That mattress over there—' He nodded his head to the opposite corner. '—that belongs to Zarin, just be careful. He don't take too kindly to new kids. He's the Master's favourite. Won him plenty of gold and silver in the ring. No one has ever beat him. He's a bully, and big, bigger even than you.' With that Ridley turned and shuffled off, chains clinking, leaving Jaydon alone in the shadowy room.

Jaydon collapsed onto the mattress. The candlelight flickered as his movement disturbed the air, shadows danced over the stone walls. He brought his knees up into his chest, hugging them tightly, burying his head into his folded arms. He resolved to push out any despair, he needed to be strong, not show any weakness. His grief would be a burden that he could no longer carry. He needed to grow into a man and show the doggedness his father had always taught him. *Be strong, be brave and above all be ever mindful.*

Jaydon had to be ready for any opportunity to escape. He thought back, remembering words of advice his father always gave: *If shadows are all you see in front of you, my son, turn around to face the light.* Jaydon pictured his father's face, the familiar weathered features, greying beard and the tone of his voice, when he was abruptly yanked out of his memory.

A sniggering.

A dark shape stood in the doorway of the cell, it's face remained in shadow.

Stepping forward into the candlelight a tall broad-shouldered boy, the dim flames slowly revealing his features. A tough face, about sixteen years old and a mop of thick black hair sat atop his head, the wispy beginnings of a beard covering his chin.

'So, you're the new meat then?' he sneered at Jaydon, his lips hardly moving, his voice though, strangely high pitched. 'Well, gonna be fun teaching you a lesson on the training ground tomorrow. Stand up.'

Jaydon took in the taller boy before him, his skin the colour of an almond shell, and his narrowed pupils like cold pewter. Jaydon sized him up, then sighed inwardly, knowing this must be Zarin, the boy who Ridley had warned him about.

'I said stand up,' Zarin demanded, the pitch of his voice rising higher still. He took a step towards Jaydon, fists clasped tightly by his sides.

Slowly Jaydon rose warily, never once removing his gaze from the bigger boy. With sudden speed that belied his stature, Zarin flew forward, grabbing Jaydon around his throat and squeezed, pinning him against the cell wall.

Using all his weight and strength he leaned into Jaydon, who couldn't move, gasping for air as Zarin tightened his grip on Jaydon's throat. Bubbles of spittle foamed at Jaydon's lips.

Zarin's face contorted. 'If you want to get on here, then you better start listening. The Master may not let me kill you, but I can cause you pain. I will hurt you. I run the cells for The Master. What I say, you do. Understand?'

Jaydon's could hardly breathe, his head felt as though it would explode as the flow of blood remained trapped between Zarin's tight grip. Specks of light danced in front him, like tiny stars, his vision blurred and his head pounded. The weariness of the last few days taking its toll. He felt weak, too weak to push back. Zarin tightened his grip further, sneering back into Jaydon's face. Summoning all the inner strength he could he stared defiantly back. Zarin's face turned to fury, he pulled back his free arm, hand balled into a tight fist. But before he got any further another voice boomed out from the cell.

'ZARIN. ZARIN. STOP. NOW. RELEASE HIM AT ONCE!' Jaydon felt the grip on his throat loosen, then Zarin finally released him.

Sliding down the wall, falling onto his mattress, gasping for air, the world around him swaying in and out of focus.

The voice spoke again, 'The Master wants you, Zarin. Now get over to the hall.'

He heard Zarin shuffle off. Still gasping for air, Jaydon slowly dragged himself upright. One of Malin's guards, loomed above him. Within his hands he held a pair of rusty chains. In the doorway, behind him, stood Ridley.

'Right, boy, you gotta wear these. Sit still, feet apart.' The man clamped the cold, heavy chains around his ankles, checking their tightness, but not too tight. Then hammered in the pin. Grunting with satisfaction that they were secure, then stood.

Lifting Jaydon's chin, he peered down at him. 'Listen, boy, don't get on the wrong side of Zarin. He rules these cells. The Master will have you fight him tomorrow to see what you're made of. Don't give him any reason to make it worse than it need be. Okay?' The jailer's face shifted, kindlier. 'My name's Rodrick, any questions then Ridley can find me. But do not think me a friend. I'll kick yer backside as good as anyone else. No liberties.'

With that he turned and left. Ridley remained in the doorway, silent.

••◆••

Supper was what passed for stew but tasted like dirty water with scraps of carrot, turnip and whatever sinews of meat were left over from what the guards and jailers ate. Jaydon would not have fed his pigs food like this.

In all, sixteen boys sat around a table in a room at the end of the kitchens. Jaydon sat next to Ridley, who rarely spoke, keeping himself to himself. Jaydon slurped on his stew, wolfing it down with hard bread, his throat still tender from Zarin's attack. Rodrick stood in the corner watching over them, growling at anyone who spoke too loudly. Zarin sat at the table head, glaring silently at Jaydon as he sipped his stew.

They were served by a girl with hair as black as night that covered most of her face, hiding her features beneath. She leant over Jaydon to pour water into his cup, as she did her hand brushed his arm. The girl gave a sudden intake of breath and hesitated for a mere moment, missing the cup, spilling water across the table.

'Stupid girl,' growled Rodrick. 'Get a rag and mop it up. Go on Raven, off with yer.'

She scurried away into the kitchens, but she left Jaydon with a strange feeling of familiarity. He dismissed it quickly, turning his thoughts back to Zarin, another enemy, and tomorrow he will have to fight him on the training grounds.

CHAPTER 9

BREAKING BONES

S leep did not come easy for Jaydon that night, despite his exhaustion he lay awake anticipating an attack from Zarin, expecting to be jumped on, punched and kicked at any moment. He would be too weak to fight back for sure. He kept a watchful eye throughout the night, yet Zarin snored loudly on his straw mattress, tossing and turning – and each time Zarin moved Jaydon expected the attack to come. But to his relief it never did. Eventually, Jaydon dozed before they were woken by the clanging of copper pots and shouts from down the cells corridors to get their lazy backsides out of bed.

Following a breakfast of watery porridge, rye bread and hard cheese, Rodrick gathered all the boys required for the training yard. Bound at their ankles, they were marched in line through a battered wooden gate and into a rectangular yard. Grit and sand scattered the ground within the yard, a ten-foot-high wooden palisade surrounded all four sides.

Malin waited in the centre of the yard for the boys. Rodrick brought them to a halt, releasing each one in turn from their chains, and had them line up in two rows, facing each other either side of Malin.

'Right, you stinking mongrels,' Malin bellowed. 'In three days we have some special guests, the Lord of West Scar will be here. He's expecting some entertainment, he pays well enough for it. A rich lord like him comes with an entourage, which means more silver to be wagered. Four of you will be put to fight against the lord's own fighters. I want you ready, all of you. But first—' Malin shot a sideways glance in Jaydon's direction. '—we have some new blood to break in.'

A sense of inevitability overcame Jaydon, he resigned himself that he would have to fight Zarin, training yard or not. He recalled the coaching and exercises he used to go through at the lake with his father, hours and hours of practice, the repetitive drills, the endless aching and pain he went through.

At the time Jaydon could never understand why a farmer's boy would need to be trained to fight given the old wars had ended and peace had reigned throughout the lands of Calaria and the Thulian Isles. *The wars are never over, son,* his father would say. *One day you may need to protect those that you love, and I would be a failure of a father if I had not prepared you.*

Jaydon studied Zarin's face. It contorted into a scowl, feral. His dark eyebrows knitted together as he jigged up and down as though full of nervous energy. Jaydon wondered why Zarin had so much hate? What was his story to be here in this yard?

'Rodrick, hand them a training sword and a shield each,' Malin said, nodding toward a rack of swords to the side of the yard. 'Zarin, Jaydon, step forward. The rest of you spread out, form a wider circle.'

As the rest of the boys shuffled into position, Rodrick passed Jaydon and Zarin a battered training sword each. Heavy steel, blunted edges, rounded points, but dangerous enough to bruise limbs and break bones. Jaydon felt the weight of the weapon in his hands, gauging its balance as he held it firm, swinging it around in a circle.

Both were then given oak shields with steel rims heavily dented from years of abuse. The face of Jaydon's shield emblazoned with a faded dog in flaky black paint.

Jaydon thrust his left arm through the shield's hoops, it felt loose on his forearm, not ideal, but he could grip a strap with his hand. It would have to do. They wore no armour, just sleeveless leather jerkins for protection.

Hush descended into the yard, only the distant sound of barking dogs from within The Wyke could be heard. The drab skies above pressed down like a heavy blanket. Jaydon's heart pounded, this was not training with his father, but a real fight, time to put what he learnt into practice, and hope all those hours would pay off.

He focused his attention onto Zarin, keeping his knees slightly bent, poised and balanced as he had been taught. Zarin shuffled to his left, a spiteful grin smeared across his face. Lifting his sword arm he rapped the weapon against his shield's rim, *clank, clank, clank*.

Jaydon ignored him, focussed, breathing slowly through his nose. *Clank, clank*, Zarin continued, stepping slowly to his left once more.

'Come on you turd. Are you scared? That sword too big for you? Maybe we should give you a stick instead?' Zarin laughed at his own joke. Jaydon ignored the taunts, knowing Zarin wanted to goad him into making the first move. Patience was needed. Zarin had strength and no doubt had greater experience as a fighter. Jaydon knew he would need to use guile and wait for the right moment.

Zarin side-stepped again, Jaydon mirrored him, watching. *Clank, clank, clank*. Again, Zarin beat his sword on the steel rim of his shield. Then held both his arms out wide. 'Come on, what are you waiting for? Strike me, attack. Here, I don't even need my shield!' he shouted as he tossed it to one side. 'Surely that gives you the advantage now? Come on turd face, attack me.'

Not rising to the bait Jaydon shook his own shield from his left arm too, flinging it behind him. Zarin let out a loud howl of derision, laughing in disbelief as he turned to face the other boys, who all laughed back.

'You really are as stupid as you look. Right then, let's see what you have.' Zarin sprang forward, both hands gripped around his sword hilt, bringing it down, firm and fast.

Jaydon stepped backward, dropped to one knee and parried the blow with his own sword. Quickly, he rolled to his right, the dusty ground beneath still damp from the morning dew, as Zarin swung again, missing the side of Jaydon's head by inches. Getting to his feet again Jaydon crouched, his sword held firm in both hands and readied himself once more.

The other boys in the yard started shouting *Go on Zarin do 'im in. Break the bastard's leg Zarin.* Again, Zarin broke forwards, swinging left, right, then left again. Jaydon continued to deflect, block and dodge each swipe. Steel on steel rang out as Zarin attacked once more, forcing Jaydon backwards. He parried each one, blow after blow, sending vibrations down his arm from the force of each one of them. Zarin grunted in surprise at Jaydon's continued speed and resolve, but he continued to force Jaydon on the backfoot.

Yet again Jaydon parried as he stepped backward, but instead of the grit and sand, Jaydon's heel caught the edge of his discarded shield. The healing blisters on his feet chaffed. He yelped aloud, then stumbled, arms flailing, trying to keep his balance. The watching boys laughed and urged Zarin on, who quickly seized the opportunity and drove low with another swing of his weapon.

Instinctively Jaydon defended the blow before parrying another upper thrust, regaining his composure as both swords locked, wedged at the cross guards, bringing the two fighters face to face. Jaydon could smell Zarin's breath, snot streamed from his nose like wax dripping down a candle. Zarin's face grimaced as he tried to use the advantage of his weight to force Jaydon backwards.

The other boys were chanting now. '*Zarin, Zarin, Zarin.*' But still Jaydon stayed strong, using every fibre of his body to hold the larger boy. Then from somewhere deep in his gut he summoned a last reservoir of strength and started to push back. Slowly at first, but then he got purchase on the ground as his feet dug into the grit, and stepped forward. Zarin's eyes widened in disbelief.

'Is that all you've got?' Jaydon hissed through gritted teeth. 'I thought you were supposed to be the champion?'

A mere moment of uncertainty crossed Zarin's face, but Jaydon saw it, using it to his advantage. Like a shot he dropped again onto one knee, at the same time twisting his arms, the locked swords loosened, as Jaydon thrust his head forwards hard and low into Zarin's stomach.

Letting out a loud grunt, Zarin's grip slackened on his weapon. Grabbing the chance, Jaydon hooked his other leg across the back of Zarin's knees, wrestling him down and onto the ground. Tiny clouds of grit puffed outwards from the impact as Zarin lay winded.

Zarin's sword fell and bounced out of reach. In the same instance, Jaydon swiftly arced his own sword around. Instinctively, Zarin raised an arm to protect himself from the blow, but without any weapon to block it his forearm took the full impact. A dull crack could be heard as bones broke.

Dragging in heavy breaths, his chest heaving and eyes stinging with sweat Jaydon stood over Zarin, who cried with pain, clasping his deformed arm with the hand of his other. Jaydon placed his blunted sword point to Zarin's throat. He blinked, and took a moment to wipe the sweat from his eyes with the sleeve of his undershirt and started to push the blade harder, depressing Zarin's skin. Jaydon felt no emotion, adrenalin rushed through him, but his mind remained clear as the yard descended into silence; the other boys watched on in shock at the fight's outcome. Should he push harder? End this for good?

'STOP THERE. STOP RIGHT NOW.' A bellowing, red-faced Malin marched over and grabbed Jaydon by the scruff of his neck.

Hauling him backwards he took the sword swiftly from his grip with the other. 'That's enough, boy. Now stand over there. Rodrick, keep him to one side.'

Rodrick took Jaydon's arm and led him away from the rest of the boys. The adrenalin still rushed through his veins as he panted heavily through his open mouth. He glanced back at Malin as he dragged Zarin to his feet, still groaning in agony clutching his broken arm to his chest, now turning a deep blue from where Jaydon's sword struck.

'Stop your whining, boy,' Malin growled as he cuffed Zarin around the head. He didn't shout, but snarled, loudly enough for them all to hear. 'You just got bested by that mongrel. I was to make good silver from you when the Lord of West Scar gets here. You may have cost me and I won't have that. D'you hear? I won't have that.'

He turned to Jaydon and Rodrick. 'Boy, you stay there. Rodrick. Take this worthless turd and have Carla patch up that arm. I don't want to see him again this week. Move him into another cell. I want him on dung pit and cleaning duties until that arm of his is better. Ask Lewen to stop what he's doing and come in here to ensure the rest of these miserable sods carry on their training.' Then pointing at Jaydon, he said, 'You, boy, you'll be coming with me.'

•••◆•••

Jaydon was taken into a gloomy room, the only light from a couple of candles that cast flickering shadows on the walls. Malin sat behind an oak table that had seen better days, slicing and eating an apple with a knife. He leant back in his chair, feet stretched onto the table top. Rodrick had returned and stood behind Jaydon, whose ankles were shackled once more in the rusty chains.

'So, what is it about you, boy? Where did you learn to fight like that?'

'What do you mean, Master? I, erm, I don't know. It just came to me.'

'By the gods, I am not having that. You've been trained. Where did you say you were from?'

Jaydon hesitated before answering, 'Hardstone Woods, Master. A small farming village south of the Moray Hills. We, erm, we had a traveller who used to help with the harvest. He fought in the old wars. He used to teach me and some of the boys to fight.' Jaydon lied—still unsure if revealing the truth of his father would be a good or bad thing. Better to keep himself unknown.

'Hmm, he must have been some teacher, no one has ever beaten Zarin before. Ever!' Malin continued, watching Jaydon with suspicion as he sliced off another piece of apple and put it into his mouth. 'That sword that I bought from Brennand. Where did you get it? It's a bloody fine sword. Not from some farmer, that's for sure.'

'Stole it, Master. It belonged to the traveller. That's why I was running away you see. That's when Brennand and his group caught me.'

Malin waved the knife blade towards Jaydon. 'I don't trust you, boy. But you can fight, and fight well. You'll be taking Zarin's place in the arena in a few days. Win silver for me and I won't care where you're from, or how you got that sword. D'you understand?'

Jaydon nodded. 'Yes, Master.'

'Good, ah, Raven. Fetch me some ale,' Malin called towards the open doorway.

The same dark-haired servant girl, who had served the boys the night before at supper, entered the room. She carried a horn of ale and placed it on the table in front of Malin. Slowly she moved her gaze upwards towards Jaydon. Her jet-black hair hung loosely around pale features, but her eyes were as dark as two pieces of coal.

Jaydon felt the hairs on his arms and the back of his neck stiffen, prickling. An unnerving sensation as though he already knew her, a memory from where he did not know. He had only ever spent his life in his village, and she certainly did not come from there. Raven held his gaze for a moment, but to Jaydon it felt like minutes, hours even.

'Right, get on, girl. On with your duties,' Malin broke the silence.

'Yes, Master,' she replied, her husky voice full of confidence. A voice that remained in Jaydon's mind as she glided out of the room, almost as though she floated on a cloud.

'Right, be off with you, too, boy. Rodrick, see that he eats well the next couple of days. I want him strong. The Lord of West Scar is bringing a couple of his own fighting boys. I owe him after the last meeting we had.'

Rodrick, tugged on Jaydon's arm, leading him out of the room, whose thoughts remained with the dark-haired, black-eyed Raven.

CHAPTER 10

THE TRAINING YARD

———————•··•◆•··•———————

'Come on you miserable whelps. Speed it up a little,' Rodrick bellowed. They were jogging around the outer edges of the training yard. Jaydon led the group, the healing blisters on his feet still sore, yet he wasn't going to let that hamper him as he pushed himself onwards, picking up the speed despite the burning in his lungs. Behind him were the other boys, six in all, training for the fights in the arena.

All they had done since arriving in the yard after breakfast was run in circles, round and round the edges of the yard.

'Two more circuits,' Rodrick yelled from where he stood in the centre. 'Best effort now, sprint finish.'

Jaydon lengthened his stride, behind him he could hear the heavy panting of one of the other boys, he could feel his presence as he started to catch him. Jaydon pushed himself harder. Reminding him of the times he and Ober used to race each other. He always fought to beat Ober then, he wasn't letting this stranger beat him now either. He forced himself to go faster, even though it felt as though his chest would explode.

One more lap was all he needed. He glanced over his shoulder, the boy at his heels, the others now straggling behind the two of them. Jaydon pushed and pushed, not relenting. The finishing line now in sight. Jaydon dug deeper one last time to fend off a final attack from the other as he crossed it ahead of him, screaming with the exertion.

Jaydon collapsed into a heap on the damp ground, wheezing heavily, but thankful he had held on. The other boy flopped next to him, gasping for air. Jaydon rolled onto his back, staring up at the overcast sky. The fog still clung to the day. though it had lifted from the yard and the blanket of drizzle had ceased, for now. He burst into laughter. He turned his head to see his competitor, who now lay beside him. A red-headed boy, of similar age to Jaydon, with grit and sand stuck to his sweaty face. The boy glanced back at Jaydon, a look of bemusement on his face, then he too erupted.

'Alright you two. You're not here for fun. On yer feet,' Rodrick hollered.

Gradually, they both stood. Jaydon bent over, hands on his knees, catching his breath a little before bringing himself to his full height. The other boy stuck out a hand. Jaydon observed him. He stood a head above Jaydon, yet, where Jaydon had wide shoulders, the boy's frame had a slender, leaner frame.

'My name's Corren,' said the red-head as Jaydon grasped his hand and shook it.

Panting still, Jaydon replied. 'Jaydon. Good race.'

'I'll have you next time.'

'You can try.'

Both boys laughed again.

'Alright, alright, you two. Enough,' Rodrick demanded. 'Okay, all of you. Get yer'selves some water. You've warmed up enough now. Then the hard graft starts. There's a couple of buckets against the wall. Don't take all day about it either.'

The boys made their way to the corner of the yard. Jaydon welcomed the cool water, drinking straight from the ladle, dribbling streams of it down his chin. He didn't care though as it refreshed him.

'So, you're the new boy?' Corren asked. 'I saw you beat Zarin. Never seen anyone do that before. You'd better watch your back though. He'll want his revenge.'

Jaydon shrugged. 'I could be dead in a couple of days. Not sure he can do much before that.'

A flash of apprehension crossed Corren's eyes, then he curled the corner of his mouth. 'True. We could all be. How did you wind up here?'

Jaydon paused before answering, again wary on revealing his true identity. 'I was kidnapped by bandits in the grasslands. They sold me to Malin. If I ever get out of this place I will kill them. What about you?'

'I don't blame you…my parents died, my grandmother was too sick to look after me. The witch sold me to Malin, said I had to earn my keep. Make my own way in the world. She died a week later, so I'm stuck here. But I can swing a sword well enough I s'pose. Malin says if I earn him good silver then he'll free me. Somehow, I doubt it, I've been here about eight months now. But what choice do I have?'

'That's shit. Sorry, Corren…my parents are gone too.'

They stood in silence for a few moments, a small bond forming between them.

'You seem alright, Jaydon. I can help with Zarin too if you like? Most kids are too scared of him. He don't scare me much, so if he starts causing any trouble, we can both stand up to him.'

'What's his problem, anyway?' Jaydon asked, wiping the water from his chin.

'Malin gives him a hard time, believe it or not. I guess he takes it out on the rest of us. I think Malin does it to ensure he has someone to keep us all in check when he or the guards aren't around. Most of the kids are younger, like Gurnar over there,' Corren pointed to a smaller boy with a mop of dirty blond hair. 'Zarin's always having a go at him. Tell you what though, the little runt is quick with the sword. He's a real fireball when he gets going. Ain't that right, Gurnar?'

'Faster than you, Corren.' The group of small boys responded with more laughter. The merriment in the group surprised Jaydon, despite what they were here for, they could find amusement with each other. Jaydon began to understand the comradeship his father had always spoke of.

'Alright, enough now. Come on, grab yourselves a sword and shield each,' Rodrick broke up the chatter. 'I want you in three pairs. Jaydon, Corren. You two are the best matched. You form one pair. The rest of you match up too.'

Rodrick had them practising their drills, using the training swords and battered shields. For the next hour he pushed them hard. Taking them through attack moves, defensive stances. What to look out for with their opponents. Then he would stop them and make them do the moves again and again. Attack. Defence. Parry. Move. Repeat.

Jaydon had gone through many training sessions like this with his father. Corren could never outwit him as they sparred. Throughout the training Jaydon could feel Rodrick gauging him with cold eyes. But he would keep barking out orders, calling words of encouragement to the boys.

'Right, lads. Time for a breather,' Rodrick shouted out as the boys started to tire. 'Lunch will be here soon. Rest your muscles, go and sit on the benches until it arrives.'

Almost sighing in unison, the boys trudged back to the benches. Dragging weary bodies for a hard-earned break.

'Not you, Jaydon,'

What now? Jaydon thought, rolling his eyes skywards. He felt drained, and at the mention of food his stomach complained, growling with hunger.

Rodrick took his arm, and led him further away from the others, ensuring they were out of ear-shot. 'You're good. I've been training lads to fight for many years. It comes natural to you, Jaydon. I know what you told Malin yesterday. But where did you really learn?'

Jaydon pondered a moment, tight lipped. 'As I said, it was a passing traveller who used to help on the farm. He used to teach me in secret. My parents didn't know. He took a shine to me.'

'Really? You said he fought in the old wars. Calarian?'

'Erm…yes. He fought for Calaria.'

Rodrick chewed his lower lip, studying Jaydon's face. His eyes scanning him for the truth in his words. 'And the name of this traveller?' He asked.

'Ober,' Jaydon replied, the name of his old friend the first to come from his lips.

'Ober, eh? I fought with the Calarians too, boy. Not sure I remember an Ober. Did he have a family name?'

Jaydon had to think quickly, no easy task when he felt so emotional and physically weary. 'Don't know. He never told me. I only knew him as Ober.' He had to change tact. Get away from this questioning, and quickly. 'Where did you fight, Rodrick? Were you at Winter's Harbour? I heard it was a great battle, Ober told me that. He fought there apparently.'

Rodrick sniffed, then his face shifted into a slight smirk. 'No. I wasn't there. Not at Winter's Harbour. I stayed in the north east in the main. Up by West Scar.'

Behind them the gate to the arena crashed open. Both of them turned their heads at the sound. two of the slave girls, from the kitchens, entered, pushing a barrow. 'Very well then, Jaydon. Off you go. Looks like lunch is here. I'll be keeping an eye on you though.'

•••◆•••

That afternoon the boys went through more sparring drills; learning to defend with a shield and without one, when to spot an opening to attack, when to wait, how to move, how to lure an opponent in. Honing their skills and movements. The day began to darken, the fog, that had hung around in clumps earlier, had disappeared but the sky remained overcast and the air cool, causing steam to rise from their sweaty bodies.

Finally, Rodrick called them to halt. 'Right, lads. Time to pack it in for the day. Some good work out there. Keep that up tomorrow and you'll be ready. Remember, it ain't just about being able to wield a sword. It's about training your muscles, not just in your arms, but your brain too. It's your lives at stake in the arena. All I teach you now is to give you the best chance to win. To survive. To live. D'you all understand?'

Tired heads bobbed up and down, a few mumbled a response. Rodrick seemed satisfied enough.

'Okay, put your swords back in the racks. Shields in a pile then sit and wait on the benches whilst I fit your chains again.'

The boys followed his instructions, wearily making their way to where he indicated before slumping onto the rough wooden benches. Heads drooped with fatigue. Jaydon sat on the far-end, Corren next to him. His arms ached, he would have bruises the colour of blueberries tomorrow.

Jaydon gazed at the pile of shields. The flaking emblems on their faces barely legible. One particularly grabbed his attention. It had the clearest emblem of them all, the shield Corren had been using was painted all black, and in the centre what looked like a white cup or a goblet.

Jaydon nudged Corren with his shoulder, then with a flick of his chin toward the shields he asked. 'What are the paintings on the shields, Corren. That one you had, the black one. What is it?'

Corren looked up. 'It's a chalice. For Mieses. You must know that, Jaydon?'

Jaydon tried to remember back to what little schooling he had back at home. His mother would teach them words, his father, aside from swordcraft, would teach him the ways of the farm. When crops should be sown. How to milk the goats. Knowing when the sow had gone into labour and what to do. Odric, the village elder told them about the gods. Jaydon knew who they were: Onir, Radnor, Mieses and Elokar. He knew Elokar had been banished by Onir for plotting to overthrow them all. But that's all he knew. His father never mentioned the gods, not much. They never prayed to them. He knew some people in the village did, especially to Mieses, as the goddess of fertility. Believing that prayer would help with the growing of the crops.

He wiped a bead of sweat away from his forehead then absentmindedly cleaned his hand on his trousers. 'I don't think I was ever taught that. Not sure my father was that religious to be honest.'

Corren considered him for a moment before replying. 'Well, the symbol for Mieses is a chalice. That shield would once have belonged to someone who followed or worshipped her. All the gods have symbols. Onir's is the sun, Radnor's a sword, and Elokar an eagle. Other shields have different symbols too. I think the one for the soldiers who fought from The Wyke had a black boar?'

'I understand,' Jaydon thought a little. 'It's funny. My father was a soldier once. He never told me any of this. Yet he had a shield, with a red sword on the face.'

Corren nodded his head in recognition. 'Maybe men don't like to be reminded of war,' he said. 'You know Jaydon. I shouldn't admit this. But I am scared you know. For the arena. I've never fought for real before, have you?'

Jaydon glanced at his new friend. 'Only training, with an old soldier. You'll be okay, Corren. You can fight well enough.'

Both boys remained in silence until Rodrick arrived with the chains.

CHAPTER II
THE BLACK STAG

———•··•◆•··•———

The *Black Stag* was bustling with noise, the inn dark and smoky. A fire from the central hearth provided the main light and heat against the cold and damp evening. Groups of men sat around tables, drinking ale, playing dice; piles of copper and silver coins lay on table tops. Others leaned into each other, sharing jokes, tales or bragging about their days trading. Brennand, Morgen and the twins sat in a corner, tankards half-empty.

'What's taking Wilfrec so long?' Morgen asked, taking a swig from his ale. 'He only went to see Jowan to see if any news had arrived from home.'

Brennand sighed. 'You worry too much Morgen. You know old Jowan, never one to say something in a few words, not when he can say it in a hundred. Besides I could do with some time without Wilfrec, I'm starting to question my judgement, allowing him with us. He's becoming more and more of a burden, too unpredictable.'

Korban and Gordar nodded their blond heads in unison. 'I trust him less each day Bren, we should ditch him,' Gordar replied.

'I agree, send him on an errand then let's leave him behind,' Korban added, 'He's trouble, that one. I have said it before and I will say it again. Trouble.'

'I know, but he has his uses, we need that wiliness sometimes, lads. I know how to handle the likes of him. You needn't worry.'

'He was muttering earlier, Bren, when he thought no-one was listening. Cursing and swearing about that wretch we sold to Malin. Calling you all the names under the sun too, y'know. Saying you had no respect for him.' Morgen added.

'See, Bren. He's bad news. I feel it. Why did we bring him with us? You saw him outside Malin's. Wanting to kill that boy. Could have cost us good silver. He's a liability.'

Brennand played with the twine in his beard and thought. He had only hired Wilfrec as a favour to an old friend. Wilfrec had gotten himself into a spot of trouble and needed to get away from Ironbrook for a while. He had always had faith in his own instincts and he too had had a bad feeling about Wilfrec. It wasn't like him to go against what he felt, and he certainly didn't trust him much either. Morgen and the twins had been with him many a year, and if they felt the same he must listen. He would mull it overnight.

'I hear you, lads. Let me chew it over a for a while. I can pay him off if need be.'

A group of men, sitting close to the hearth, broke into laughter. From the heavy leather jerkins they wore, some even wearing mail, they had the look of warriors, each man armed; short swords, seaxes and knives hung at their belts. Brennand had clocked them when they arrived earlier that evening, men to be wary of, especially when ale flowed freely.

He discreetly nodded in their direction, and quietly asked his men. 'You see any of those here before? I smell trouble.'

Morgen turned his head slowly, taking a sip from his tankard as he glanced over his shoulder. 'No, Bren, they ain't from round these parts. The one on the left concerns me. The markings on his left wrist, seems to be a tattoo of a hawk, or an eagle. I am sure that's a mark from the Mirenian tribes.'

Brennand nodded. 'You're right, but what are Mirenians doing here in The Wyke? We would be well advised to stay clear of them tonight, lads. I want no trouble. We head out first thing in the morning, once we have the news from Jowan.'

A cold blast of damp air washed into the room as the door to the tavern swung open, causing the men within to turn in their seats. A tall, broad figure appeared in the doorway. The glow from the fire outlined an eagle tattoo on his forehead and a scar running down the left side of his face. Landis Thornheart. Brennand's heart skipped a beat as he saw who stood behind him—Wifrec.

Whispering into Thornheart's ear Wilfrec scanned the room, before pointing in the direction of Brennand and the others. Thornheart scrutinised them before striding toward their table. Wilfrec followed, a smirk curled beneath his scarred nose.

Brennand placed his tankard on the table, and took in the huge man now standing before him. It was Wilfrec who spoke first. 'Lord Thornheart, this is Brennand. He can give you more information on the boy, I'm sure. Bren, this is Landis Thornheart, he's been asking about that wretch we found in the grasslands.'

'And how would he know we found a boy, Wilfrec?' Brennand asked. Then turning his attention to Thornheart. 'I know who you are. Please, take a seat,' he waved an arm at an empty chair. Then turning to his men, he added, 'Lads, can I ask that you leave Lord Thornheart and I to talk? Alone.'

Inwardly Brennand despised calling him 'Lord', Thornheart wasn't a lord of anything or anywhere, just a self-given title to justify his own importance. In reality, he was a glorified mercenary, as were all Mirenians, selling themselves to the highest bidders. During the old wars the King of Vorania had paid Thornheart to dispel the Calarians, either killing them or forcing them back into the grasslands, however he lost the battle at Winter's Harbour. But here he stood, back in central Calaria, with an army of men. No doubt trouble followed and Brennand had his guard up.

Wilfrec spat onto the straw laden floor. 'Bren, we…'

'Quiet Wilfrec,' Brennand interrupted harshly. 'I will catch up with you on the news I hope you brought from Jowan soon enough. But for now, leave us be.'

Wilfrec stared back at Brennand with daggers in his eyes, then took a breath, as though he would speak again. However, Morgen grabbed the sleeve of his tunic and ushered him out of the way. The others following on behind.

Brennand gestured again towards one of the vacated chairs and Thornheart unbelted his fur coat and joined him at the table. Brennand ordered more ale from Wendell the inn keeper and poured Thornheart a frothing tankard, shunting it across the table towards him. Thornheart raised it to his lips, tipping his acknowledgement to Brennand before taking a gulp.

'I see my reputation precedes me,' he said, 'Your man, Wilfrec, tells me you found a boy walking the grasslands?'

'Everyone round here knows of Landis Thornheart and who you are. What brings you to these parts? Are those Mirenians your men?'

Landis shrugged. 'Yes, but that's unimportant. The boy, tell me of him.' A menacing edge clung to his voice as he leant across the table. 'What was his name, who did you sell him to?'

Suspicious, Brennand traced his finger through some spilled ale on the table top before slowly taking another mouthful, giving himself a moment to gather his thoughts. 'He was just a boy of no importance, on the run. We never ask turds like him their names. He was just silver to us. A useless runt that could hardly carry his own weedy body weight. What interest would you have in such a boy?'

'That's my business, now tell me what you know.'

Brennand remembered the boy's evasiveness. The slight shift in his expression on that narrow face, which still had the contours of a child, but beginning to firm and broaden into the man he would become. The way his green eyes—curiously old for his years—had panicked for a moment when Malin had asked his name. 'As I said, we didn't ask, didn't care. I think he said he came from North Point, or thereabouts.'

'And did he carry any belongings? Anything of value?'

Brennand slowly shook his head. 'No, nothing but a hunting knife and a bag full of mouldy cheese and stale bread.' Brennand's thoughts raced, alert. His instincts telling him to spin a tale, even though that could mean death as Thornheart's reputation for dealing with those who got in his way usually ended with a tortured corpse. 'We sold him on the markets, to a farmer from outside of the village. He needed a worker for his fields.' Then waving his hand in the air, he said, 'Somewhere back in the valley.'

Thornheart narrowed his eyes as he gauged Brennand's story, his dirty nailed forefinger absently stroking the scar on his face. Taking a final draft of his ale he said. 'Very well Brennand. Very well.' Then pausing, revealing yellowed teeth within his thick black beard. 'I am curious, though. Your man, Wilfrec, said you sold him to Malin.'

Quick in thought Brennand responded. 'We tried to,' he replied, palming away the puddle of ale on top of the table. 'But Malin didn't want him. Thought him too weak and that he had enough boys. He didn't want to part with anymore silver. I felt we could get a better price for him down the markets,' Brennand shrugged. 'Wilfrec had left by then to help see to the horses.' Brennand's impulse to lie remained, his instincts alerted in mistrust.

If Thornheart wanted the boy, then it would be for reasons that were not good. Brennand understood the precarious position he found himself in. Curse Wilfrec and his big mouth. His life would be forfeit if his story were not to be believed. Brennand recalled the fearsome reputation of Thornheart, stories of men sent to slow agonising deaths.

For a moment he felt the tug of fear at the base of his gut, the same fear he'd experienced when he had faced Thornheart's forces during the old wars. Brennand had been a sergeant in the battalions of Calaria, he had fought in the final battle of Winter's Harbour and remembered facing Thornheart and his armies when they were finally defeated. His battalion, led by his former General, Stefan Riler, who had overcome Thornheart, slashing that immense sword of his in the final throes of the battle. That sword with its stone, a majestic red-eye shining brightly in the gloomy, wet day, like a fireball. Brennand's heart stopped.

A sword with a red stone? Why had he not realised before? Could the boy be Riler's son? If so, was that why Thornheart sought him out, some form of retribution? Brennand masked his thoughts, hoping his face would not give away the lies.

Thornheart nodded and stood, his enormous frame casting a dark shadow across the table. 'Thank you for the ale, Brennand. I will send some of my men to Malin in the morning. A word of warning, you may not want to be around if your story doesn't stack up.' The threat in his voice clear, as his bear paw of a right hand fingered the hilt of his sword. Then he turned and left the tavern.

•••◆•••

Brennand had called Morgen and the twins down with him, leaving Wilfrec back in his room. It had gone past midnight, the stables of *The Black Stag* were pitch black, a resting horse nickered behind them. Following the conversation with Thornheart he had sent Morgen to seek out Rodrick from within Malin's hall, with a flask of ale, to try to discover what had happened to the boy. What plans did Malin have for him?

'What did you discover, Morgen? Is Rodrick able to help?'

Morgen kept his voice low, barely a whisper, 'Aye, Bren, he wasn't too happy being disturbed at the late hour, but the offering of ale helped. We chatted a short while. The boy is to fight tomorrow. The Lord of West Scar arrived earlier with his own entourage, including some of his own slaves for the bouts. The lad is to be pitched against them. Malin thinks he'll earn him good silver and gold. He bested that brute he always uses. Broke his arm apparently.'

Brennand nodded in the darkness. 'Why doesn't that surprise me? Did you warn him that Thornheart is in town, looking for the boy?'

'I did, he seemed doubtful about the story. Have to admit I am too, Bren, and I don't much like getting on the wrong side of Thornheart. But I have always trusted you, and I will again. What do you two think?' Morgen aimed the question at the twins.

Gordar spoke first, 'We always trust you Bren. You really think it's General Riler's son? Why?'

'Gut feeling. Something about that sword he had on him,'

'He could easily have stolen the sword, Bren.' Added Morgen.

Bren shook his head. 'No, the more I come to think of it, he has the same green eyes of General Riler. We need to get him out of there before Thornheart sends his men over.'

'An impossible task, but Rodrick has agreed to keep any of Thornheart's men away from Malin, should they go sniffing around and uncover our story. For now, at least until the day's fighting has finished, a lot of coin and silver will change hands, and we know how important that is to Malin.'

'Indeed. Good, it'll give us time to forge a plan. Can he get us into the arena at all?'

'No, but he'll meet us by the back gates, the entrance to the cells. But Bren, I have to urge caution, old friend. I don't know what yer thinking, but we can't afford to have both Thornheart and Malin on our backs.'

Brennand patted Morgen's upper arm. 'I know, Morgen, I know. But if he is Riler's son, then we owe him. We all fought by his side in the old wars. We were there at Winter's Harbour. If it wasn't for him, his bravery and leadership, we may not be here now. We would be corpses left to rot in the stinking mud. I just cannot stand by and see his own son in Thornheart's grasp. Especially if I helped put him there. I would never forgive myself if that happened. Never.'

CHAPTER 12
A CURIOUS NOTE

————•••◆•••————

'Jaydon, Rodrick asked me to give you breakfast, here you go,' Ridley entered Jaydon's cell with a plate of sausages and freshly baked bread, the sweet aroma filling his nostrils. 'He also said to make your way to the armoury to choose your weapons and get fitted for armour as soon as you've eaten.'

Jaydon took the plate from Ridley, smiling warmly. Yet inside his stomach churned as though a hundred sparrows were fluttering within his guts. By the end of the day he would be alive or dead. And even if he did survive, what would happen to him? More fights until he got killed in another bout, or constant misery, pain and hurt at the hand of Malin and his men. Would he be maimed, injured in a way that would impact him for the rest of his life? Only the gods knew his future, and Jaydon had no trust in any of them, not anymore.

His life under Malin had improved in the few days since he'd defeated Zarin in the training yard. He now had the cell to himself. Plus, he had no chores, just the constant and repetitive sparring in the yard with Corren and the other boys.

Jaydon knew this improvement in his living conditions wasn't out of any act of kindness—Malin clearly had no kindness about him—but the more comfortable Malin made life for Jaydon before the fights, the better chance he stood. And that meant Malin would make more silver. Malin would be back to being callous and treating him with disdain after the fights—if he lived. He placed the plate of food on a table. 'Thanks, Rids, what chores do they have you doing today?'

'We've to go to the arena and sweep out the awning for the Lord of West Scar and her Ladyship.' Ridley replied, then tugged at his right ear lobe before reaching into his trousers pocket, where he pulled out a small piece of parchment, folded into a tiny square, then said in a quieter voice. 'Raven asked me to give you this.'

'Raven?' Jaydon's heart quickened at the mere mention of her name. 'Why has she given me this?' he asked, taking it from Ridley's outstretched hand.

'I don't know, Jaydon, she said it was important. I did as she asked. She frightens me a little, you know, Jaydon. It's like she wants to be here. Sort of, there's a purpose to her. I dunno, I can't explain it.'

Jaydon nodded, taking the note from him. 'Did you read this, Rids?'

Ridley shook his head. 'No, no. Of course not. Raven said I shouldn't. But—' Ridley lowered his voice. 'I…I couldn't anyway. I never learned the words. No one has ever taught me.'

Jaydon smiled kindly at him. 'Well, maybe if we have time in the evenings here, I could help? My mother taught me and my sister. She insisted that we had to have lessons after our work back home in our village. *A person will go far in life understanding their words. You are both more than farming children,* she used to tell us. I would come in from cleaning out the pigs, then had to sit learning how to read and write for many an hour.'

A pang of grief quickly rose inside his stomach at the thought of the charred and burnt remains of his mother and sister, which he quickly pushed back down. Ridley waited patiently, with reverence, as Jaydon unfolded the note slowly, the paper, thick and yellowed, crackled softly in his hands.

He scanned the note and said, 'Thanks, Rids. Tell Rodrick I'll see him in the armoury as soon as I've finished my breakfast.'

Ridley hesitated, shuffling the straw on the floor with his chained feet.

'Is there something else?' Jaydon asked.

'No, Jaydon. Well yes, I...er, I just wanted to say that I believe in you. I believe you'll win, and to wish you the luck of the gods.'

Jaydon placed a hand on the younger boys' shoulder. 'Thanks, Rids, that means a lot to me. Don't worry...I'll still be here this evening and we can relive the story over our evening meal. I'll be back to sweeping horse-dung with you again tomorrow.' They both laughed, though the strain showed through eyes that did not shine – Jaydon knew too well he may not make it to the end of the day alive, yet it remained unsaid.

Once Ridley had left the cell, Jaydon read the short note from Raven, the handwriting scrawled in black ink across the piece of yellowed parchment. Jaydon had no idea how she had acquired either. The servants were never allowed out of Malin's ground without a guarded escort. He had a feeling Raven had a way of always getting what she wanted.

Jaydon. I need to speak with you urgently. Meet me behind the kitchens before you speak to Rodrick and I will explain all. Raven.

Jaydon stared at the note as he shovelled the last hunk of bread into his mouth. He knew he should ignore it, burn it with the flame of the candle that lit up his cell before anyone caught him with it. He closed his eyes and brought Raven to his mind, her pale face and dark eyes that drew him in. He felt compelled to follow her instruction.

He gathered himself, then hurriedly left the cell, stopping only to splash water onto his face and slick back his matted hair from the water barrel outside the cell block.

CHAPTER 13

THE WINTER CHERRY TREE

———•·•·◆·•·•———

J aydon walked through the grounds toward the back of Malin's hall. The morning autumn air had turned bright and warm, replacing the fog and drizzle that had persisted for the last few days. Jaydon could hear the bustle of the town from beyond the walls; a distant barking of dogs and the calls of market traders. He shuffled along a narrow stone path to the kitchens to meet Raven, his ankles still bound in the chains Rodrick had fitted.

He approached the sandstone-coloured kitchens, which were detached from the main hall. The walls were in much need of repair, crumbling at the corners where the rough mortar had come loose. The greasy smell of breakfast still hung in the air whilst the clattering of pots broke what would have been a peaceful morning.

He wondered what his mother and Jenna would have thought of such a place. Stone buildings, tiled roofs? It did make him wonder why their village lived so simply, when only a few days ride into northern Calaria the buildings were much grander. But then life seemed to be more complicated further north, at least he imagined so.

'Oi, watch out, young 'un.' A voice called out, returning Jaydon from his thoughts. Mildreth, one of the kitchen hands almost crashed into him. A middle-aged woman, small in stature, wide in girth. In her hands she carried a greasy bowl of steaming water, which she'd almost thrown over Jaydon.

'Oh, sorry, Mildreth. My mind was elsewhere. I'm just heading to the armoury…' his voice trailed as he thought on the direction he was heading and why.

Mildreth's faced warmed. 'Of course. I hope the gods are with you today, son. We have chicken broth for you tonight. I'll throw in a few extra pieces of breast just for you.'

'Thanks, Mildreth. I'm sure it will be delicious,' Jaydon nodded and continued down the path.

Raven waited in the shade of a winter cherry tree, its pink flowers in full bloom – they had a few winter cherry trees back in his village, adding a contrast to the colours of autumn, and the golds, browns and reds of the surrounding woodland. Folk said they were magical trees, which was why they always blossomed in autumn, rather than spring.

The petals from the tree were scattered on the ground like a thin carpet, the air heavy with their sweet scent. Raven stood beneath its boughs, almost trance-like. She wore a long black linen robe, the colouring had faded to a dark grey. The hems frayed and worn. Around her shoulders she had a woollen cloak, tied together beneath the nape of her neck.

As he approached, she turned to face him and smiled, parting her lips to reveal clear white teeth, glistening like snow on a winter's morning, such a contrast to her jet-black hair and drab clothing.

Jaydon hesitated, his heart beating hard. Why does she make me feel like this? He wondered to himself.

Her voice was husky, yet full of warmth. 'Jaydon, you came. We must be quick. Please sit.' She indicated toward the bench beneath the tree.

'What if we are seen?' he asked. 'I'm supposed to be fighting to-day. Rodrick is expecting me in the armoury. What's the urgency? And what's the meaning of this note about the gods?' He held the folded note out to her.

She turned toward him and said firmly. 'There is no other way to say this, so I will get straight to the point. You are Jaydon Riler, son of Stefan Riler, and the Guardian of the Stone of Radnor. I am here for a reason, Jaydon, and that reason is you. Evil times are afoot. I have been sent here by the High Priestess of Resas, from the temple of our goddess Mieses, who herself has guided me here to you. You are the true guardian of the stone, Jaydon.' The serene expression on her face never once faltered as she spoke.

Jaydon sat in silence for a moment, breathing slowly as he gathered his thoughts. A flash of light caught his eye, she wore a thin silver chain around her neck, at her throat a pendant, in the shape of a chalice.

'H...how do you know who I am?' he stammered. 'I haven't told anyone who my father was.'

Raven reached out toward him, placing the palm of her hand to his cheek, brushing her thumb across his face. Her touch felt unnaturally warm. 'I have always known who you are, Jaydon. It has been my destiny to find you, to take you to the High Priestess. I have been waiting here for many weeks now for you to arrive. And here you are, just as Mieses told me.'

The warmth of Raven's palm remained on his cheek, but Jaydon felt a cold shudder in the pit of his stomach. He felt the truth in her words, yet doubt and confusion came from his lips. 'Why? What do you mean I am the Guardian. Guardian of what stone? Radnor? Our God of war? The gods have no interest in me. They have forsaken me, to bring me here, my family all dead, butchered, murdered. I may even die this very day. How is that the will of the gods?'

'Yet here you are Jaydon, just as Mieses told me, so here I am too. The gods have their plans. Your father was a good man, a great warlord. Yet it is you they have chosen. It has always been your destiny, and mine to find you and take you to the High Priestess. We must leave tonight; the threads of our fates are being woven as we speak.

'Now go to Rodrick, he waits with what you desire the most.' With that she took away her hand, the heat from it still imprinted on his cheek and walked away, clearing a path through the fallen pink petals, without turning back.

Jaydon sat in bewildered silence, yet within him a fire began to burn.

CHAPTER 14

RODRICK'S REVELATION

————————◆·◆·◆·◆————————

J aydon entered the armoury, still mulling over his conversation with Raven. Within the entranceway the other boys, who were also fighting that day, waited silently, nervousness drawn across each of their faces. Nearest to the door stood Corren, who dipped his chin in recognition of his friend.

'At last, what took you so long, Jaydon?' Rodrick stood from a bench in the corner. 'Did Ridley not tell you to come straight here? I need to get you all kitted out. Right come on lads, leather jerkins are on the shelves behind you, breast plates to their right. Find ones that fit then we'll pick out your weapons. Corren, the master wants you to fight with a spear. Go on then, sort yourselves out.'

The boys started pulling the armour from the shelves, trying them on for size. Jaydon grabbed himself a leather jerkin and a breastplate from the haphazard piles on the shelves that ran along the stone walls. The jerkin felt cold, stiff and stank of stale sweat and old ox hide. He tied the leather fastenings and then struggled into the battered metal breast plate.

A brass snake, curled into an S-shape was embossed on the chest. Luckily, it fit snuggly enough. After fumbling with the fastenings, he turned to help Corren, who had started to struggle, his hands trembling, causing his fingers to slip from the buckles. Jaydon placed his hand over Corren's to calm him.

'These straps are awkward,' Jaydon said, as he tightened one into place for him.

Corren smiled back. 'Thanks, Jaydon. How're you feeling?' Corren asked. Jaydon could see the anxiety etched on his face. 'My legs feel like aspic, and now that bastard wants me to use a spear? I haven't even trained with that, only swords. See...' Corren showed Jaydon the palms of his hands, which still shook. 'My hands are blistered from the tattered handles on the training swords.'

Jaydon felt lucky, from years of working on the farms at home, and from the sword practice his father had put him through, his hands were calloused and hardened to manual labour. 'You'll be fine Corren,' he replied with a reassuring tone in his voice. 'It will give you an advantage with reach. Just don't let whoever you are against get inside your head. You're a good fighter, and can defend well with your shield. You must counter attack. Stay focussed and you'll do well. Pick a good shield, and get a seax too if you can; tuck it into your belt. Just don't thrust too early, bide your time for the right opportunity.' Jaydon slipped the last strap into the bindings on Corren's breast plate. 'Right, there you go... all done. Just jump up and down a little, make sure it's snug.'

Corren followed his instruction. 'Thanks, Jaydon, I guess you're right. But it ain't easy keeping calm, changing my weapon at the last moment. I could be dead tonight, this could be the last place I ever see. I may never lay with a girl, or have children...' Corren trailed off.

Jaydon placed a hand on Corren's shoulder, 'Stay focussed Corren. The other fighter will be feeling the same as you. Remember that.'

Corren nodded. 'And what about you, how do you feel? And how come you fight so well?'

'I had a good teacher.' Jaydon felt his eyes well slightly, he inhaled deeply, filling his lungs to supress his emotion. 'Besides, nothing I can do about it really Corren is there?' Jaydon shrugged. 'If that is the will of the gods then so be it. After all that has happened these past weeks maybe I will join my family in the heavens and be free from this place. Come on, better to choose our weapons before the others. Get the best we can.'

They made their way to Rodrick, who waited by the rack of swords, their steel blades reflecting the flames from the torches on the walls. The armoury had no windows, just plain stone walls. Aside from the torches, the only other light inside the dark building came from the open door, as daylight poured in dimly across the cold flagstones.

The room had a musty aroma, a faint waft of the oil, used to clean the armour and weapons, hung in the air. The weapons in the rack were not the sparring swords they had used in the training yard, but battle swords, edges sharpened, bright steel with menacing points.

Within the rack sat *Devil's Bane*. Jaydon's heart skipped. The red stone gleamed brightly in the meagre light. Jaydon reached out and stroked the stone, as always it felt warm to his touch, he could feel the heat from the stone pulsate through his skin. He closed his eyes as the words from Raven echoed. *You are Jaydon Riler, son of Stefan Riler, and the Guardian of the Stone of Radnor.*

Radnor? Jaydon looked upon the stone set into *Devil's Bane's* pommel once more – could this be the Stone of Radnor? Surely his father would have said if he had such a stone in his possession? He had heard stories of god-stones. Not from his father, but Ober had mentioned these to him. Neither his father, nor his mother, had ever talked of the gods, not unless they were blaspheming or cussing. He knew of the gods, who they were, but not much else. He had never really listened to the stories, and his father had never been a religious man. Jaydon felt there were many things in this world he did not yet understand.

'You would like to fight with your sword, Jaydon, I guess?' Rodrick, emphasising the word 'your' as he saw Jaydon with his fingers still clinging to the stone at the pommel.

'Yes,' he responded with longing, then defensively, 'I know its weight, how it feels in my hands. It will give me a better chance of defeating my opponent. Surely that will be what Malin wants?'

Rodrick's face remained impassive, unstirred, he glanced at the sword, at the red stone, deep in thought, then turned back to Jaydon. 'Of course, I'll put it aside for you. You'll collect it in the arena later. Now pick out a shield…assuming you want to use one today?' he added, with a wry smile.

Jaydon's brain spun, first Raven had discussed leaving, tonight, and now *Devil's Bane* would be back in his grasp again. Maybe the gods were looking out for him after all? But then, maybe he would be dead before the afternoon had worn itself out? But how would he escape if he survived? Rodrick would have them back in chains as soon as they left the arena. Jaydon felt any hope Raven had given him evaporate like spilled water on a hot summer day.

What games had Raven been playing? Why had she sought to give him such hope? The questions ran around his mind, swinging one way then the other. Corren broke his thoughts, leading him forwards by the arm, choosing solid oak shields for them both. Each with an iron boss in their centres, and painted brightly with coloured emblems. Corren chose one with a yellow chevron for himself. Jaydon, who could barely focus as his mind swam in confusion, failed to recognise that Corren had given him a shield with a red sword boldly displayed on in its face.

The boys were now ready, kitted out, weapons selected. Rodrick sat them down by the entrance to the armoury, he poured each of them a cup of wine. 'Sup up, lads, not too much, you need to be focussed, your senses sharp. But this will take the edge off any nerves,' Rodrick said, his voice friendly. 'Then back to your cells to rest. Take your armour off, don't wear it any longer than necessary, you can put it back on at the arena. I'll send for you when it's time. There'll be a crowd in the arena today, let the atmosphere feed the adrenalin inside you. You've all trained for this, you are good fighters, strong, quick and agile. Show no fear. Show no emotion to your enemy. Strike hard. Strike true. I believe in you all. Now be off with you.' The boys drank down their wine and stood to leave.

Jaydon swirled his in the cup before gulping down the red liquid. His face grimaced as the sour wine hit his tongue. It tasted foul and warm as it hit his palate and slid down the back of his throat.

'Not you, Jaydon, stay here will you please?' Rodrick asked as Jaydon made ready to leave.

Once they were alone, Rodrick sat Jaydon back down on the wooden bench and poured himself another cup of wine, which he slugged down in a single gulp. Patiently Jaydon waited, not sure why Rodrick had held him back. His mind had already been muddied from his conversation with Raven, now he sat here wondering what Rodrick had to say.

The cup of wine he had moments earlier did not help his clarity. The torches on the wall flickered, casting dancing shadows on the floor in front of them. Rodrick remained silent, his index finger tapping the empty wine cup he held in his hand.

'You know, Jaydon, I had a visitor last night?'

Jaydon didn't respond, but waited for Rodrick to continue.

'It was Morgen, one of Brennand's men that brought you here. He had an interesting tale to tell,' Rodrick paused before continuing. 'I fought with them, well, with Brennand, Morgen and the two twins, side-by-side in the old wars? Bren was our sergeant. I had a choice many years ago to stay with them, and seek out work in farmsteads across the country.'

Rodrick gazed into his empty cup deep in thought. All the while, Jaydon sat silently, wondering what this had to do with him? 'They fell on hard times, you know? Choosing banditry instead to earn a living. I declined their offer, and chose to come here and take Malin's silver, despite my personal feelings for him and what he does. I used to train the younger soldiers during those wars you see, teach them how to fight, hold their ground on the battlefield, work together as a team and form the shield wall. So, my services here are to ensure boys like you are all ready, prepared for days like these.'

Rodrick stood and poured more wine, then took another large draft with trembling hands. Then, he stood opposite Jaydon, his body framed dark in the doorway, his features shadowed. 'I fought for your father, you know?'

Jaydon's skin pricked as an icy shiver ran up his back. His mind fumbled to take it all in. How did Rodrick know who he was also? Did Jaydon hear him correctly? Had Rodrick and Raven been speaking about him?

'I...I, don't know what you mean,' Jaydon stuttered.

'They are right, boy. You have your father's eyes. And that sword... the red stone. There aren't too many swords like that. Bren put it together you know. He worshipped your father. If it wasn't for him none of us would be here now.'

'If it wasn't for him, I wouldn't be here now either. About to fight for my life.' Jaydon couldn't help himself, he spat out the words in anger. 'He and the others, if they had let me be. I would be almost at Everwood now, safe. And for what? A few pieces of silver to feed them for a day or two? I don't care what they thought of my father, I may not live to see this day out. I hope they rot in the fires of the underworld.'

Rodrick nodded; the truth had been laid bare, Brennand had been right. He sat down next to Jaydon, keeping his voice low. 'Does the name Landis Thornheart mean anything to you, boy?'

A shadow passed over Jaydon's face. Then he responded in a low growl, 'Thornheart? Yes, I will have him if I ever leave this place. I will run *Devil's Bane* through his guts, twisting them round in a knot. That evil bastard will pay.' Jaydon's fists clenched into tight balls, his knuckles white, as he spoke. 'He will pay for what he did. He killed them, you know?'

'Killed who?'

'All of them. My father, mother, Jenna. Everyone in the village. And for what? All those innocent lives. Why? For revenge?' Any grief Jaydon felt earlier became engulfed by hatred.

'Riler's dead?' Rodrick asked, surprise on his face. 'Sorry to hear that, Jaydon. Now I know who you are and why you were wandering about the grasslands with that sword. Your father was a man of enormous stature and well respected. But listen, I can't set you free, not before the fights. Malin would have my guts for that. You still need to step inside that arena today. You need to be focussed. Survive Jaydon. Live and we will get you away this evening. Bren is coming to take you away. He owes his life to your father.' Rodrick ran his hands through his hair, slicking it backwards. 'This is important, you need to fully concentrate on the fight at hand, beat your man. Thornheart has sent his men here this morning, searching for you. I have delayed them with a tale I agreed with Morgen. But we need to get you away. Leave the how with me.'

Jaydon said a single word in acknowledgement. 'Raven.'

Rodrick nodded with understanding. 'Raven,' he repeated.

CHAPTER 15
EVERWOOD

—◆—

As they approached Everwood the rain started, heavy and unrelent-
ing. Nyla cursed the gods as she wrapped her cloak tightly around
her body – she hoped Thornheart was right, and Arthek Mulliner would
be found here, in this godforsaken town. Her mare snorted but trotted
on with the men following behind on their steeds. Traders were hastily
packing up their wares as the rain brought a halt to the day's bartering.
Deep in thought, Nyla thought back to the expression on Thornheart's
face back at their camp after he had spoken with Elokar. Not many
things shook Thornheart to his core, nor Nyla for that matter, but the
banished God chilled her soul. Just the mere mention of his name would
freeze her heart with dread.

The road was a quagmire of mud beneath hoof and foot despite the
cobbles and, although only late afternoon, the dark clouds gave they
day the look of an evening sky. Nyla thought to head for an inn first
for shelter, food and warmth. Seeking out Arthek Mulliner could wait
until the morning, her men were tired and hungry after the ride from
Bleakhorn Forest.

Thornheart should be at The Wyke already, so word could be sent
quickly enough if she heard anything tomorrow or saw any sign of the

boy. She pulled up beside a trader pushing a barrow full of furs towards them, no doubt heading home now the rains had come.

'Sir,' she called out, 'Is there an inn or a tavern in this town?'

Wiping the rain from his face the man stared up at Nyla. 'Aye, lady.'

Thunder rolled in the distance. He had to raise his voice above the beating of the downpour. 'Down the road, *The Hatchett*, don't worry about the name though lady. It's a safe place to stay and drink.'

Nyla noticed his eyes shift to the weapon at her side, and those of her men.

'Not that you would worry, all the same.'

'Thank you, sir.' She reached an arm into the velvet purse that hung at her belt, pulling out a silver coin, handing it to him. 'For your trouble, no doubt a day's trading finished early because of this weather?'

'Aye, 'fraid so. Thank you, lady, most kind. Ask for old Harrin at the inn. Tell him Thomos Cordray sent you. He'll give you good board and food.' He placed the coin inside his heavy cloak, tipped his hat and moved onwards with his barrow down the muddy street.

Nyla kicked her horse on toward *The Hatchett*, looking forward to the warmth and dryness that beckoned her and her men. Her thoughts wandered again, wondering why Thornheart had gone to The Wyke, and why had she been sent to this miserable place?

Later that evening Nyla, and her four men supped on beef stew and ale. She relished the local beef Harrin's wife had cooked up for them, as tasty as he had promised, and rich from the lush grasses of the valleys that surrounded Everwood. The ale and wine, though, tasted like they had been sieved from the latrine pit.

Harrin gave them good rooms, as the trader had vowed, with thick straw mattresses and clean blankets. The hearty food lifted their moods, as they filled their stomachs. The bar was close to being empty, the storm kept most folk in their homes, just a few locals sat alone drinking, keeping themselves to themselves. Harrin spoke to each one of them in turn, regular punters no doubt, no wives or mistresses to return home to. The rain could still be heard outside, lashing hard as the wind continuously rattled the shutters, threatening to whip them open as it whistled through the gaps.

Thunder rolled in the distance as flashes of light occasionally lit up the street outside. Nyla was thankful they had arrived when they had, glad not to have been fully caught in the storm that had followed them into Everwood. Harrin returned with more tankards of ale, a stout man, with thinning grey hair and a heavy moustache beneath a red bulbous nose.

His cheeks were rosy and his demeanour pleasant and full of humour. 'More ale?' he offered, as he placed the tankards on the table.

Nyla smiled her thanks back at him as her men reached across, each grabbing a drink. She observed Harrin for a moment before speaking, 'Quiet tonight. Is it always like this?'

'No, lady, it'll be the storm. But some folks have headed down to The Wyke for a day or two. A spectacle of fights in the arena there, money to be won you see. What brings you here on a day like this?' Then eyeing their swords, he added, 'We usually get traders, or tinkers passing through Everwood. Not soldiers, not these days.'

Nyla paused for a moment and took a sip from the tankard, masking her distaste at the foul liquid before responding, 'Just searching for someone. A boy. Probably about fourteen years. He would be travelling alone, not from these parts.'

'Cannot say I have seen nor heard of such a boy, lady; I usually hear of such things. Any stranger is usually talked of round these parts so I hear it soon enough, and especially a child. Would he be your son?'

'No, the son of a friend.' She replied. 'I have been asked to find him. He ran away from home, you see. He may be here searching for someone who goes by the name of Mulliner, do you know him?'

'Oh, poor lad. But I know Arthek Mulliner, he runs the smithies on Carter's Lane, we do each other favours, I send travellers to him for any horses that need re-shoeing. He sends them here for food and ale. He's a good man, Arthek. Why do you think this boy would go there?' he asked.

'My friend knows him from the old wars. He seemed to think him likely to head this way. Some travellers we met yesterday said they saw him on this road, so it tallies up.' The lies came easily for Nyla, her quick wits sharpened and tuned, yet her demeanour remained friendly towards the innkeeper, the affable expression on her face never faltering. 'Maybe we'll visit this blacksmith tomorrow morning, when this storm has passed.'

'Aye, you won't want to be out there tonight that's for sure. Can I get you anything else? My wife has baked some plum pudding.'

'No, thank you, Harrin, you've been more helpful than you can imagine.'

•••◆•••

The next morning the storm had broken and the heavy clouds gave way to blue skies. Everwood started to come to life with the sounds and smells of a market town. Traders were setting up stalls, shouting and joking with each other. Smells of burning fires were punctuated with that of roasting meat and baking bread. The street outside *The Hatchett* remained muddy from the previous day's downpour, but already the morning sun had started to dry patches of ground around them.

Harrin's wife, Martha, had given Nyla and the men a good breakfast of sausage and fried potatoes, washed down with watered down mead.

Nyla gave her men their instructions for the day. 'Kartis, you are to come with me and see this Mulliner. The rest of you tend to the horses. Ensure they are rubbed down and have plenty of hay and water. Get some apples from the market too for them.' She paused to scratch at an itch on her upper arm. 'They need good rest, it was a long ride from Bleakhorn Forest. We may be here for a few days yet too. Just keep an eye out in the town. Have a look at where things are, get your bearings. You all deserve the rest too. Here,' she handed a few coins to each of them. 'Treat yourselves.'

Her men acknowledge her generosity, nodding their acceptance of her orders. Nyla understood the need to keep them happy, something that Thornheart sometimes struggled to do himself, leading by fear instead.

Nyla suggested to Kartis that they leave their swords behind, so as not to arouse any suspicion, knowing they would be noted as strangers. Better to let people think they were travellers or traders. But more importantly she wanted them to appear non-threatening when they met with Mulliner.

They followed the directions to Carters Lane given to them by Harrin, it was only a short walk from the inn, so Nyla and Kartis strolled casually, instinctively taking in their surroundings. Checking outside streets and alleyways, to get their bearings and keep their senses sharpened; always on alert should anything take a turn for the worse.

'Nyla,' Kartis broke the silence as they walked. 'Why exactly are we searching for this boy? Why does Thornheart want him? What is it about this stone he killed Kitto for?'

Nyla knew of the full story of the stone, Thornheart had confided in her, *don't tell the men. No one must know exactly what we seek...not yet at least. All they need to know is that it's a great treasure,* he had warned her. She understood the importance of it, but she trusted Kartis, he had earned her confidence. 'He has a very precious artefact, Kartis. It is worth more than any gold or silver we have plundered before. Lord Thornheart will reward us in time. Our men must be patient.'

Kartis huffed. 'Aye, but they grow restless. Sacking Hardstone Woods wasn't enough…it had meagre pickings anyway.'

'I know, and Thornheart knows too. We must be patient and put our trust in him. Haven't we always?' But doubt niggled at the back of her mind, a dark presence that she couldn't quite shift.

'Listen, Kartis. We need to pass as non-threatening when we speak to Mulliner. We will be a husband and wife, searching for a friend's boy who's run away.'

Kartis nodded.

'You lead the questions, I'll jump in if needed,' Nyla continued.

Ahead they heard the smithies workshop before they saw it. The familiar clanging of the heavy hammer on steel ringing out like the bell of a clock relentlessly sounding out the hour of the day. They entered a square, the buildings seemed desolate empty shells, with the exception of the workshop, which was well kept.

As they approached the blacksmith stopped his work and looked up. 'How can I help you folks out then?' Beneath his leather apron he wore no shirt, his muscled torso, heavily scarred beneath. He had heavy thickset arms that were already greased and dirty despite the early morning. His long-greying hair, tied back into a ponytail, strands had fallen loose and hung in front of his face. He sported A trimmed beard on a hard weather worn face that glowed with years of working the hot forges. Yet his smile remained friendly and welcoming.

He stuck the iron rod he had been working with the hammer into a bucket, which hissed and steamed as the water cooled the metal, before plunging his hands into another barrel of water, cupping them together to splash away the sweat from his face.

'Morning sir,' Kartis called as they approached. 'We're looking for Arthek Mulliner, would that be you?'

'Aye, that's me,' Arthek replied, wiping his hands on the back of his breeches. 'What can I do for you?'

'My wife and I are seeking a boy. We were told he'd travelled here, to Everwood. Harrin, the innkeeper at *The Hatchett*, suggested you may be able to help.'

'And why would I be able to help?'

'We met some travellers enroute, they saw the boy and he mentioned your name. He ran away from his family. Apparently, our friend, the boy's father, knew you in the old wars. Silly lad has heard lots of stories and wanted you to teach him to fight.' Kartis laughed. 'You know how young boys get their heads filled with such fantasies. But his father would have none of it, so the lad ran away from the village; Lower Dontan. We were travelling here to trade and agreed to come help and seek out the lad.' Kartis raised a hand to the height of his shoulder. 'He's around fourteen, tall for his age, probably this tall. Dark hair. Don't suppose he made his way here, did he?'

Arthek's face screwed. Shaking his head, he replied, 'Nope, not seen any boy. And I don't know anyone in Lower Dontan, not anyone with a boy that age at the least. Now, I got work to do, sorry I can't help, but good day to you and I hope you find him.' Arthek picked up his hammer and tongs, ready to start back with his work, ending the conversation.

'Wait,' Nyla interrupted, causing Arthek to face them once more. 'Sorry, I know you're a busy man Mr. Mulliner, but you see our friends are very upset. Should the boy arrive we're staying in *The Hatchett* for a few more nights. Please send him our way. Just to warn you though, he has a reputation for fantasising. The old wars fascinate him. He makes up stories and battles about them, in fact spends too much time in make-believe sword fights with a branch or a stick than he does working on the farm. His parents' despair.' Nyla rolled her eyes. 'I will never pretend to understand you men. However, should he come your way it would be appreciated if you could let us know.' Nyla's eyes shone with mock tears as she spoke. 'Please, all I ask is that you just bring him to us safely, or keep him distracted for us to collect him.' Again, her face broke into the same innocent, friendly smile as she had the night before with Harrin.

Arthek nodded, his face open with concern. 'Very well lady, I can do that if I see him.' He took the iron rod from the bucket once more and thrust it into the hot forge behind him.

'Thank you, sir,' Kartis replied.

'I want the men to do shifts, and watch out here for the boy, or anyone else who might arrive over the next couple of days,' Nyla instructed Kartis as they walked away. 'They mustn't be seen. Use one of these empty buildings. We will find him. In the meantime, we need to get a message to The Wyke and tell Lord Thornheart we've found Mulliner.'

CHAPTER 16
CRIMSON SAND

—— •••◆••• ——

The cells beneath the arena felt cool despite the autumn sun that lanced through the narrow-barred openings in the walls. One bout had already ended, Jaydon had watched on along with the other boys, who stood on tip-toes as they strained to see the fight unfold. Gurnar one of Malin's younger fighters won his fight, he'd ducked, weaved and darted gracefully, almost like a dance. Cutting and slicing his opponent before finally thrusting the blade of his short sword through a gap above his breast plate and into his throat.

The rest of the boys were now sat on long wooden benches, waiting for their names to be called. Outside the crowd roared for more, their thirst for blood raised, relishing the spectacle of young boys pitting themselves against each other in battles to the death.

Corren nervously jiggled his knees rapidly up and down, silently staring ahead. On the next bench sat their opponents, the Lord of West Scar's boys, most nervous; with hunched backs, or sat with arms folded across their chests, leaning forward and chewing nails or picking at scabs and scars. All except one who oozed confidence, he reminded Jaydon of the way Zarin carried himself, self-assured, arrogant. He appeared to be around fifteen or sixteen years, with strong arms and a head above Jaydon in height.

Rodrick's voice boomed across the cells breaking the silence. 'Corren, Jakor, you boys are up next. Come on, lads. Grab your weapons by the gates, helmets on, shields in hand.'

Corren shot Jaydon a last nervous glance, Jaydon responded as reassuringly as he could. 'You'll be all right Corren, remember all we spoke about. See you when you return.' Corren gave a feint nod back at the words of encouragement but his eyes belied the confidence he showed.

The two boys made their way slowly to the iron gates, Jaydon could see the whites of Corren's knuckles where he gripped his spear. As they fastened their helmets, Rodrick gave them both final instructions before whispering words of encouragement to Corren, as the iron gates swung open into the arena.

The noise from the crowd thundered once more, deafening, as both fighters walked nervously forwards and strode into the sunshine and the commotion of the arena. The gates shutting behind them as they disappeared from view.

The taller boy remained seated, impassive; Jaydon knew he would be his opponent out in the arena, he sighed inwardly hoping the gods, if they had any compassion left for him, would get him through the day.

Jaydon crossed the cell to watch Corren's fight, with clenched fists as he prayed for him, then a blast of a horn rang out, Jaydon jumped at the sound as it jolted him out of his thoughts. The horn indicating the start of the bout.

Corren started well, using the spear and shield to good effect, keeping Jakor out of reach, despite the lack of training he had received with the weapon that had been forced upon him.

Come on Corren, you can do this, Jaydon thought to himself and then he roared, willing Corren on as he swung his spear, drawing blood on his opponent's upper arm. Jaydon lost all sense of time, the fight seemed to have continued for an age, but Corren had begun to tire, lowering his shield more and more, and he was slower with his thrust and parries.

Then Corren stumbled, as he did his opponent hacked down, cutting the shaft of Corren's spear in two. The other fighter moved quickly on his advantage and thrust his sword deep through the gap beneath Corren's armpit. Jaydon watched on in horror, as Corren screamed, crimson blood oozed from the wound and over his silver breastplate. Corren, wide-eyed, spat more blood from his mouth as Jakor withdrew his weapon and Corren slumped to the ground. As his life ebbed away Jakor dipped his fingers into Corren's blood and smeared it across his face, before triumphantly raising his arms aloft. Playing to the crowd. Jaydon screamed in rage.

Jakor returned to the cells, roaring in victory, the taller boy stood and greeted him, gloating, then with two fingers of his right hand he wiped some of the blood from Jakor's face and daubed two bloody stripes down his own, sneering at Jaydon as he did so. 'You're next, maybe I will mix your blood with that of your friends?'

Jaydon clenched his fists, rage coursed through him. He stepped forward but checked himself, not yet, not yet, Jaydon.

The two boys snorted and embraced again, clapping each other on strong arms laughing in the joy of victory. Jaydon turned and sat, his head bowed, and fumed silently to himself. What had Corren done to deserve this? He shook his head, he knew little about him, only their brief exchanges in the training yard. At least he would be at rest with his parents now. Did Corren have any other family somewhere who would want to know what had become of him? Would they know, or care, that he took his last breath here, on the dusty ground with the crowd baying for his blood, and that bastard crowing over his victory?

'Ercan, Jaydon, you lads are up next. Same drill, collect your weapons. Helmets and shields on. Let's put on a good show for these bastards,' Rodrick shouted across the cells.

Ercan, the taller boy, pushed against Jaydon, barging him to the side with his shoulder, Corren's blood still smeared across his face. Jaydon remained unmoved, thoughts of his dead friend running through his mind, tears welled, he could hear Ercan laughing, mistaking the tears for fear.

'Jaydon, up you come, lad. I have your sword here.'

Jaydon trudged forward, taking *Devil's Bane* from Rodrick, gripping the leather hilt firmly, feeling it like an old friend and readied himself, shutting out the noise from the crowd as the gates swung open once more.

•••◆•••

The two boys strolled side by side into the arena. Tattered sun-bleached flags of red and blue atop wooden masts ran around the top of the concourse, gracefully flapping in a gentle breeze. Immediately Jaydon felt the warmth of the late afternoon sun on his body, contrasting with the coolness of the cells from which they emerged. The crowd erupted as they strode into the centre, feet crunching on the grit and sand that covered the ground beneath them.

Jaydon clasped *Devil's Bane* firmly in his right hand, his left gripping the shield, which had been strapped to his forearm. The cries of the baying crowd were now drowned out by the beating of his heart and the blood roaring like thunder through his body.

He wore his helmet, chinstrap fastened beneath his chin, and cheek pieces lowered; he had chosen a good helmet that fitted well and with an open face to ensure his vision would not be impaired, in contrast to his opponent's, whose helmet finished below his eyes and across the bridge of his nose; two slots providing the openings for him to see.

The two boys marched in to the centre of the arena, Jaydon noted the dark patches of blood to his right, the spot where Corren fell to his doom. He fought back tears at the death of his friend, not tears of sadness but of fury. An anger which he would use to channel for his own fight as he strode toward the dais at the far side of the arena.

Jaydon picked out Malin sat in the dais, beside him another man, dressed finely in reds and golds, with a dark trimmed beard, groomed with oils that glistened in the sun. A man who exuded wealth—the Lord of West Scar. Jaydon glared as Malin whispered something into the ear of the Lord, who nodded and laughed before standing to clap the two young fighters before them.

The Lord of West Scar then raised his arms and the crowd fell silent. He took a moment, taking in the atmosphere around the stands before speaking in a clear voice, 'Ladies, Gentlemen. It is time for the third bout of the afternoon. Two more brave young warriors will pit themselves against each other in a fight to the death. I bring my own champion, Ercan, winner of nine bouts, never defeated. Today he will win his freedom. I say this to you all here that I promise to release him from his bonds this very day when he defeats his opponent. I have wagered good silver and gold on him myself, and I urge you all to do the same.'

The crowd cheered. Laughter erupted as men and women waved arms and fists into the air, jangling purses and beating their feet on the wooden stands.

The Lord of West Scar waited for the raucous to subside before continuing, 'My good friend, Malin, tell us about the poor wretch whose life you are wasting on this bout today?'

Again, the laughter spewed from the crowd as Malin waved them to silence. 'My Lord, alas, it's with a heavy heart that I say poor Ercan will not win his freedom today. I bring Jaydon, who defeated Zarin this very week, a conqueror of champions, a bone cruncher, who is as swift as a deer and as cunning as a fox. Good People of The Wyke, don't waste your hard-earned silver on a dead boy. Wager on Jaydon to be your champion today.'

More cheering as the excitement of the onlooking crowd reverberated around the arena. Both Malin and the Lord of West Scar clapped enthusiastically, revelling in their own jokes at the expense of Jaydon and his opponent.

The crowd beckoned the bookkeepers to them, frantically wagering silver and life savings. Moments later a loud blast from a horn broke through the noise of the crowd, who again fell silent. The signal to end their betting as the bout would soon commence.

As briefed by Rodrick beforehand, both boys raised their swords in front of their faces in a salute to the Lord of West Scar, then turned to face each other.

Beads of sweat trickled down the inside of Jaydon's helmet, running down his face and neck, yet despite the heat goosebumps covered his skin, causing a shiver to run down his spine. The blood pounded through him, a dull *dum, dum, dum,* in time with the pulsing in his veins.

He had to concentrate, calming his breathing, just as his father had always said to him many times: *Keep your mind sharp, Jaydon, breathe in through your nose, exhaling through your mouth, lips pursed. Control your heart rate. A calmer head can react quicker. Remember, your enemy will be scared too. The more composed you feel, the bigger the advantage it will give you.*

Jaydon remembered the lessons, he slowed his breathing, the pounding in his head subsided, his heart rate eased. Ready, he peered up, into the face of his opponent, Corren's blood across his cheeks still visible beneath his helmet. Ercan poised, ready to strike, he had the advantage of height, strength and experience.

Yet, Jaydon told himself, he was the son of Stefan Riler, and he had *Devil's Bane* clenched in his right hand and he would prevail. He pushed away all thoughts of escape and focussed on the foe in front of him.

The boys waited, the crowd silent in anticipation, then another blast of a horn, sent the crowd into a frenzied roar. Jaydon could hear the cheers, some calling his name, others his opponents, but he blocked it out and focussed. Ercan shifted his body, swaying right to left. Jaydon stepped backwards, one step, then two, watching, waiting.

Both boys sized each other up, then Ercan feinted to his right, but Jaydon saw it for the bluff it was and stepped back once more. Another feint and again Jaydon anticipated it. His opponent smirked, no doubt thinking he had Jaydon worried, scared.

Again, a feint, this time to the left, Jaydon backed off again. Just like against Zarin he knew patience would be needed, so he waited, ever mindful, watching leg movements, trying to gauge his opponent's eyes for any tell-tale signs of his intentions within the shadows of his helmet.

The boys shuffled around, circling. The sign came, Ercan grunted and sprang forward, slashing his sword high and hard. Jaydon blocked it with his shield, but the force sent him backwards. Again, his opponent leapt, which Jaydon once more blocked with his shield. A dull thud as the heavy steel sword beat down on the oaken wood. His arm throbbed from the impact.

A third blow, hard onto the shield with enough force that drove Jaydon to collapse onto one knee. Ercan spun around, using his body weight to force his shield down onto Jaydon's, swinging his sword arm around he arced the blade around toward the back of Jaydon's neck.

Jaydon allowed the weight of his opponent and their shields to force himself onto the floor, then he rolled across the ground, and brought himself back up onto one knee, raising *Devil's Bane* to block Ercan's sword. A loud clanging rang out as steel hammered on steel, the vibration sending a tremor down Jaydon's forearm. At the sound of the swords clashing the crowd roared once more.

Quickly Jaydon stood and stepped back and up onto both his feet, just as Ercan swung his sword toward him. Once more *Devil's Blane* blocked and parried each thrust. Ercan rushed forward into a feverish attack, pounding Jaydon with his sword. Jaydon retaliated as both boys exchanged blows, blocking each other with their weapons and shields. Sweat poured down Jaydon's face, his vision began to blur. He fought on instinct, block after block, swing after swing, crash upon crash of steel.

Unexpectedly, Ercan changed tactics and flung himself shield first into Jaydon. The force from the heavier boy rocked Jaydon backwards, he stumbled, staggered off-balance. Ercan's shield flew towards him again, smashing Jaydon full in the face between the cheek plates and cracking his nose, blood sprayed across his face.

Jaydon's world turned fuzzy as he toppled backwards, hitting the ground in a cloud of dusty sand and grit. *Devil's Bane* bounced from his grip and out of reach. Winded, Jaydon groaned loudly, spitting blood, as the dark shape of Ercan loomed above him, sword arm raised. The crowd screamed for blood; *kill, kill, kill,* they chanted.

Ercan pumped his shield arm into the air in a victory salute, basking in the glory of another win and his impending freedom. It was a moment, but Jaydon sensed the opportunity, thrusting his own shield up as hard as he could into his Ercan's groin.

Ercan grunted, his face distorted. Jaydon thrust once more, again striking his opponent in the same place who this time doubled. Knowing he could not hesitate Jaydon rolled in the direction of where he thought *Devil's Bane* had fallen, flinging out a hand onto the ground, grasping in hope.

With his vision blurred he struggled to see, but as though the gods themselves were with him, the red stone on the pommel began to glow, like a guiding beacon. Jaydon found the hilt and held it firm. Half-blinded, he gathered himself up onto his knees. He no longer felt any pain, just a burning surge of fury that churned from his stomach and up through his throat into a scream of rage.

It was now or never. He swung his arm, sword firm in hand, and thrust *Devil's Bane* across the back of Ercan's heel, slicing tendon. Ercan screamed as his leg gave way. Jaydon did not waver, lunging once more, this time through the back of the knee of Ercan's standing leg. Blood poured as ligaments and muscle were sliced in two, his leg gave way and he crumpled onto the ground.

Yet again the crowd wailed for blood, this time recognising the tide had turned they screamed Jaydon's name. Jaydon staggered to his feet and loomed over Ercan. Grabbing Ercan's helmet, he pushed it upwards, jerking it from his head and tossing it to one side. Jaydon regarded the remaining stains of Corren's blood, smudged with sweat and dust, on his enemy's face before thrusting *Devil's Bane* down hard into his throat and releasing it in a jet of crimson turning the yellow sand around him red.

Jaydon collapsed onto hands and knees, exhausted, the blood from Ercan dripping from *Devil's Bane*. The noise from the crowd like a distant echo.

He had never killed a person before. Bile rose in his throat as he flung his sword and shield to the floor. He wrenched off his helmet and vomited a vile red liquid onto the sand, remnants of lunch and the wine he had drank earlier spattered onto the ground. Snot, sweat and blood trickled from his face. His broken nose throbbed.

He knew he had avenged Corren, however the shock of the kill wrenched his stomach. He bent forward and retched again onto the floor, specks of vomit covering his legs and feet.

CHAPTER 17
SACRIFICE

———◆———

Thornheart had brought some of his men along to the arena for the entertainment, allowing them to relax while waiting to hear of news from Nyla at Everwood. He sat three rows behind the dais where he could see that fool Malin roar in delight, clapping the Lord of West Scar hard on the shoulder. He enjoyed the bouts himself; seeing young boys kill and maim each other brought him enormous delight.

But, just as the underdog had seemed doomed, Thornheart had noted how his fallen sword had shone when it fell from his grasp. It gave him a jolt, as a slow shiver ran down his spine. A memory conjured from the recesses of his mind, many years ago during the battle of Winter's Harbour a sword, just like that shone in front of him. Unconsciously, he fingered the scar running down his face as it itched at his mind. It could not be, could it?

The guards had dragged the victor away, back towards the cells at the far side of the arena. If he was right then Wilfrec had been too, meaning Brennand had lied to him in the *Black Stag*. For that he would pay with his life. Thornheart turned to one of his men who sat by his side.

'Terren, we need to get into those cells, under the arena. Gather some of the men and meet me on the far-side. And hurry, no delay. I want them armed and ready to fight,' Terren nodded and stood. 'Oh, and Terren, have someone search for that Brennand and his men, The ones I spoke with last night in the tavern. Just find out where they are, nothing more, then report back to me.'

Thornheart gathered his thoughts, he needed to get into the cells, he would have to fight his way in no doubt, not a problem, he knew his men could do that easily enough. Then get the boy, surely he must be Riler's son? And that stone, shining on the sword…had to be the Stone of Radnor. Had it been on the sword all those years ago when he faced Riler in battle? Not hidden away, kept somewhere safe, but fitted to the pommel of his weapon? Thornheart knew it for certain, he felt it pull at him. The boy could die, but the stone would be his at last.

His thoughts drifted back to his last conversation with Elokar, he gave a shudder. At least this time he would bring him good news, and Elokar would give him his due rewards. One step closer to all that power, and the world would be his along with immortality.

••◆••

Back in the cells Rodrick pulled Jaydon to one side, guiding him around the corner from the main area and handed him a grubby rag. 'Here boy, wipe yourself clean.'

'Ow!' Jaydon winced as he wiped the blood and vomit away from his face, the rag making contact with his tender nose. 'By the gods, I hope it's not broken.'

'Here, get some fluid in you first. Then I'll have a look,' Rodrick handed him a cup of water.

Jaydon grasped it with trembling hands and gulped down the cool liquid, spilling droplets down his chin.

'How do you feel boy?'

'Sick, I just feel sick.'

'You'll be fine, Jaydon, we all break noses and bones in our lives, you'll live,' Rodrick continued, inspecting Jaydon's face.

'It's not that, I…I killed him, Rodrick. I took another person's life,' Jaydon could feel more tears welling, he wanted to vomit again. 'He was alive this morning, looking at the autumn sun just as I was, talking with his friends…now he's dead and I did it.'

'Stop it. Listen to me, Jaydon. If you hadn't, it would be your blood soaking into the sand out there. Your body being dragged to a nameless grave. You fought, you won. You've got a survival instinct…' Rodrick paused. 'But we can't hang about. Now, sit on the bench near the rear doors. Once I have called the last two boys into the arena, we'll get you out of here. Raven should be waiting outside with Brennand and his men. You gotta be quick, lad. Here…' Rodrick handed *Devil's Bane* back to Jaydon. 'Now be off with you. I'll be back shortly. Malin will have my guts for this boy, I hope you understand that?'

Jaydon nodded, still wiping the blood from his nose, though the flow had slowed. 'I know, and thanks. I won't forget this, Rodrick. Aren't you coming with us?'

'No, Brennand will have one of his men give me a little beating, make it appear like they broke in and took you away. Still, Malin will have me for it. Probably lose a week's pay…if I'm lucky. We've just got to get you out of here. Right, wait by the doors, I'll be back shortly.' Rodrick disappeared into the main cell and called out the final two boys. Jaydon heard the crowd roar again as the gates into the arena swung open for the final bout of the day as he waited clutching *Devil's Bane* close to his chest.

A short while later, after more jeering from the audience in the arena, Rodrick returned. He unlocked the rear doors with a heavy iron key. Outside, Raven and Ridley were waiting. They were joined by Brennand and his men – Jaydon felt relief that Wilfrec wasn't with there. Raven, though, made no acknowledgement, but instead she muttered quietly, in a low voice, staring upwards. Jaydon glanced up to see what had caught her attention. Above, a single grey cloud was forming in the blue sky, growing thicker and darker, deepening from smoke to charcoal to ebony. A massive bruise engulfing the sky above their heads like nothing Jaydon had ever seen before, almost as though it had a life of its own.

Rodrick shoved Jaydon forward. 'Come on, Jaydon, stop gawking. Bren, quick, take the lad before the next bout is over. Good luck, may the gods be with you.'

Brennand grabbed his arm, ushering him along to hasten their escape 'C'mon, lad,' he said. 'We need to get out of here. Looks like a storm is coming.'

The cloud above, now a dark shadow falling over the arena blocked the light from the sun. A gentle breeze picked up, dust balls swirled and wafted in tiny clouds across the street.

From the corner of his eye Jaydon noted movement behind a crumbling stone wall on the opposite side of the road. Ridley had moved to the wall, gaping at the large forming cloud. Jaydon waited for more movement, was that a shadow or just a trick of light that he saw? But before he had chance to check, a shout came from their right – a group of men had appeared from around the corner of the arena and began jogging towards them; their swords withdrawn.

Rodrick had seen them too. 'Bren, behind you,' he called. 'Thornheart's men.'

Brennand turned as his men drew their weapons, plans thwarted. They must stand and fight. Jaydon had yet to fully recover from the arena, but still he clutched *Devil's Bane* tightly in his fist.

Time seemed to slow, the sky almost black now that the sun had completely disappeared behind the strange cloud, then heavy rain burst from above, beating heavily down.

The wind grew stronger and whipped across them, towards the approaching warriors who seemed to falter in the strong gust. Brennand yelled aloud, as did his men as they streamed forward to meet Thornheart's soldiers. Steel swords clashed, as thunder ripped through the skies.

Jaydon remained by Raven's side, ready to protect her. She still muttered the strange language, not once taking her eyes from the sky.

As the groups of men clashed, the first of the enemy fell under Gordar's sword, his twin engaged with another who too was felled.

The freak weather seemed to push back the onrushing enemy, yet it spurred Brennand's men forwards as though an extra sword and shield fought and pushed at their backs. Rodrick too ran into the foray screaming a war cry as he engaged them.

Jaydon frantically scanned around him, only to see Raven still calling to the dark clouds above. Her eyes had turned from dark black to a misty glaze, 'Raven, get behind me.' He screamed, his thoughts were to protect her as the wind ripped through them both. The heavy downpour starting to soak them all, plastering Raven's meagre clothing to her skin. But she didn't move, continuing to call to the sky; to the gods.

Across from where he stood, Ridley cowered against the wall. 'Rids—Ridley, this way. To me. Quickly!' he shouted, holding *Devil's Bane* out in front of him with both hands. 'I'll protect you.'

Ridley turned his head to where Jaydon called, but before he could move, a shadow rose from behind the low wall. A shadow with greasy hair billowing in the wind and rain – Wilfrec. Jaydon shouted a warning, but too late as Wilfrec grabbed Ridley with one wiry arm, putting a knife to his throat. His twisted face held a triumphant grimace.

'Drop the sword, boy, or this snivelling runt dies.' Wilfrec bawled through the storm. He pressed the knife harder into Ridley's throat.

Without thinking Jaydon sprang forward, *Devil's Bane* held high, raging. As he did Wilfrec brought his knife slowly across Ridley's throat, a sneer smeared across his face. Ridley's eyes widened in shock, his mouth flopped open in a silent scream as dark blood gushed down his tunic.

'Noooo!' Jaydon yelled as he leaped forward bringing his sword with force down onto Wilfrec's forearm, breaking through skin and bone.

The older man yelled, then stumbled backwards and released Ridley who slumped to the ground. But before he could defend himself further, Jaydon swung *Devil's Bane* again, striking Wilfrec across his head. Then struck again and again. Blow after blow as Wilfrec sagged to the ground in a bloody heap. Still Jaydon screamed and swung his sword; all wrath and fury.

In his rage he hadn't noticed the storm around them had petered out as suddenly as it began. Not until he heard Raven's voice cutting through his blood lust did he cease striking the dead body before him. 'Jaydon. JAYDON…enough. He's dead. JAYDON STOP!' she commanded.

He stared back at her, panting, tears streaming, smearing blood and sweat. Her eyes were now returned to their normal dark colour.

'Enough Jaydon. We must go,' she said, kindlier this time.

Jaydon dropped his eyes to the body of Wilfrec, his face destroyed, the insides of his skull leaking onto the ground. Then his senses returned, he spun around and fell to Ridley's side, dropping *Devil's Bane* into the mud as he cradled the dead boy's head in his arms, crying in sadness and rage. He recalled crouching by his dead father and holding his mother and sister in his arms too, in what seemed a lifetime ago, feeling the same despair.

'Why?' he said aloud. 'Why Rids? What did he ever do?'

Raven placed a hand on his shoulder. 'He died to help rescue you, Jaydon. And he is avenged. He is with the gods now.' She acknowledged Brennand and Gordar's approach, faces grim. 'We must leave here. Right Now. Thornheart will be here any moment.'

Brennand nodded. 'Come, lad, we must go. Gordar, pick the lad up will you? Raven's right. Thornheart wasn't with his men, but he won't be far away.'

'Too late,' Gordar replied, as he nodded behind them, where Thornheart had arrived, striding over the dead bodies sprawled across the road.

Gordar swept Jaydon away from Ridley, pushing him onto one of the horses. Brennand grabbed *Devil's Bane*, thrusting it into Jaydon's arms. 'Quick,' he shouted. 'No time to waste. Leave the other horses and ride hard. Don't look back, just ride.'

They all mounted, swung the beasts around and headed toward the road that led out of The Wyke at full gallop. Jaydon still sobbed in his saddle, but held firm as he followed on, leaving behind the bodies, including those of Korban and Morgen who had both fallen in the melee.

•••◆•••

'By the gods,' Thornheart cursed, the storm seemed to have sprung from nowhere. 'What devilry is this?'

He jogged forwards, struggling against the wind and rain. Only moments earlier he had heard the familiar clashing of swords, but that had stopped. As Thornheart rounded a corner the storm broke and he stopped in his tracks. Bodies were strewn everywhere, lying within pools of water that were coloured red with blood. He recognised his own men.

The whinnying of a horse drew his attention, then disbelief turned to anger as he spied four riders making their escape. The boy amongst them, along with Brennand. 'Brennand, you dog,' he cursed loudly as he hastened toward them. 'No, you don't,' he screamed as they started to ride away.

Hurriedly he untethered one of the remaining horses and made chase. He kicked the flanks hard and pushed his steed onwards, but it did not have the speed and strength of his own beast, who could cope with his heavy frame. Regardless, he urged it on all the same, hoping to gain ground. He would not give this up now, he was too close. He yelled at the horse, kicking it again as he urged it into a full gallop, leaning low in the saddle.

From behind he heard shouting, someone screaming his name.

'THORNHEART. THORNHEART, YOU SWINE.'

Turning in the saddle, Thornheart cursed once more. Malin's guard, Rodrick, had followed behind, screaming at him. No doubt Rodrick had helped the boy escape and he was gaining on him too.

Thornheart grunted with frustration and turned the horse, pulling hard on the reins to steer it towards the on-rushing Rodrick, then drew his sword. Rodrick drew his too as they sped towards each other, both horses snorting heavily as their hooves thundered on the ground.

Each of the men swung their weapons as they approached, steel rang out. Thornheart put all of his strength into the blow, knocking his enemy backwards. Rodrick slumped, then fell from his saddle as his horse ran on ahead riderless. You're mine now, thought Thornheart, as he steered his horse back around and headed for him again, at speed.

Rodrick staggered onto one knee, his weapon still in hand. Thornheart bared down upon him and swung again. His opponent parried the blow once more, the force flinging him onto his back and onto the dirty ground.

Incredibly, Rodrick somehow stood, staggering to his feet in defiance. Thornheart could not believe it, he swore loudly as he rode in for a third attack. This time Rodrick made to feint to his left, but Thornheart read it, and steered the horse into him, knocking him down, trampling him under the hooves of the beast.

As he did, his horse screamed, throwing its head backwards, eyes rolling wildly in their sockets. It staggered on a few more paces before rearing up with another ear-splitting cry. Thornheart was thrown from his saddle, landing on the ground with a heavy thud, as the horse sagged onto its knees then fell over onto its side.

Winded, Thornheart took a moment before hauling himself upwards. The horse, still screaming, thrashed its legs wildly. A deep red wound on its belly, from where its insides dangled, opened to the air.

Thornheart growled in frustration, then turned toward Rodrick, who still lay prone on his back, gasping for air, ribs crushed, blood seeping from a wound on his head. Unable to move. As Thornheart approached Rodrick laughed, spitting pink frothy blood from the corners of his mouth. Then he winced and bawled as Thornheart placed a boot on his ribs and pressed them down, deeper into the man's lungs.

'What do you find so amusing, dead man?' Thornheart grunted.

Rodrick coughed, spat more blood and replied hoarsely. 'He got away. He got away, you bastard.'

Thornheart raged, then brought down his sword.

PART TWO

CHAPTER 18
RAVEN'S STORY

They rode in haste, pushing their horses as fast as they could to escape from The Wyke and Thornheart. Only when Brennand was sure they were not being followed did he slow the pace. He guided them on a circuitous route away from the trade roads, doubling back around the south of the town, then westwards.

They used the cover of the trees and woodlands to their advantage, eventually finding somewhere to rest within a ringlet of hills, overshadowed by a copse of ash trees. As darkness fell, Raven set a fire, blocking the flames with rocks so they could not be seen from afar.

Jaydon sat, withdrawn and exhausted. His broken nose throbbed, his body, covered in deep purple bruises, ached from head to toe. The others left him to rest as they made camp. Raven stirred a pot over the fire – a stew made from squirrel meat infused with herbs. Jaydon welcomed the aroma, focussing his senses on that rather than smell of his own grimy and sweaty body, and the stench of death on his hands.

Gordar sat, head bowed, no doubt mourning the loss of his brother and racked with guilt for leaving his body behind. Brennand too, appeared downcast, Jaydon assumed he felt the loss of his men as much as

Gordar did his brother. A pang of guilt tore through Jaydon—he never asked them to help him, but they did it all the same, putting their lives at risk for him. Yet if it wasn't for Brennand he would not have needed to be rescued, Brennand and his men had kidnapped him and sold him to Malin. He could have been near Everwood by now if they had let him be.

'We need to agree on a plan,' Brennand said, breaking the silence. 'We can't stay here, Thornheart will have the rest of his men out searching for us. We need somewhere safe.'

Raven continued to stir the pot, the scent of the herbs lingered in the air around them, 'We shall head to the High Priestess of Resas,' she replied confidently. 'Jaydon will be protected there. We'll all be safe.'

Brennand shook his head. 'That's over three-days ride, across open plains and hills. We cannot risk that. No, we need somewhere closer. If we head back east, Everwood is just over a day's ride from here, maybe two if we keep to the northern forest tracks rather than open roads. We can seek somewhere to stay there. I know an old farmer on the outskirts of the town. He can shelter us for a while, until we decide our next steps.'

Raven stopped stirring, her dark eyes lit unnaturally red from the flame. 'No, it is not safe there,' she answered. 'The High Priestess will protect us all. Mieses has led me here and will guide us to her Temple. Everwood is too dangerous. Especially for Jaydon.'

At the mention of Everwood Jaydon stole his eyes from the fire and spoke. 'I was heading for Everwood,' then shooting a sideways glance at Brennand before continuing. 'Until I was captured and sold. My father had an old friend there, Arthek Mulliner. He'll help us. I'm certain of it.'

'I've heard of Mulliner. Was he a captain under your father? I think he was. I was led to believe that he was a good man. Then it's settled. We ride to Everwood,' Brennand decided.

'No, Brennand. I have said it's not safe.' Raven raised her voice. 'I've been shown the way by the goddess Mieses, we must take Jaydon to the Priestess, immediately. She will guide from there.'

'Listen, girl, I don't believe in all this magical godly drivel. I believe in what I see, my sword and my men. We'll have allies in Everwood, that is clear. You go to your priestess. But we take the boy to Mulliner.'

Raven glared at Brennand, her right hand unconsciously touched the silver pendant at her neck, fingering it between forefinger and thumb. Brennand stood, as though challenging her to disagree with him further.

'Bren's right,' Gordar interrupted. 'We need allies. Thornheart has an army behind him. We cannot risk getting caught out in the open. I agree to ride back eastwards and onto Everwood, seek safe shelter. We can hide the boy at the farm we know. Let Bren and I ride into the town and seek out Mulliner. If it's not safe then we ride to Resas.'

Raven fell silent, her eyes closed, then eventually she said, 'Let the Guardian decide. Jaydon, there are bigger things at play in this world. You are the Guardian of the Stone. The High Priestess has asked that I bring you to her. There is evil at work and we cannot allow the Stone of Radnor to fall into the wrong hands. Elokar is behind all of this, I feel his presence out there, in my soul. But it is your choice and I will remain with you regardless.'

Jaydon glanced at *Devil's Bane*, the flames from the fire danced brightly within the red stone, like tiny shooting stars flashing across a crimson night sky. He sighed. 'We go to Everwood. But, if it's not safe, then we go to the Temple at Resas. And I promise, Raven, we will go afterwards and see the High Priestess. But I need to speak with Arthek, in my heart I know that is where I must go first.' He exhaled loudly as he stared into the fire, remembering the dream he had at Lake Blackheath and the face and voice that rose from the flames – giving him Arthek's name. 'It's something I must do.'

Raven took a deep breath, then nodded. 'Then so be it. Now, the stew is ready. We must eat.'

'Good, I'm famished,' Brennand said, sitting back down. 'Then we get some sleep. Gordar and I will share watch tonight. Jaydon, you must rest. We leave at first light.'

•••◆•••

From a clearing on a hill, Jaydon sat atop his horse, a chestnut mare with a white star shape on the bridge of her nose. She reminded Jaydon of the horses he rode back in his village, especially the one he raced against Ober, his father had named her Bella.

'Her name is Frugo,' Gordar had told him earlier. 'She was my brother's horse. He would be honoured that you ride her now, as I am too.'

From the clearing, Jaydon took one last look back towards the town of his enslavement. He took in the view of The Wyke where the arena sat on the eastern side. He could make out the coloured flags scattered around the outer walls, flapping in a slight breeze. It seemed peaceful from here, yet only yesterday it had been full of death. The memory filled him with sadness, the bloody murder of Ridley played heavily on him, but a sadness dampened with hatred. Hatred of Malin, but more so of Thornheart whose actions and attack on his village and family had brought all this upon him.

He became aware of the weight of his sword, *Devil's Bane*, and the red stone fixed so innocently at the pommel, yet a stone that had suddenly become a heavy burden. A stone of the gods. He had yet to be convinced of this guardianship that had passed onto him, and he was still unsure of Raven, but more dubious of Brennand.

Yet, they had set him free, they had fought for him, and Brennand had lost two of his men in the melee that preceded their escape. Resentment, for now, overridden by gratitude. He hoped that Arthek would help him, maybe take him in, at least until he had decided what to do next and work out his plans for vengeance.

It was a slow trek to Everwood, the group kept away from the trade road that ran between there and The Wyke. Instead, they navigated ancient tracks through the dark forest north of the town. The heavy canopy above blocked out the sun, which cast dappled light back down onto the damp ground beneath them. The forest, a mixture of twisted oaks and birch trees, trunks lined heavily with moss, underfoot fallen acorns crunched under the horses' hooves. A musty aroma hung in the air from the decaying leaves. From the tree tops woodland birds called out, sounding warnings at the strange travellers on the ground below. The horses struggled through, at times the riders having to dismount and climb fallen trees and large rocks. Regardless, the horses plodded on, uncomplaining.

Brennand had asked Gordar to lead the group, keeping a watch ahead for oncoming travellers, or worse, a search party sent by Thornheart who would no doubt have dispatched his men around the area searching for them. Brennand explained that Gordar was an experienced scout, who knew the lands of Calaria in intricate detail. In the old wars he had led the scout section and could recall at any moment his precise location from the shape of a hill, the way a stream ran through a valley or from how a wood blended into the plains.

Brennand rode to the rear checking they were not followed, ever watchful, ever on alert. Raven rode just behind Jaydon, who had remained silent for most of the day. What little sun that reached the forest floor had shifted, creating long shadows as they moved into late afternoon, they would have to make camp again before they arrived at Everwood.

Raven kicked her horse forwards, and rode alongside Jaydon as the track ahead widened. 'It's a mistake, Jaydon,' she said. 'Going to Everwood. I fear evil in front of us. It is not too late to change your mind.'

Jaydon sighed then glanced across at Raven. As always, transfixed by her beauty. Black hair, dark eyes, such contrast to her milky white skin. 'I appreciate your concern, Raven. But I need to find Arthek. I can't explain it but his name came to me in a dream. It was dream full of fire but I remember that a face came from the flames, a woman who gave me his name and that I would find him in Everwood. So, I must seek him out.'

'I understand, I have sought the answers from Mieses and she tells me to trust you, Jaydon. But I do feel the evil on the road ahead, my blood runs cold when I face eastwards. We must be ever cautious. Brennand and Gordar are here to protect us, the gods have deemed their worth. Use them to seek out Arthek for you. It is too dangerous for you to enter the town.'

Jaydon sat silently for a few moments before finally responding. 'Why me?' he asked. 'Why am I the Guardian? Why did Mieses guide you to me? What does the High Priestess want with me?' His brows furrowed as he spurted out the questions.

'I can't answer all your questions, Jaydon. The Priestess has the answers you seek. When we are finished at Everwood, we must go to the Temple, she will tell you all. That I promise,' she smiled weakly at Jaydon. 'It's not a simple burden you now carry, this stone,' she said pointing to the sword at his hip. 'The guardianship is of great importance and your life and mine are now entwined. The gods are with us and together we're stronger. The world is at a crossroads. Calaria and all the Isles of Thulia are in danger of descending into a blanket of evil. The banished Elokar is all around us, I feel his presence like a dark mist that clings to life and suffocates it. He seeks all the god stones, something we can't allow to happen.'

'And what of Thornheart? What does he seek?'

'He is just a pawn, Jaydon. Elokar uses him in the physical world, corrupts his mind for his own purpose. No doubt promising an abundance of rewards. But they are lies. The fallen god is all lies and deceit. A malevolent presence who is using Thornheart for his own purpose, and will just as soon discard him when he has what he desires.'

Jaydon thought on this for a while; stones, gods, a guardianship? A sense of unease pricked him like a healing scar. A small voice inside him that nagged: *Why didn't your father tell you all this, Jaydon?*

He shook his head. Confused. Too much to take in and even more to understand, plus he was exhausted. He glanced at Raven again, her natural beauty beguiling him. Her features were so different from anyone he had met before.

'Raven, where are you from?'

She hesitated for a brief second, before responding. 'I have served the High Priestess since I was an infant. I cannot remember my parents, or the land I came from. All I know is that once every ten years, one family from the island of my birth gives their eldest female to the service of Mieses. I was born on an island called Qetha, it lies at least a three-day sail east off the coast of Vorania.'

Jaydon thought of how much he missed his own parents, yet Raven had never known hers. 'That's really sad, Raven. Do you miss them?'

'How can I miss what I have never known? I was born to give my service to Mieses. The people of my land have been providing for the goddess, and the High Priestess for generations. This is my destiny, as the Stone of Radnor is yours.'

'But still, you must have wished to have been with your mother, to have known her?'

'I have never wanted nor longed for anything, Jaydon. But—' Raven thought a moment or two, screwing her eyes so she looked like a mouse. 'I do have a hazy recollection of a woman with dark hair, and of sailing on a narrow ship. It was propelled by two lines of men, who rowed with great oars through the sea. It had an enormous white sail that the captain raised when the winds allowed. I can remember the sea water spraying my face with the dipping of the ship as it cut through the murky waters. And a pod of dolphins that swam beside us as we raced along. Yet, I cannot recall any of her features, nor her voice…' Raven trailed off in thought.

Ahead Gordar halted, the rest of the group drew up alongside him. 'We rest here tonight,' he said pointing to the right of the narrow track where an enormous oak tree stood, with a trunk as tall and wide as any Jaydon had ever seen. 'Up there, around the back of the old oak. It gives us cover from the track. Tether the horses together, behind the tree are some heavy bushes, that'll keep them out of view.'

'Thanks, Gordar,' Brennand replied. 'Let's make some shelter and rest. Again, we leave at dawn. How far now to Everwood?'

'We can be there before the town awakens. There is a hill to the west we can use to scout out the surrounding area before we enter. We'll have cover.'

'Good, let's set camp and leave in the morning.'

The morning sun rose as the group dismounted, turning the clouds from grey to pink. They stood at the edge of the forest on a rise overlooking Everwood. From this distance the town appeared still, except for the wisps of smoke rising from homes as the townsfolk began their daily business.

Fields surrounded the town, their patterns broken by the occasional tree and hedgerow, that were left to grow in peace. Cattle and sheep grazed in the pastures, and snaking its way through the landscape ran a dusty old road that led back to the town. Brennand had the group tether their horses to a tree behind them as he scanned the ground below.

'All is quiet, as I would expect,' Brennand said after a short while. He ran his fingers through this beard, twisting the twine that kept it tidy. 'But, let's wait awhile yet. If it's safe we can make our way down to Lothar's farm.' He pointed to the north west of the town, where a farm, a pale speck in the morning sun, sat a half-mile from the outer edges of Everwood.

Gordar nodded. 'Why don't I head closer, scout things out a little? We don't want to head into a trap.'

'I agree. We'll wait here. Then if all's clear we can make our way to Lothar. We have silver, so I am sure he'll feed and bed us for a day or two.'

'Can we trust him?' Raven asked. 'We cannot put Jaydon into danger.'

Brennand scowled. 'I trust him, that's all you need to know. He's an honest man and has helped me in the past. But to be safe, Jaydon, we can't let him know your name. For now, we all call you Mikon. And hide that sword. Here—' Brennand unfastened a dirty blanket from his saddlebag and flung it toward Jaydon. 'Wrap it in that. Keep it out of sight, especially that stone.'

They waited in silence for a while, each lost in their own thoughts, until Gordar returned; giving the nod that all was safe.

CHAPTER 19
THE TAPESTRY WEAVES

The farmyard had seen better days, broken fences, rusting tools slumped against walls. The farmhouse itself looked like it would only stand one more winter. The wattle walls were crumbling, the wooden shutters, cracked and broken – one hanging on its hinges. A chicken coop stood next to the building, the scrawny birds clucking away, scratching at the dusty earth searching for scattered scraps of corn.

Stacked against the walls of a dilapidated barn lay a pile of logs. By the barn, a small pond where a couple of white geese sat side by side in the long grass. Jaydon compared it to the farms around his own village, they may not have been as big, but they were always well maintained. Should any of the local farmers or villagers hit hard times, the others would always rally round to assist. Yet, here it felt as though there was no community. Farmers left to fend for themselves, Jaydon felt a stab of sadness for the world he had left behind.

'Lothar, my friend,' Brennand and the farmer grasped each other's forearms. 'Good to see you again. I'm afraid we need your help.'

Lothar seemed ancient, reminding Jaydon of old man Odric back at Hardstone Woods. His hair white and wispy with a weathered face, but he had the strong arms of a farmer. A man who had spent his life tilling the lands. 'Good to see you, too, Bren. Gordar, you too, young fella. What brings you this way? What help d'you need from an old man?' Lothar glanced over at Jaydon and Raven as he asked the last question.

'We need a place to rest up for a day or two, some food. Ale too if you can provide? I have silver, we'll pay our way. We shouldn't be around for long. We need to attend some business in Everwood, but have to lie low and not draw any attention.'

Lothar nodded, scratching the stubble on his chin. 'And these two young 'uns? Who are they? Not yours, are they, Bren?'

'The lads name is Mikon, my nephew, our Henrik's lad. The girl is just a servant.' Jaydon dipped his head at Lothar as a hello. He noticed Raven bristle in her saddle, obviously insulted, thankfully she kept her thoughts to herself.

'Mikon, eh? Never knew you had a nephew. And a servant girl? Going up in the world, young Bren.' Lothar let out a raspy laugh that erupted into a phlegmy cough. 'Sorry 'bout that. Damn chest playing up these days,' he said, a curled hand thumping his breastbone 'There's always a home for you here though, Bren. But I guess I'd better let you know I've seen a few bands of Mirenians round these parts the last couple of days. I s'pose you want to avoid them? Rumours are that devil, Thornheart, is roaming the land again.'

'Thanks, old friend, and as I said. Just a day or two, no more. And yes, we want to avoid Thornheart and his men.'

A gentle nod from Lothar. 'Where are the others? Korban, where's he?'

Brennand and Gordar glanced at each other before Gordar replied, his voice catching with a tag of emotion, 'Dead.'

Bowing his head Lothar replied, 'Sorry to hear that Gordar, he was a good man. We'll have an ale to celebrate his passing to Onir and the gods this evening. He'd be welcome into Radnor's service and the battle fields of the heavens. And the others too, all dead?'

'Aye,' Bren replied. 'All of them. We, err, we ran into a bit of trouble. But the less you know the better.'

'Well, I shan't miss Wilfrec, something weren't right with that one. No idea why you took him on, Bren. Never liked him. Gone to the demons of the underworld, that's for sure.' Then he nodded toward the barn. 'This way, you can keep yer horses in there. The wife has some meat cured, and freshly baked bread. Maybe some cheese too. Yer all welcome in my home.'

'Thank you, Lothar. You're a good man,' Brennand said.

Lothar turned his head, calling back to the farmhouse. 'Ally. Ally, can you come out here a moment please, my dear?'

Within moments a frail elderly woman made her way from the house. Her legs bowed as she waddled towards them, wiping her hands on a tattered cloth.

'Oh, Bren. Nice to see you. What brings you this way?'

Brennand bent forward, taking her hand in his, pecking her on the cheek. 'Ally, good to see you too. How are you?'

'Y'know me, Bren, can't complain. But times are hard these days. Are you stopping? Do you need food?'

'Just a day or two. Not for long.' Brennand introduced Jaydon, as Mikon, and Raven to her too. Then pulled out a small pouch from an inside pocket of his leather jacket, taking out a few silver coins. 'Here, Ally. To pay our way.'

Ally, clasped his hand in hers, then took the coins. 'Thank you, Bren. I can't lie. We do need whatever extra we can get our hands on these days. Terrible harvest, this year.' Ally pocketed the coins into her apron. 'Right, let me prepare some food for you all, you look starving as well as tired.'

Brennand nodded his thanks, then, as Ally made her way back to the farmhouse, he turned to back to the group. 'Mikon, Raven. Can you take the horses? Gordar and I need to speak with Lothar about a few things first,' Brennand asked. 'Make sure they have enough water and hay, will you? We may have plenty of riding ahead of us yet. You'll find us in the kitchens when you're done.'

It took Jaydon a moment to realise this meant him. 'Of course... Uncle,' he replied before taking the reins of Brennand's horse, as well as his own and leading them toward the barn. Raven followed sullenly behind with the remaining two horses.

The interior of the barn was gloomy, Jaydon left the door open, letting in light. He tethered the beasts to a woodworm riddled joist, then found a couple of wooden pails, which he filled with water from the pond.

'There you go, Frugo,' he said, rubbing the nose of his horse. 'Drink up and I'll get you some hay.' Stacked to one side of the barn sat a loose pile, Jaydon grabbed large handfuls for the horses, so they could feed as he unfastened their griths and removed the saddles.

When he had finished, he stood watching Raven admiringly, as she started to rub down the flanks of her horse with a handful of straw. Jaydon sensed her mood, a cloud seemed to have crossed her face as she worked at the horse.

'What's up, Raven? You've been quiet since we set out this morning. Have I done something wrong? Or is it Bren introducing you as his servant?'

Raven continued to rub down the sweat from the horse in vast strokes, not turning to look at him. 'We shouldn't be here, Jaydon. But

Mieses said I was to put my trust in you. And I am bound to you now. However, I sense danger. It festers in the pit of my stomach. There's a menacing atmosphere around Everwood. I feel it gnawing at me. And now, Mieses is silent. I haven't heard her voice since we left the forests. Perhaps she is angry at me for not taking you to Resas? Or maybe there is a veil of evil over this land, preventing me from speaking with her?'

'I've explained my decision, Raven. I must seek out Arthek. I know it from my dream.'

Raven stopped rubbing the horse and turned to face him, the bundle of straw still clutched tightly in her hand. 'Did you consider that may have been a trick? Elokar works in dreams and nightmares. He is the master of deceit, a liar, a false god. You cannot place your faith in dreams, Jaydon Riler.'

Jaydon felt an anger build inside him and for the first time he raised his voice at her, 'I have placed my trust in you Raven. I am here with you, aren't I? I have to trust you all, even Bren and Gordar. They sold me into slavery. I never planned any of this,' Exasperated, he waved his arms in the air. 'Only a short while ago I was happy. At peace in my village. Helping my father in the fields, playing with Jenna. Learning my words with my mother. All that is gone. Ripped away from me. And the three of you are all I have. But Arthek is a link to my father's past. He was his friend, his companion. Don't you see? I have to seek him out. I have to understand more about what he knows of my father and his sword. He can help me, he has fought Thornheart before.'

Raven sighed, a thin smile appeared beneath her dark eyes that shone in the gloomy interior. 'Of course, I understand Jaydon. I'm sorry, I didn't mean to upset you. We both carry great burdens. Yours is the stone, and mine? Well, that's you.'

Jaydon felt a pang of regret for his outburst, it wasn't Ravens fault what had happened to him. 'I know, I'm sorry too...for getting cross.

My mind doesn't feel my own these days. I do know you're here to help me, Raven...I really do.'

Raven released the straw, letting it fall gently to the floor as she moved toward Jaydon, then placing her arms around his neck she embraced him, bringing him closer to her. Jaydon could smell the sweet scent of her hair as he breathed in. He could feel the shape of her body, her heart beating hard against his chest. He closed his eyes as he placed his own arms around her waist, clutching her tightly into him.

Her warmth transferred to his body, seeping into his muscles, bones and his insides. Without warning the tears came. Streaming down his face as he held her firmly. He sobbed uncontrollably, shoulders heaving. Thoughts of his family flashed through him. All the while Raven held him in silence, letting him release his emotions whilst her fingers stroked the back of his neck beneath his thick matted hair.

Eventually Jaydon's weeping waned and he slowly released Raven. She stood back, giving him a moment to compose himself. Jaydon looked back at her, through his grief another emotion rose from the pit of his stomach as he became lost in the dark pools of her eyes. The most beautiful eyes he had ever seen. Raven raised a hand and brought it to his right cheek, tenderly brushing away the tears.

Jaydon winced as her thumb touched his nose, still tender and bruised. But then his chest tightened. He had an overwhelming urge to kiss her, Raven's face was all he could see, everything else a blur.

In that moment, coming out from his grief nothing else existed. He bent his face towards her, but Raven placed the palm of her hand onto his chest, tenderly pushed him backwards. Jaydon blinked, confused.

'I'm sorry, but I can't give myself to you, Jaydon. I am a servant of the High Priestess and made sacred vows to Mieses. I have known and loved you all my life. However, my existence on this earth is to guide you. We mustn't do anything that could jeopardise all we are fighting for.'

Jaydon blinked again, he felt sick, what had he done? Seeing the hurt on his face, Raven took his hand in hers, softly stroking her thumb over the ridges of veins.

'Listen, when all this is done. When we have reunited the stones and thwarted Elokar, my task will be done. I will be released from my vows. Then…well, let's see.'

'What if we fail? What then?'

'We can't fail, Jaydon. If we do…if we do all is lost. The world as we know it will fall into shadow. Elokar will manipulate those who are weak minded. Others, like Thornheart, will do his bidding. A blanket of the darkest night will lay over these lands for an eternity. So, we must not fail.'

Jaydon stood silently, taking in her words. It was a cruel world to have this burden fall on him and yet take so much from him too. What could he do? Just a boy, he had not yet entered manhood. Just him, Raven and two failed soldiers who scraped a living by kidnapping children and selling them into slavery. Men who stole from good, honest folk. Just the four of them against an army of seasoned killers, led by a malevolent giant of a man. He felt desperate, yet, observing Raven once more, taking in the splendour of her black hair framing her pale face. The way her dark eyes glistened and shone, and the confidence she exuded when she spoke. He felt a kindling of hope, a dull flame that burned in his gut. A grin curled at the corner of his mouth.

'Then we had better not fail, had we?' he replied. 'Maybe we should've gone to the High Priestess after all? Sorry, Raven. Have I brought us closer to danger?'

'You've no need to apologise, Jaydon. We share our burdens together. You did what you believed to be right. The gods weave their tapestry and all we can do is follow. Now, we should join the others. I'm hungry.'

CHAPTER 20
ARTHEK

・・・◆・・・

A chilly morning mist still clung to the ground as the sun rose, struggling to find a way through the heavy cloud. Brennand and Gordar had left Lothar's farm soon after breakfast. Traveling on foot to Everwood, leaving the horses to rest. Under Brennand's instruction Jaydon and Raven had stayed behind, knowing Thornheart's men would be seeking four people on horseback. He ordered them to keep a low profile, though they had insisted on helping Lothar and Ally on the farm, to keep themselves occupied and also to repay them for their hospitality.

Just before he left, Brennand grabbed Jaydon's arm and guided him to a quiet corner of the farm yard.

'This Mulliner? What d'you know of him? Where can we find him?'

'All I know, Bren, is that he's a blacksmith. Or at least that's what my father said. I think it was his family business before he joined the Calarian forces?'

'I may recognise him when we find him. We'll have to make some discreet enquiries when we get there.'

'Can I not come?' Jaydon had asked, but Brennand remained resolute. The boy had to stay out of sight. He and Raven had to stay at the farm and hide, especially if they saw any strange groups of men or riders in the valley.

Everwood was not too far a distance on foot, regardless Brennand and Gordar took their time. Gordar remained quiet, unusually so, Brennand assumed he still mourned his twin.

'Korban was a good man. So sorry, Gordar. I loved him as a brother too.' Brennand said, eventually breaking the silence.

Gordar did not respond immediately, waiting a short while before speaking. 'Thanks, Bren. He loved you also. He died the way he would have liked, sword in hand. He'll be drinking ale with Onir and Radnor now in the heavens.' He shook his head, his blond hair swaying in the breeze, 'He'd always been a better fighter than me, but at least he took two of Thornheart's men down with him before he fell. I hope this is all worth it, Bren. Do you believe Riler's son is who the girl claims him to be?'

'I've no idea. You know me, not one for the gods really, am I? I do know we owed him for all his father did for us. Who knows what Calaria would be like now if Thornheart and the Voranians had won? We wouldn't be here now that's for sure.' Brennand shrugged. 'But the girl seems convinced.' Brennand picked up a small pebble from the ground, throwing it across the fields ahead of them. 'If Mulliner is here we can see if he will take Jaydon into his care. Both of them in fact. We need to get to Ironbrook. You need to let Korban's wife know she is widowed. Poor Leesa – she's pregnant too isn't she?'

Gordar nodded. 'She is, Bren. Not a task I'm going to enjoy.' He paused for a moment. 'Maybe I'm putting it off... but perhaps we should take them to see the priestess, as Raven asked? I know you're not a godly man, Bren. I guess I feel responsible for the lad now. He reminds me of Korban when we were boys. We ran away from home to join the Calarian armies, that's when General Riler took us under his wing. You looked after us both then, too, remember? Maybe we should do the same with his son. For sure it will be safer than here.'

'Maybe. Let's seek out this Mulliner first, look,' Brennand pointed ahead as they approached the boundaries of the town. 'People are starting to rouse. We can find this smithy and see what he has to say.'

The two men walked the rest of the way in silence, only stopping to seek directions. The town of Everwood was comparable in size to The Wyke. The buildings were familiar, with white weather-beaten walls, spattered with grime and dulled to a light-grey. Roofs were red-tiled or thatched. The main roads in the town were cobbled, muddy side streets spoked off every few yards.

Eventually they arrived in a quiet square, the surrounding buildings were lifeless and empty. However, in the corner sat the blacksmith's yard, they could see the forges were burning already, charcoal coloured smoke rising from their chimneys. The yard was empty, so Brennand and Gordar waited silently by the entrance, leaning against a wall.

As they waited, Brennand scanned the rest of the square. It seemed strange to have a blacksmiths yard in such a desolate spot, surely not good for business he thought? The buildings around them were definitely abandoned, they were in such a state of disrepair.

Window shutters hung loosely, or had fallen onto the ground, leaving broken window slats uncovered. Tiles were missing from their roofs, black holes staring to the sky. A slight movement from within one of the buildings caught his eye, a shadow from the darkness within. Did he really see that? His hand instinctively went to the hilt of his sword. He observed the window once more through squinted eyes, as he opened his mouth to tell Gordar he heard another voice call out.

'Mornin', gents.' An older man approached, a leather apron tied around his waist. 'How can I help?'

Brennand cast the shadow from his mind, moving his arm from his weapon. He vaguely recognised the man approaching, a face he had seen from the old wars. Hopefully they had found their man. 'Ah, good morning. Are you the smithy, Arthek Mulliner?'

The man raised his chin, gazing at them both with slanted eyes. 'I am, and, may I ask, who might you be? Not seen you around Everwood before.' He glanced down at their swords, standing with his hands on his hips.

'Forgive me.' Brennand held out his palm, to shake Arthek's hand. 'My name is Brennand, Bren Derowen. My friend here is Gordar Crowe. Could we talk? Somewhere quiet, away from this square?' Brennand glanced over at the building opposite again.

Arthek squinted and scratched his chin before replying, 'I'm a busy man Mister Derowen.' Then nodding towards his yard and forges. 'Got a heap of work to do. Have to get the wheels for a cart finished this afternoon. Can this wait, maybe tomorrow, or this evening at best over an ale?'

'It's about your former general. Well, in fact our former general. Stefan Riler.' Bren put the emphasis on the word *our*, hoping this would bring him favour.

At the mention of Riler's name Arthek relaxed slightly. 'Our general? You served under Stefan? Where? When?'

'I was a sergeant in one of his infantry units. I fought at Winter's Harbour. Gordar here led the Calarian scouts. But we come with bad news, and a request for help. Your help.'

Arthek nodded. 'Very well, follow me,' he led the men into his barn, closing the door behind them.

The inside of the barn was dimly lit, shafts of light splayed across the floor from the gaps between the wooden panels on the walls. Dust from the hay floated between the shafts from the bales that were stacked in one corner. Blacksmith tools hung on the walls and an anvil sat in the centre of the barn. A barrel of water sat to one side of the anvil, a pair of tongs poking out of the top. Discarded, beside the closed door lay a pile of rusty horseshoes. Arthek indicated to the corner, for them to sit, using the bales of hay as seats.

'Now, tell me what news you have. There are a lot of strangers in town at the moment. Groups of Mirenians have been arriving and I hear Thornheart has been seen?'

Brennand waited a moment or two before deciding to get to the point. 'Riler is dead, sorry I know you were old friends. We were shocked, too, but you're right. Thornheart is around and I fear dark times are ahead of us again.'

Brennand saw Arthek's face change, his eyes widening and jaw sagged open, as he sat silently for a moment, absorbing the news.

Finally, Arthek gave a sharp intake of breath before exhaling through puffed cheeks. 'How did he die? Where? I have known Stefan most of my life. We fought side by side for many years, as young lads then later as leaders. I haven't spoken to him for an age. Twenty years maybe? Tell me, what happened?'

'It was at Thornheart's hand, back in his village where he lived with his family. The whole village was destroyed, we don't have all the details, but none survived. Except one. We have his son.'

'You have Stefan's son? Where?' then he paused, his brow creased in thought. 'I had two strangers here a coupla' days ago searching for a boy. It seemed odd, but I didn't think much of it. They send men to watch over my yard. They think I don't know, but I see them all the same.'

So, Brennand thought, he had seen someone in the building after all, it was not just a shadow or his mind playing a trick on him. He nodded but kept silent as Arthek continued.

'The boy, his son, does he have any belongings with him? Anything unusual, maybe even a sword?'

Bren and Gordar stole a glance at each other. Brennand explained that Jaydon had travelled with them. That they had come to Everwood for his help. And their concerns that Thornheart was hunting down Jaydon for the stone. Arthek listened, taking in the news before replying.

'I can't take in the lad. If what you say is true and he has the sword, then with Thornheart and his army in town he won't be safe here.' Arthek stared down at the strands of hay on the floor between his feet, his toes scuffed them to one-side making marks in the dust. 'But I will ride to meet him. I will need to lose those watching me though. They will have seen you visiting me here now. I suggest you make haste and leave. There's a river north of Everwood. If you follow it eastwards you'll come across an old ford. I can meet you there with the boy, after nightfall tonight. Make sure you're not followed. I'll do the same.'

Gordar replied, 'I know the ford. We'll wait on the northern bank, there's a copse there. We'll be hidden within.'

Thank you, Arthek,' said Brennand. 'We'll see you after nightfall.'

Jaydon felt relief when Bren and Gordar returned and confirmed that they had found Arthek, who had agreed to meet with him. But that relief was countered by fear. Fear because Arthek said there were men watching over his yard. Maybe he should have listened to Raven and let her lead them to the High Priestess after all? He hoped he had not put Arthek in danger too. It seemed to Jaydon that everyone he encountered, or those he befriended, were at risk, or worse wound-up dead.

He thought of poor Ridley, his throat sliced open like a slaughtered lamb. Jaydon's family were all murdered. Ober too, who had been guilty of nothing other than living in Jaydon's village – who were also butchered. Even Brennand and his men had not escaped the dark shadow that followed him. Gordar had lost his twin and Jaydon had no idea if Rodrick was dead or alive after helping him escape. So much death in such a short time. He shook his head. Even he himself had added to that, taking Ercan's life in the arena. And he remembered Wilfrec. Jaydon had butchered him in a blood lust he could not control. Finally, his thoughts drifted to Jenna. How he missed his younger sister. Never again would he gaze into her green eyes that were always bright. What had she done wrong? She brought only joy wherever she went. Death hung over Jaydon like a shadow, and he feared for those still around him.

Jaydon considered leaving. He thought about waiting until nightfall, when all were asleep, then he would creep off in the middle of the night. Surely, they would all be safer without him? Yet, he had no idea where he would go. Maybe just him and Raven then?

'So, we meet him after nightfall,' Brennand confirmed and turned to their host. 'Lothar, many thanks for your troubles. I can't thank you enough. You too, Ally. I don't suppose we could trouble you for some food for our journey. I can spare a little more silver for you both, to help?'

'Of course…of course, Bren. I'm just happy to help. But, where will you go?' Lothar replied.

Brennand glanced over at Jaydon and Raven, 'I guess to the Temple at Resas after all? Seems logical. We'll meet with Arthek first though, as agreed. We better get ourselves ready.'

'If there's anything else you need Bren, just ask Ally. I have to run a few errands first. There's sheep to feed in yonder field and a trader in town I've have to do some business with. We've had such a bad year, heavy rains in the spring, the crops have struggled. Only money we'll make this autumn is from the sheep and cattle. The trader I know can help.' Lothar shook his head. 'Maybe this life isn't for us nowadays, getting too old fer it. Ally, can you provide them what they need?' he nodded toward his wife, then turning back to Brennand. 'If I'm not back before you go, fair travels my friends.'

Ally's face reddened and her gaze remained fixed on the ground in front of her. Jaydon thought it odd, she had been so affable the day before. Maybe she felt embarrassed at their plight? Old folk can be so proud.

'We don't have much,' she mumbled. 'I'll spare what I can.'

Lothar shook hands with Brennand and Gordar, then waved a farewell to Jaydon and Raven as he walked towards the eastern fields. Jaydon felt relief, knowing they were doing something and that he would get to meet Arthek. It seemed to bring him out from the melancholy he had felt earlier. He smiled at Raven, surely, she would be glad that they would be on their way to the High Priestess after all? But she seemed troubled still, clutching pensively at the pendant around her throat.

'Good news Raven? Finding Arthek…see, I was right.' He said a short while later.

Raven barely looked up. 'Yes, but something plays on me, Jaydon. I don't know what it is. But the sooner we're away from this place the better.' She paused, her face screwed, before continuing. 'I still haven't heard anything from Mieses. I worry that Elokar has more power in this world and stronger than we thought.'

'Don't worry, Raven, we'll get to Resas. Besides, I'll protect you… with *Devil's Bane*, just as you protect me with your magic.'

'Right, you two, come along. We need to ready the horses. Gordar, take Raven with you to the barn. I want us well on the way before it gets dark,' Brennand ordered. 'Jaydon, see Ally, get what food she can spare and fill the skins with water.'

Jaydon found Ally in her kitchen. She had readied some old cheese and freshly baked bread for them. Her mood, though, seemed a little dour.

'There you go, Mikon,' she said, adding a couple of apples to the rest of the food.

'Thanks, Ally. Is everything alright?'

Ally looked at him earnestly, her watery eyes exploring his face. 'No. No, I'm fine. Come on now, take the food. You'd better get off. There's a few more days riding ahead of you now. No time to dally about.'

Jaydon thanked her and scooped the food up into his arms. As he did, Ally placed a frail hand onto his. 'Take care, Mikon. You travel safely now,' she said, before hurrying out the kitchen and disappearing from the farmhouse.

CHAPTER 21

THORNHEART'S VISITOR

———◆———

Thornheart had arrived from The Wyke at first light, full of rage, making it impossible to speak with him or get him to see any reason. Nyla had tried asking him what happened at The Wyke, but Thornheart had exploded, hurling abuse at her, the men and his servant, Petari. What she did understand, in all of his ranting and raving, and from querying Terren afterwards, was that the boy had been in The Wyke all the time Thornheart had been there. But he had slipped through his fingers yet again; this time with a girl and two men in tow. Two men whose descriptions matched the ones who stood across the street from her now as she watched over Mulliner's yard.

Nyla waited inside an empty building hidden within the shadows, watching from the wooden-barred openings within the walls. She pondered whether to approach them or wait. She decided on the latter. Mulliner had only just left after lighting his forges, so would be back soon enough. Best to wait patiently and see what unfolded first.

Nyla had learned to bide her time over the years, keeping patient. As a young girl she had endured the hardships of slavery. Then pulled on her inner-strengths as she gradually found ways of earning Thornheart's trust, winning her freedom. Through all the suffering she had learned perseverance and the strength of character to slowly rise through Thornheart's ranks, becoming his lieutenant. She shuddered as she recalled all she had tolerated.

She had lied, stolen and killed for him…and worse. This should not have been her life, certainly not one she would have chosen. She had never known her parents, nor the country of her birth. All she knew was that she had been taken as a child. Kidnapped by the Mirenian mercenaries and forced into slavery. She had been beaten, punched, kicked and made to work. Cleaning horses, polishing armour, serving the men their food and ale.

Then later, there were far worse things she had to endure as her body changed and she grew into a young woman. The men's advances changed entirely. She had learned to defend herself, viciously and used her cunning to trick her way out of trouble. Thornheart had noted how she handled herself, and then her freedom came when she had saved his life, foiling plans of mutiny. Killing two traitors who planned on luring him into a trap.

She had gained his trust, always showing loyalty to him, and him alone. He protected her in return, freed her and raised her up above others.

But things were coming to a head, Thornheart had clearly been shaken from his conversations with Elokar, He drank heavily after using the stone to converse with the fallen god. She had seen him tremble in fear afterwards, and he would drink until he could no longer speak. He would just sit there rubbing the tattooed eagle on his forehead as though trying to erase it, or the memories of Elokar away. She doubted his ability to lead too. Recently he had not seemed the warlord he once was. The ale affecting his ability to think clearly. It concerned her, as she tried to comprehend Thornheart's actions.

Nyla watched Mulliner walking back down the street toward his yard. The two men waiting by the gates greeted him as he arrived. She would see how this unfolded before reporting back to Thornheart, so they could plan a way forward—if he stayed sober long enough.

Mulliner and the two visitors went into the barn, closing the door behind them. Nyla considered creeping across the square, to eavesdrop, but no, that would be too much of a risk. She had no idea how long they would be, minutes or hours? She remained in the old building. As it turned out she made the right choice, they were not long and after only a short while the door opened and the three men emerged into the morning sunshine.

She continued to watch as the two visitors headed northwards, taking the road that led out of Everwood. Nyla squinted her eyes into thin slits, deep in thought, as she watched them leave. Mulliner remained behind and began stoking the forges to commence his days' work.

Thornheart's men had taken over *The Hatchett*, the atmosphere becoming raucous as the ale and wine flowed, filling the air with songs of battles. Nyla spotted Kartis to one side and beckoned him over as she caught his eye.

'Kartis, can you ensure a couple of the men stay reasonably sober? We don't need any trouble tonight, you know what it's like when bored warriors drink too much.'

Kartis nodded. 'Aye, Nyla. I already have. Deved and one-eyed Fletcher have agreed to keep an eye on things.' Kartis smiled at his own joke.

Nyla returned a small laugh. 'Good. But any trouble and bring them my way to be dealt with. Any sign of Thornheart, has he surfaced from his room yet?'

'He's been in here for most of the day,' Kartis nodded his head to the far corner of the inn, where, in a partitioned off area, Thornheart sat alone, a tankard of ale in one hand.

'Thanks, Kartis,' she said, then sighed. 'I suppose I had better sit with him. See if I can get any sense of what we do now.'

Kartis gave her look of sympathy. 'Aye, listen. I will stick around for a while yet too. Let me know if you need anything.'

Nyla patted Kartis on the shoulder. 'Thanks, old friend. I'll be okay though. You go and have a drink.'

Nyla picked her way through the throng of men and women, and joined Thornheart. She noted the table already had several empty tankards scattered on its surface. Nyla grabbed the attention of one of the serving girls, a young girl, probably around sixteen, with curly brown hair that fell across her face. 'Fetch me a flagon of wine will you please, girl?'

Thornheart sat with his head down, not moving, already drinking his way through another one. She had seen him like this many times before, but the frequency had increased of late.

As she waited for her wine she regarded him with disgust, he stank of booze, his breath as foul as manure. She wasn't even sure he had washed since his arrival from The Wyke.

The serving girl returned with the wine. Nyla stared at it with distaste, the wine Harrin served tasted like horse piss. It was all she had drank through the week. She sat gazing at the foul liquid, how she missed a good wine from the golden valleys of Vorania or from the Southern Isles on Thulia. She idly wiped away beads of condensation from the outside of the flagon of wine, not really in the mood to take a sip.

Bored of waiting for Thornheart to realise she was sat across from him she coughed aloud, in hope to grab his attention and bring him from his state of semi-unconsciousness.

It worked, he drew his gaze upwards and tried to focus with eyes surrounded by dark circles, like cess pits in a muddy battlefield.

'Ah, Nyla. My good friend. You're here?' he slurred.

'I've been here for some time, my lord,' she forced herself to smile, despite wanting to vomit as she regarded him. 'You spoke with Elokar then? What did he say?'

Thornheart bowed his head once more, staring into the half empty tankard that sat before him. 'Yes. Yes…we spoke.' He paused, as though waiting for the ale to give him inspiration. Then bringing his head back up he hissed. 'I fear him, Nyla. More than I have feared anything in my whole life. I cannot express the rage that torments me inside my head. It's pure hatred. Pure…evil. And why? Because a boy. A child has thwarted me again. I am feared in these lands, Nyla. Men quake at my name. Yet this son of Riler defies me…' Thornheart hesitated a moment.

Nyla knew that he had said too much, he never liked to show weakness, yet he continued.

He tapped his temple with a stubby finger. 'My head burns, Nyla. Burns from Elokar's vile anger. I have known evil, but this is a level I cannot express. Pain sears my mind like…like a hot poker. Burning my eyes from the inside.' He shook his head then drained the remaining ale.

Droplets dribbled through his dark beard. Nyla could not help but notice the silver hairs, more now than there were a few days ago. He put the tankard down onto the table, and glanced around for one of the serving girls. Nyla placed a palm over the top of the empty cup.

'No more, lord. Landis. Look at me. No more,' she said softly, with a shake of her head.

Thornheart took in a deep intake of breath, his immense chest heaving. 'You're right. Of course. You always are Nyla. Now, tell me of your news.'

Nyla hesitated a moment. She'd been deliberating all day as to whether she should tell Thornheart of the two guests that Mulliner received that morning – knowing he would rage once more. She paused briefly before replying. 'Mulliner had company this morning. Two men, they matched the descriptions that Terren gave me of this Brennand and one of his men.'

At the mention of Brennand's name a shadow crossed Thornheart's face, he scratched at his scar with a thick dirty fingernail. 'Go on,' he said, 'Tell me more. What did they talk about?'

'I couldn't get close enough to hear. They shut themselves inside his barn. They weren't long though, and seemed to part on good terms. I would wager they had come to an agreement of sorts. This Brennand and his companion, they left on foot taking the north road out of Everwood.'

'The boy wasn't with them?' Thornheart asked in hope.

Nyla shook her head. 'No. But he can't be far if they were walking.'

A voice interrupted them. 'Lord…Nyla. Sorry to disturb you both. But there's a man who claims to know the whereabouts of the boy. Says he has spoken with him. Shall I bring him to your table?'

'Thank you, Kartis…what man? Where does he claim to have seen them?' Nyla asked. 'I believe I saw Brennand this morning at the Blacksmiths yard?'

'He claims they were at his farm, Nyla. But left late afternoon. They're heading to The Temple at Resas, so he reckons. There were four of them. A man called Brennand, someone called Gordar and two others. A boy going by the name of Mikon and a strange dark-haired servant girl.'

Thornheart, stopped fingering his scar and sat upright in his chair. 'Bring him to me, Kartis.'

Moments later Kartis returned leading an old man to their table. He had the rugged face of someone who had clearly fallen on hard times, like one of the beggars that hung around the market stalls. He wore a threadbare jacket and, in his hands, a filthy woollen cap that he held by the rim, turning it nervously between twisted fingers.

'This is the man, lord.'

'Thank you, Kartis. You may leave us now.' Thornheart waited until he had gone. 'Now, tell me your name and what you know, old man.'

The man hesitated before stuttering. 'My…my name is Lothar, lord. I …I believe you're offering silver for information on a boy?'

'It depends on the boy, Lothar. How do I know it's the boy we seek? That you are not hoping to make some quick silver from me? You seem desperate enough.' Thornheart said, a look of revulsion across his face.

'He travelled with a man named Brennand Derowen. I have known Bren for many years. We go back a fair way. But this boy, Mikon he called him, claimed to be Bren's nephew. Well…I… err…well I overheard the girl call him a different name…they were helping mend some fencing for me. She called him Jaydon, which I thought odd…then I remembered a visit I had from some of yer men a coupla days ago who said to come to *The Hatchett* if we were to come across such a party passing through the land, 'specially if a boy travelled with 'em. If I did, I would be rewarded.' Lothar smirked, staring at the straw scattered on the stone floor, gripping his cap tightly in his hands, tight enough for the whites of his knuckles to show through the filth.

'So,' Nyla asked. 'If you have known him for many years, why would you betray him? How do we know this isn't a ploy to turn us off his scent?'

Lothar responded quietly. Nyla could hardly hear him over the din from the inn. 'I…I'm ashamed. But…but I need the money. We've had a hard harvest. My wife and I are not getting any younger. Good silver will see us through the winter. Allow us to buy more crops. More cattle. We can pray to Onir and Mieses for a better spring next year. But without your silver we may not survive a harsh winter.'

'You will turn in an old friend for silver? Is that what you would have us believe?' Nyla asked.

Lothar bowed his head, then nodded slowly, staring at the floor, yet she could see his cheeks flush as his eyes glistened in the candlelight.

Thornheart spoke again, 'Thank you, old man. You will have your silver. Nyla, see the man is paid, will you?' Then he stood slowly. 'But, a warning. If you have given me false information I will return to your farm. I will hang your wife slowly, then slice ribbons from her skin whilst you watch on. Do you understand?'

Lothar dipped his head again, 'Y…yes, lord. Yes, I…I understand. Thank you.'

Nyla reached to her belt, from the pocket-sized velvet pouch she pulled out five silver coins, placing them on the edge of the table towards Lothar, who reached out a quivering hand to take them. Without warning, Thornheart withdrew the knife from his belt and slammed it through the back of Lothar's hand. The old man screamed, loud enough to silence the inn, shrieking like an owl in the night. Blood spread across the table top, over the coins and dripped onto the stone floor. Thornheart brought his giant frame forward, grabbing tufts of Lothar's wispy hair he yanked his head backwards and whispered into his ear. 'I don't trust any man who would betray a friend. You could just as easily betray me.' Then, withdrawing the knife from Lothar's hand he let it slide smoothly across the old man's throat. Dark blood gushed across the table, Lothar gurgled, spitting blood that dribbled down his stubbled chin. His eyes widened in shock before turning lifeless, like a snuffed candle.

Nyla stared impassively at the old man's body. 'He may have been able to give us more information,' she said to Thornheart.

Thornheart shrugged, 'Maybe, maybe not. But I have all we need. I sensed the truth in his story. He seemed desperate enough.' Thornheart wiped the blood from his blade on Lothar's ragged jacket. 'We must ride for Resas.'

Nyla peered down at the dead man as his body slowly slumped onto the floor in front of them. Retrieving the coins, she wiped the away the blood and placed them back into her pouch. 'How can you be sure, lord? It would be a gamble. I can order some men to ride out. Seek out this Temple and watch over it? I can have them ready before midnight. Maybe best to see first. To be sure.'

The kill seemed to have sobered up Thornheart. 'Thank you, Nyla. No, we cannot delay. We take everyone. I'm sure of it. I'll send some scouts on the road ahead of us in the morning, but it makes sense to me now,' then lowering his voice to a whisper, as his men were all now watching on. 'If Elokar is seeking to bring all four stones together. Would it not make sense for the High Priestess to do the same? She works for the gods. She is the voice of Mieses down here on this earth. Mulliner would know this for sure. He spent many years at the side of Riler. He would know, and I wager he told that to Brennand today.'

He banged the table with a heavy fist, Nyla's flagon of wine jumped, the liquid splashing onto the table, mixing with Lothar's blood. 'I want the men ready at dawn, every last one of them and we ride. We ride to the valleys beneath the mountains of Resas.' Thornheart waved a hand at Lothar's corpse. 'Tell Kartis to have someone clean up this mess, and give the inn keeper some silver for the trouble.' With that he pushed his chair backwards, scraping the legs on the cold stone floor of the inn and walked away.

CHAPTER 22
THE OLD FORD

G ordar found a spot within a thicket of bushes and trees that sat on
a rise and allowed them to overlook the old ford. The ford itself
was just a narrow and slightly shallow bend on a river the locals called
the *Living Run*, which ran down from the distant Scarlet Mountains,
before meandering eastwards through Calaria and across the borders
into Vorania. The rush of the *Living Run's* waters in the night seemed
loud, as did every sound they made too.

Jaydon heard a fox barking in the woods behind them and a river
owl screeched further downstream. They had walked their horses further into the shadowy thicket, dampening any noise they would make.

'Are you sure we've not been not followed Bren,' Jaydon whispered.
'What about earlier when you left Everwood? These watchers – they are
likely Thornheart's men. How did they know to watch Arthek? What if
I've led you all into danger?'

'Don't worry, lad. I'm sure. Gordar and I would have spotted them
by now. Now keep quiet, not a sound.'

Jaydon hoped this to be true. Paranoia had caught hold of him. He
thought back to the behaviour of Ally in the kitchen, before they had

left the farm. It felt odd, as did the way Lothar had quickly disappeared too. He could not be found in his fields. He had said he had business in Everwood. But what business?

Jaydon knew Brennand felt guilty and troubled by it too, but Ally had convinced him all was fine, telling him that Lothar often did the rounds on other farms too. Finding ways for them to make any extra money to ease their troubles.

Another screech from the owl made Jaydon raise his head, he scanned the river, and listened. Raven lay beside him, Brennand and Gordar too were concentrating, gazing into the dark night. Then, another sound could be heard beyond the river, a horse nickering. Brennand and Gordar heard it too and became alert, hands instinctively moving to the hilts of their swords.

'Someone approaches,' Brennand hissed. 'Let's wait until we know if it's him. The moonlight is good tonight, so we should know soon enough.'

Under the silvery night a man on horseback slowly approached the old ford. As he got to the water's edge he stopped and waited. Jaydon's heart beat fast, when he left Lake Blackheath it had been with the goal to seek out Arthek Mulliner. This could be him, waiting just a few yards in front of them.

All Jaydon had been through these past few days, the doubts he had, the anguish, fear and pain he had suffered. He hoped he'd been right. The dark shape dismounted, patted his horse and waited. The rider wore a hood, his face hidden in shadow, making it difficult to discern his features and know for sure if the rider was Arthek, or not.

'Gordar, your sight is sharper than mine. Is that him?'

'I can't tell Bren, shall I creep down and get a little closer? The moon is behind these trees, so I'll have the shadow for cover.'

'Aye, but slowly and not too close.'

Gordar removed his sword and belt from around his waist, handing them to Brennand. 'Here, just in case I make any noise. I have my knife,' he said patting the blade at his hip.

Gordar crawled slowly forwards, sliding like a snake through the grass on his stomach the short distance to the river, yet to Jaydon it seemed to take forever before Gordar eventually moved into position. Just a dark silhouette, hunkered behind a grassy mound. The horseman still waited patiently by his steed. The horse, standing, head bent low, eating the fresh grass by the water's edge.

After a short wait, which seemed to expand for minutes, the man turned towards them. The brightness from the full moon caught his face, as it did Gordar stood and called out in a low hushed voice. Jaydon could not hear what was said, but the rider waved an arm, then mounted his horse again to cross the ford.

Gordar led him to where they were concealed within the treeline, as they approached, Brennand emerged from the cover of the corpse and greeted him, clasping his forearm with a strong grip.

'Arthek, thank you for meeting us,' he kept his voice low. 'Bring your horse into the treeline. We've got good cover tonight. The boy is here, waiting.'

Jaydon watched silently as Arthek led his horse to where the others were tethered, before returning to join the group. Raven too watched on, clasping the pendant at her throat as though for reassurance.

'This is the boy, Jaydon. Riler's son.' Brennand said, indicating to Jaydon with an outstretched arm.

Arthek stepped forward and lifted Jaydon's chin into a chink of moonlight that had found its way down through the trees, 'You have yer father's eyes Jaydon. I'm so sorry for yer loss. He was a good man, I loved him like a brother. I too mourn his death.'

'He loved you too,' Jaydon whispered back, he had to fight back the tears once more. 'He told me many stories of the battles you shared. Of many nights with ale in your bellies and the adventures you had together.'

Arthek looked kindly at Jaydon, 'Aye lad, they were good times. Dark times too though. But yer father led us through them. He always did.' He paused a moment, eyes glistening in the silvery moonlight. 'Tell me, how did he die? Was it Thornheart?'

Jaydon dipped his head, 'Yes. He killed them all.'

'Then sit, tell me about it. Tell me everything.'

The group seated themselves on the ground as Jaydon proceeded to tell the full story of that early morning raid on his village. Of the fires raging, the killing and brutal murder of his father, of his family and his friends. He recalled the fiery dream when Arthek's name came to him. Then how, whilst heading for Everwood, he'd been captured. He paused here, as he explained the part Brennand had to play in that. Glancing sideways at him and Gordar, who both sat in silence, listening. Allowing Jaydon to unburden everything from his mind. He told Arthek about Malin, and how he fought in the arena, killing Ercan. He recalled of how Rodrick had plotted with Brennand to help him escape, and of the strange storm that Raven seemed to have conjured to help them defeat Thornheart's men. Finally, he brought up the stone and Raven telling him he was the Guardian of the Stone of Radnor, and of their journey to Everwood to seek him out. All the while Arthek sat, taking in the tale, not interrupting, not saying a word.

When Jaydon had finished, he let out a sigh. He felt like a huge weight had been lifted from his shoulders. It was the first time he'd spoken aloud the full story of his journey, and all that had happened to him. Jaydon could not believe it had only been just over a couple of weeks, it felt a lifetime, he shook his head silently in the darkness.

Jaydon's eyes moistened, but the tears did not come. Instead, he felt a relief that his story had been told; all of it. The group remained silent, in thought, eventually Arthek spoke, breaking the hush.

'Thank you, Jaydon. I'm sure that was hard for you. Firstly, don't be too hard on Bren and Gordar. They lived off the lands, and had to do what they needed to support families back home. It's tough being an old soldier. As you said, Bren realised his mistake and has made amends since. Aside, he's lost good a couple of good men too in a bid to get you here.'

Brennand nodded his head in thanks at the kind words from Arthek, but did not speak. Allowing Jaydon time to reflect, no words of remorse nor any apologies were needed.

Arthek drew his cloak tighter around his shoulders, keeping out the cold night air. 'As I said, I loved yer father Jaydon. I will tell you more of those stories and of the man he was in time.' He paused a moment, drawing in an intake of air before continuing. 'Do you have the sword now Jaydon? Is the stone safe?'

Jaydon had slung the sword over his back, still wrapped in the dirty blanket that Bren had given him the day before, 'Yes, it's here and safe. Do you want to see it?'

Arthek smiled weakly. 'No, lad. No. It's your sword.' He, again let out a sigh, then fumbled at a leather purse that hung on his belt. From within he withdrew a gold coin. Arthek clasped it with sadness as he held it upwards between thumb and forefinger before tossing it towards Jaydon.

'Yer father gave me that coin many years ago. We were rooting out some Voranians near West Scar. The lord there gave it to your father, it's an old Calarian gold piece. A gift from the lord for a battle which saved his fortress from the raiding enemy forces. Yer father gave it to me instead as I had led the force out that day. The battle had been tough, we lost many men, but the enemy more as they flung themselves at us.' Arthek paused, reaching for a skin, that he had brought over from his horse, and took in a draft before continuing. 'I have kept it since, despite its value. But it's yours now, lad. You keep it. Something old, once owned by yer father.'

Jaydon held the coin up into the moonlight, he had never seen a gold coin in his life. He held it with awe, the moon made it appear a deep yellow. One side of the coin was cast with a castle with two towers at each end. Turning it over he could make out the outline of the face of a man wearing a crown. He had a thick beard and flowing hair. The face of the coin smoothed from years of hands and fingers rubbing away at its surface. 'Who is this man on the coin, is it a king?' he asked.

'Aye lad, we no longer have a king in Calaria. But many years ago, way before the old wars we did. That is King Ethon. He ruled almost five hundred years ago. Many said he was a heroic king. His death sparked the beginning of the old wars.'

'King Ethon,' Jaydon repeated. 'Where is this castle? Why was he such a heroic king?'

'Ah, that is a story for another time. But we can't stay here any longer. Bren, what are yer plans? The boy needs to get away from here. Thornheart's men are everywhere. I heard *The Hatchett* was full to bursting with them this evening.'

Brennand, who until now had been sitting silently, scratched his head. 'Well, the girl here—' he pointed toward Raven, who still clutched the pendant at her throat. '—says we should take the boy to the Temple of Resas. To the Priestess there. I had been hoping you would take the lad to be honest Arthek. But it's clear now you can't do that. Maybe the Temple it is?'

For the first time Arthek acknowledged Raven, looking her over with narrowed eyes. 'The girl is right,' he replied. 'That would be the safest place to head. I have a feeling the High Priestess has some explaining to do? What's your name, girl?'

'My name is Raven. And yes, the High Priestess wants to speak with The Guardian. To Jaydon. We are already delayed and we are in more danger.' She released the pendant from her grasp before continuing. 'Mieses welcomes you, Arthek. You must come with us. It's your fate to join us on our paths. The High Priestess will want to speak with you also.'

Arthek creased his brow, but grinned warmly back, 'I'm not sure about my destiny at all, Raven. But right now, I'm here for Jaydon, another sword for him and hopefully, if he allows, I can be like an uncle to him too, as like a brother his father was to me.'

CHAPTER 23
THE HUNT BEGINS

⋅•⋅•⋅◆⋅•⋅•⋅

The next morning Thornheart and Nyla led the one hundred strong army through the chilly autumn morning and out of Everwood, taking the northern road from the town. Nyla had dispatched two of her men to Mulliner's yard the previous night, but he had disappeared. She sent others to search the local taverns but no one had seen him. Nyla had hoped to question him, but it was too late, she feared he'd departed with Riler's boy and Brennand. She cursed herself. She'd dithered instead of acting. Not a mistake she would make again.

The army cut a muddy path out of the town, locals stood in doorways and hung out of windows, watching the host of men depart. Thornheart had dispatched a couple of scouting parties ahead, hoping to catch sight of their prey.

Nyla kept an ever-watchful eye over him, his mood had lightened, which gave her some relief. Maybe he would be more focussed on the task in hand. She prayed to the gods this would not be another bad call. Thornheart had made too many of them recently, his focus blinded from the drink, and from Elokar.

After an hour of marching northwards, she caught movement on the road ahead. A man on horseback cantered toward them; one of the scouts returning. Had they found them already? Surely not? They would be long gone by now.

The scout reined in his horse alongside Thornheart, Nyla joined them to hear his report first-hand.

'Lord, the old ford, a mile or so ahead on the road. It seems like a small group has camped there overnight. At least five men. There's a thicket across the ford. The ground within trampled. No fires, but they have horses.'

'Thank you Reben. How recent?'

'Less than twelve hours I would say, lord. There are tracks leaving the woods. Heading cross-country, to the north west. Certainly, they've not taken the trade road.'

Thornheart gave a sideways glance at Nyla, a thin smirk spread across his face. 'Northwest. Nyla, I'm right. I am more sure of it now than I was last night. They are heading for Resas. Reben, keep to your orders. I want to be certain. They have the advantage of time on us and are far fewer in numbers, so they will have speed on their side too. But the terrain will be trickier than the main route and less direct. Tonight, we camp at Keenward, there is a fort. It's just a ruin now, but I will see you there this evening. Well done, lad.'

Reben nodded, kicked the flanks of his mount and sped on ahead to re-join the main scouting party.

'Lord, should we send another band of men after Mulliner and the boy? Try to head them off? I can take a few of the warriors. I will bring you the boy's head?' Nyla asked.

'No, we have time. I know where they are headed, Nyla. We will keep to the trade roads. If they are headed cross-country, it will slow them down. Also, an army this size can be seen easily from afar. They will know we would be following and no doubt change their plans. But this way they won't spot us. We'll have the element of surprise. And if they reach Resas before us,' Thornheart shrugged his heavy shoulders. 'Then we surround them. The temple sits atop a rocky mountain. There'll be no escape this time. We have the advantage of time, and far greater numbers. The scouts can follow their trail and report back. We will remain one step ahead.'

Nyla studied his words, he spoke an element of truth. Marching an army this size cross country would be too dangerous. But still, it nagged at her. They could head them off, and push them back towards the road. 'I understand, lord. But if this fails how would Elokar react this time? You cannot be sure they're heading for Resas. It might be a rouse to throw us of our tracks.'

Thornheart turned in his saddle, his face full of thunder. 'Careful, Nyla,' he growled. 'You know not of what you speak. I have raised you up. But don't think I wouldn't hesitate in putting you back down. Not for a moment.' He waved an arm at the soldiers behind him. 'Anyone of these men here would want the trust I show you. Don't take it for granted.'

Thornheart urged his horse forward, leaving Nyla to stare at his back in silence. Once a few paces ahead Thornheart reached down for a skin of ale, then throwing his head back he emptied it before tossing it to one side.

CHAPTER 24
THE TALE OF TONRAR

————◆————

'Tell me more stories of my father Arthek. How did you meet?'
Jaydon asked as they rode side by side. The sun had moved across
the sky as late afternoon bore down on them, they had decided to take a
hilly cross-country route instead of the tracks and roads that would lead
directly to Resas. Gordar rode ahead, the map in his mind guiding them
through the safest course he knew. The autumn sun cast long shadows
ahead of them.

'Ah, there's a story. We could only have been a few years older than
yerself, lad. We were training, up near the castle at West Scar. We had
an old training sergeant.' Arthek pondered this for a moment. 'What
was his name? Ah, yes. Tonrar, or something like that. A gruff man, he
hailed from the northern isles of Calaria, The Sisters they're called. Five
large islands, cold and unforgiving places of snow and ice when winter
sets in. The folk who live up there are strange too, living in tribes, always
squabbling with each other with strange customs and beliefs. They still
follow the old gods you know? But you need to be hardened to survive
in those lands. And Tonrar was harder than most.'

Arthek broke into laughter, 'He had four scars running through his hairline then down across his cheeks. The rumour had been that he'd fought an ice bear. And won. He took no prisoners on the training ground. The strongest men would be left crying as he ran us into the ground every day. Sparring until we could raise our sword and shields no longer. Drawing bows over and over again until our forearms bulged to twice their size. Every day we trained. There would be no army more impressive in all of the Isles of Thulia than those of Calaria, and Tonrar was proud that he had made it so.'

'I remember those stories. Tonrar's reputation has long outlived him,' Brennand had been listening with interest, wanting to know more about the general he had revered.

'Aye, that's true. Can you believe he died by falling from a wall? He fought off an ice bear, trained thousands of young men to become battle hardened warriors. Yet, he died climbing over a wall trying to catch a cat.' Arthek shook his head. 'We all imagined him invincible, that he was some creature that Onir had created to strike fear into us young men. A cat, killed by a cat?' Arthek let out a huge bellow of laughter.

Jaydon grinned and laughed along with him, it felt strange laughing for what was the first time in many days. Yet he delighted in Arthek's company, glad that they had found him in Everwood. The stories he told made him feel close to his father once more. Knowing he would be watching Jaydon from the heavens, proud that he had overcome the adversity he had faced and that he now journeyed with Arthek, his old friend. The burden he had felt in Everwood slowly evaporated with every minute he spent with the blacksmith.

Arthek continued his story, 'It was one training session, we were being run into the ground by Tonrar, we must have run from the castle to the *Old Lady*, an ancient oak tree that sat alone atop a steep hill, several times that day. We were all exhausted, men were dropping like flies.

Then we had to spar against each other. *Just like in the battlefield* Tonrar would say. *You could march all day then have to fight at the end of it.* We needed to be battle fit, not just fighters, but toughened warriors who would have the athleticism and resolve to continue when other armies would fail.

'Tonrar had paired me against your father. We sparred hard, muscles aching, our bodies weary. Yet neither of us would give in. We fought on regardless, with Tonrar barking at us at every moment. Eventually he had to part us to stop. We were dead on our feet. The respect that yer father and I had for each other grew that day.

'Yer father had been a better battle commander than I ever could be. As though he had inner sight on how to lead on the battlefield, like the gods themselves were advising him. And I followed him, and was proud not only to call him my general, but my friend.' Arthek raised an eyebrow. 'I had a son too you know? He's dead now. The pox took him… and my wife. We named him Stefan, after your father.'

Jaydon sat atop Frugo, his chestnut-coloured mare, astounded, His father had never told this story. 'Did my father know this?'

'No, it was a few years after we parted at the end of the old wars. I meant to write to him. To let him know. My son was still a babe when he died. Grief struck me for many months after his death. My solace came from the bottom of a cup of ale. Perhaps I should've ridden out to him, but…' Arthek trailed off in thought.

'I'm sorry to hear that, Arthek, but my father would be glad that you're with me now. I certainly am.'

'As am I Jaydon. As am I.'

The group rode on in silence for a while. They were crossing open ground. Gordar and Brennand kept an eye out behind them for any sign of Thornheart's men. They had decided to stay off the road that would have led to Resas, sure it would be a gamble, but Thornheart commanded many men. This route gave them better cover and more options for escape if they were seen.

As the day wore on, they agreed to make camp as the sun started to set behind distant hills. They found a tiny stream, where they allowed their horses to drink.

Raven struggled to light a fire, the kindling not taking hold of the sparks from the flints. Jaydon watched her, bemused. Raven, looked up, seeing the smirk on his face.

'What are you grinning at, Jaydon Riler? Having fun, watching a girl struggle? Do you want to light the fire instead?'

'Sorry, Raven. It's just...well, you can summon a magical storm from the sky, yet you're struggling with the flints. Why not magic the fire instead?'

Raven glared at him, a cloud of anger crossed her face. 'It doesn't work like that, Jaydon. I cannot just magic everything I want, you know. Here,' she held out the flints to him. 'Come on, you try.'

Jaydon burst with laughter, reminding him of the days when he used to tease Jenna. He felt a pang of guilt though. 'Sorry, Raven. Honestly, I really am. But, okay, let me have a go.'

Jaydon took the flints from her. Crouching on his haunches he tried trying to strike a spark into the kindling stuffed beneath a pile of twigs. The sparks flew, but just would not take hold. He tried again, and again, and again. But no fire.

'There,' Raven said, whipping the flints from his hands. 'Not so easy is it. Now, make yourself useful and help Gordar collect some firewood.'

Jaydon smiled at her. 'That's me scolded,' he said. Raven glared back at him, tight mouthed.

Eventually, the coppery sparks from the flints caught and the fire crackled into life as the red light from the flames bloomed.

As night started to shroud the sky, the group sat around the fire, keeping themselves warmed, eating the cheese and bread that had been provided by Ally. Jaydon took a blanket, pulling it tightly around his shoulders to keep out the night chill.

'How long a ride is it to the Temple?' Jaydon asked, poking the flames with a long branch.

The group looked to Gordar. To Jaydon it felt like Gordar knew every blade of grass in Calaria, an invisible map engraved deeply within his mind. 'Just over three days, at a fair pace, I would say. No more, maybe two if we ride harder and don't stop. We're making good progress, but we can't push the horses too quickly.'

'If Thornheart is following, what do you think he'll do?'

Arthek replied. 'For all his reputation, he ain't a clever man. I would say he'll take the main trade roads. He has a big army, so my guess is he will be confident in this and will use the speed of the road. He doesn't take risks, so I reckon he'll take his full army. That'll slow him down. Assuming he knows where we're going.'

'Do you think he'll know?' Jaydon asked, hoping Thornheart would not. That he would still be searching the lands around Everwood still.

'He knows,' Raven stared into the embers as she spoke, her face, radiant from the flames. 'He is heading westward on the trade road now. I feel it's so. But we will be protected at Resas. It's sacred ground.'

Jaydon thought on this a while before responding. 'How? If he has an army of one hundred men. How will it stop him? He could just march into the Temple and slaughter all of us there.'

'The gods protect us, Jaydon. No army can, nor has ever marched into the Temple. It has stood for a millennia. It has survived many wars and not once has any army invaded the grounds. It is sacred, guarded by forces not of this earth.'

Brennand huffed. 'Codswallop! Gods! Magic! The only thing that protects people is a good sword. If Thornheart doesn't march into the Temple, then it's because of fairy tales and make-believe stories told to make us feel safe and keep the dark night at bay.'

'Bren, if you do not believe after all that you have seen and heard, then I pity you. But you have a part to play yet and the gods have guided you to be here with us. Your story is woven in front of you. A path that has already been written that just has to play out. You were supposed to find Jaydon. You were supposed to bring him to Arthek, and you are supposed to be here now. You can deride. But the true path is here, and you are already walking down it's long trail.'

'Raven's right, Bren,' Jaydon interrupted before he could retort. 'We're all on this journey together. I know, I feel it too. I can't explain. But somehow, I know she's right.'

'Boy, you would follow her anywhere. You're not thinking with your head, it's another part of your body that guides you. I see the way you look at her. Don't blame you mind, she's a pretty girl.' Bren sighed aloud. 'But I'm a man of my word. I said I would help you, and I am. I agreed to go to Resas, and we are. But once there Gordar and I must soon depart. We have family in Ironbrook. And Gordar must tell his sister by law that she's widowed.'

Bren's words hung in the air as Jaydon felt his cheeks redden. He thought he had masked his feelings for Raven. He still felt hurt from her rejection of him at Lothar's barn. Yet he longed for her constantly. Jaydon had once asked his father how he met his mother. He had told him how they had loved one another as children, she had been the reason he had returned to Hardstone Woods when the old wars had ended. *We cannot decide who we love,* his father had said, *no more than we can change the flight of a spear once we have thrust it at its target.*

Again, Raven broke the silence. 'Our fates and our paths will be decided at the Temple. That I know. You will then be free to make your own choice, Bren. The gods will thank you for your service, no matter whether you believe or not.'

••·◆·••

Jaydon was startled awake, he groggily cleared the last vestiges of dreams from his mind. Dawn had just begun to break, Arthek stood over him, a grey shape in the dull light.

'Come on lad, wake up. We need to move. Quickly now.'

Jaydon sat upright, slowly becoming alert to the tone in Arthek's voice. 'Wha...what is it?'

'There, on the eastward hill, yonder. D'you see?'

Jaydon squinted to where Arthek pointed. On a distant hilltop, about one mile away, stood six men on horseback. Dark shapes silhouetted against an orange sky flecked with blue-grey clouds. The men weren't moving but were clearly watching their group. Jaydon instinctively grabbed *Devil's Bane* which lay at his side.

'I see them. Thornheart's men? Are we to fight them?' he asked, steel in his voice.

'Not today, Jaydon. They're just scouts. But it proves Thornheart knows where we're heading. C'mon, grab yer stuff and saddle up. We leave. Immediately.'

Jaydon nodded, the others were up and about, Raven had already started rolling up her blankets. Brennand and Gordar were mounted, watching the enemy scouts, letting them know they were spotted too. Jaydon strapped on his sword, grabbed his blanket and readied himself. Within moments they were on the move once more, heading in a westerly direction. Jaydon glanced over his shoulder and noted the horsemen were following them, making their way down the hill but keeping their distance. Then Jaydon realised that there were now only four of them, two were gone.

'Where are the other two?' he asked.

Brennand, who again was riding to the rear of the group, said. 'No doubt doubling back to Thornheart. To let him know we've been found.' He replied. 'We won't shake them off. They won't attack either. We keep to our plan and head to Resas...and hope to the gods that Raven is right.'

CHAPTER 25
KEEPWARD FORT

⬥

Thornheart placed the green stone back into the wooden box. Full of paranoia, he no longer trusted Petari with its keep – in fact he didn't trust anyone with it, so it remained with him at all times now. He breathed in deeply, letting the morning breeze waft across his face.

With a quivering hand Thornheart scrabbled at an inside pocket of his heavy fur cloak, trying to insert the box into the folds. He cussed loudly, his mind a furnace, the breeze doing nothing to abate the pain within his head. Elokar had damned him for sure. Thornheart wished he had never vowed to give his life to the banished god. He had been promised the reward of eternal life and powers he could not yet comprehend. The world would be his to rule. Yet, it felt like control constantly slipped from his fingers. His every turn thwarted with failure.

Once more, the conversation with Elokar had been full of torment for Thornheart: *I will burn your entrails in the hottest fire that the demons of the underworld can muster. Your eye-balls will be removed from your sockets with a fiery poker. But I will keep you alive for a thousand years whilst you die a slow and agonising death…*Elokar had screamed inside his mind. Menacing threats, each coming with a vision of Thornheart writhing in torment. Visions so real Thornheart could feel the pain as Elokar spoke the words inside his head. So real that he yelled in agony.

Glad that he had walked away from the encampment, ensuring that his men could not see nor hear him speak with Elokar. Only this way could Thornheart hide the pain from any mental torment he would have to endure.

He strolled back to the main camp, Nyla was breakfasting whilst she waited for his return. She sat atop a bulky grey stone, fallen from the towers of Keepward Fort. The fort had been an old burgh, set up by the Calarians, a series of early-warning systems to alert of invading enemy forces during the old wars.

Thornheart recalled ransacking the fort years earlier. It had been defended by a handful of soldiers, farmers and local men armed with pitch forks and hunting knives. Still, he had left none alive. Thornheart hung the commander from a nearby tree, then drew a blade across his stomach allowing his guts to fall and dangle toward the ground below his kicking legs as he jerked from the bough.

He had made the commander's men watch before they too were all slaughtered. Then he had ordered his army to tear down the walls, so the fort could never be used again. But here he was once more, this time for a differing task, and a different kind of war.

He did not want to talk with Nyla yet, so turned his back on her, he needed ale. His thoughts still fresh with the images of the torture Elokar had promised him if he did not retrieve the stone from the boy.

He called out to Petari to fetch him a drink. He knew Nyla's eyes were burning into his back, yet he didn't care. He hadn't liked the way she questioned his every move and each decision. Taking the tankard from Petari, he threw back his head and swallowed it down, draining every drop. 'More Petari,' he asked. 'And some breakfast too.'

Petari refilled his tankard and headed to the campfire, turning chunks of beef that sizzled in the pan, before returning with them to Thornheart, who pierced a hunk with a thrust from his knife and took a huge bite, greasy juices running into his greying beard.

'You've always been loyal to me Petari.' he said, chewing on the meat.

He slugged more ale, still stewing with anger that simmered inside him, boiling away like a pot of water over a hot hearth. The ale did nothing to abate the pain. Thornheart swallowed the remaining beef, and stared at the servant, who stood patiently, still holding the pan.

'Why? Why have you remained loyal Petari? Is it fear? Ha, you should fear me, I am the great warlord, Landis Thornheart. Do you fear me Petari? Is that it, do you fear me?' He bellowed out the last question 'WELL?'

Petari, took a step backwards, mouth agog. 'Lord? I...I serve you, always.'

'Serve me? You should fear me. Be in awe of me.' Thornheart screamed back at Petari, spit flying from his lips. A red blanket descended across his mind as he quickly advanced on her, thrusting his knife forward and before realising it he drove the blade into Petari's throat. Wide eyed, Petari dropped the pan onto the damp grass below her feet. Blood spurted and flooded down her tunic before she dropped onto her knees, falling face down onto the hot pan, which hissed as it burnt into her flesh.

'Lord, what are you doing?' Nyla, ran to Thornheart's side. 'What in the gods names have you done?'

Thornheart turned on Nyla and snarled. 'Not now Nyla.' Then he glanced at the knife in his hand, Petari's blood dripping from the blade onto the ground between his feet. Slowly, the fog within him cleared. He glanced down again at Petari, his loyal servant, lying prone. Dark red grass beneath her body. The anger receded, breathing heavily he sheathed his blade. 'Get me another servant. And, Nyla? Do not question me again.'

Nyla bowed her head. 'Lord.'

'Have someone bury her. She was a loyal woman…are you still loyal, Nyla? Do I have reason to not trust you anymore?'

Nyla responded. 'Lord, why do you doubt me? Have I not stood by you for years?'

'You have, Nyla…' Thornheart paused for a moment – his mind swirled, as he looked around wildly, some of the men had gathered and watching the furore.

He glanced back down at Petari's body again and scratched at the scar on his cheek. It itched more than ever these days. From within the folds of his cloak he could feel the stone pulsating, radiating a warmth with each throb that seared into his chest. What had he done? He thought to himself. Petari had always been faithful. Maybe he had been wrong to doubt Nyla too.

'I…forgive me.' Then shaking his head, he said, 'I don't know what came over me. It's this stone. And Elokar. I needed to let off my anger. Petari just happened to be in the wrong place at the wrong time.'

'I understand, Lord,' Nyla replied gently. 'It must be a heavy weight to carry. I can't begin to imagine.'

'It is, Nyla. But we must stick to our task. I cannot let this beat me. I cannot allow Riler's son to continually defy me.'

Within the camp something drew his attention. Thornheart could hear a commotion, men shouting and calling his name. He turned with Nyla to see the cause of it. Some of his soldiers were running toward them, followed by Reben, his lead scout.

'Reben. What brings you here? Do you have news?'

Reben panted heavily as he ran to face them both. Men surrounded the group to eavesdrop for any updates Reben brought with him. 'Yes, Lord, we've spotted them. A group of five, including the boy. We tracked them across the lands south of here, definitely headed north west to Resas, for sure.' Reben paused to take a gulp of water from a skin that had been handed to him. His face flushed red. 'I would say they're a couple of days ride from there. They spotted us and broke camp as soon as they did.'

Thornheart nodded. 'They will be ahead of us and will get to Resas before us. Send another scouting party out. They can catch and follow the others. I want regular reports…Reben, you have earned a break. Good man. Get yourself rested and fed. I will reward you well for this news.' Thornheart patted him on the shoulder with a heavy hand.

He stood in deep thought. Moving a sizable army was never quick, he cursed inwardly to himself, knowing they would beat him to Resas. They would be safe there, yet despite the powers that protected the Temple, it had a flaw. It sat atop the summit of a small mountain and only one path wound its way up to the Temple. Once there they were trapped. There would be no escape this time.

'We move as soon as we've broken camp. They won't be able to flee from Resas if we block the path that leads from the Temple. There is no other way out and we have the numbers.'

'Lord,' Nyla asked. 'Again, would you like me to ride ahead and wait with a few of the men? We could thwart them before they even reach the Temple.'

Is she questioning me again? thought Thornheart. Is she purposely trying to belittle me in front of my men? No, I haven't been thinking straight. She has always been dependable and given good counsel. It's just my doubt after speaking with Elokar…isn't it? His thoughts raced, trying to decide what to do.

Eventually he responded. 'It's a good idea, Nyla. But not yet. If they decide to change tactics, then I want you with me when the reports reach us from the scouts. I don't want to separate the men. But thank you for your advice...as always.'

'Very well, lord. As you command. I will order the men to move.'

'Thank you, Nyla.' Thornheart was sure he saw a flash of anger in her eyes before she walked away. Or did he imagine it? Again, he felt conflicted. He cursed Elokar and his damned stone. The sooner he had the Stone of Radnor in his hands the better.

CHAPTER 26
THORNHEART RELENTS

———•··◆··•———

Nyla rode on in silence. Stewing. Thornheart could be damn infuriating at times, if he allowed her to move forward with some of the men, they could head off the boy and those fools who helped him.

Kartis rode alongside her. 'What's going on, Nyla? I can see from your face something isn't right.'

Nyla turned to face him, she trusted Kartis. 'Keep this to ourselves. But I keep asking Thornheart if we can ride ahead with some of our men. Try and get a head of this boy. He constantly refuses. Only the gods know why? I don't think his mind is right, Kartis. I really don't,' shaking her head, she continued. 'You saw what he did to Petari'-

'Aye, Nyla. Some of the men are uneasy about it. Morale is low, lower than I have ever seen it. Some are scared, others could revolt but are too scared. However, there are those who are still loyal. What are you thinking?'

Nyla pondered a while. 'I will keep trying. I may convince him yet to see sense.'

Kartis nodded as they cantered onwards. They had been on the road for three full days, Thornheart had been driving the army forward at a hard and fast pace, those on foot lagged behind, stringing out miles to the rear. He told Nyla he wanted to get there quickly, so he forced his men ahead, whether they were on horseback or not. The trade roads were wide, well used and solid beneath foot and hoof, as such the going was easy for the men on horseback, but hard on the feet for those who marched on behind.

Thornheart sat at the head of his army, mounted atop his great black war stallion.

Nyla had been riding a few paces behind with Kartis at her side. She turned to examine the dark lines of straggling men. They could lose a tenth of their army if this continued, she despaired shaking her head. 'We can't continue like this, Kartis,' she said despondently. 'I'm going to speak with him again.' She kicked the flanks of her horse, heading to the front where Thornheart led.

The scouts had been giving regular reports to Thornheart all through the march. Several times a day two riders would canter towards them, pass on an update before leaving again. Nyla noted his mood had lightened as his suspicions that Riler's son was heading to Resas were proving correct. Maybe this would be a good time to ask him again? She mused.

As she approached two more scouts had reached him and Thornheart beamed in delight.

'What news?' she asked as she trotted alongside him. 'You seem pleased, Lord.'

'Ah Nyla, indeed I am. I know I've not been myself lately. These past few days my moods have been sour. Please, accept my apologies,' Thornheart patted the neck of his stallion. 'But good news my old friend. The boy is nearing Resas, and we are only a few short miles away ourselves. With Elokar behind us, we'll surely meet them soon enough. If not, then there is only one-way in, and only one-way out of the Temple.'

Nyla studied the lines of his face—indeed his moods had been sour. She still stiffened at his poor decision making. But he had not spoken with Elokar since leaving Keepward Fort, she could see a little of the old Thornheart coming back. His face appeared less haggard and the rings around his eyes had softened a touch.

'I heard stories that it's a magical place, guarded by strange forces beyond anything we know in this world.'

'Ha,' Thornheart snorted. 'We have the Stone of Elokar. What magic can stop us with all his powers behind us?'

Nyla kept her thoughts to herself, the stone had not helped so far. She let him continue.

'But our luck is turning,' he sneered. 'We should arrive at the foot of the mountains this very day.'

'Lord? I know I have asked before, but surely if we are close enough now, I could take, say twenty good men. We could head them off in the valley, with good fighting men. It would all be over then.'

Thornheart sat, considering her request. Then nodded.

Nyla inwardly sighed in relief. 'Thank you, lord. I will bring that stone to you.'

'Wait, Nyla. Bring Riler's son to me alive. Kill the others.'

Nyla dipped her head. She looked ahead at the Resas mountain range, despite the cloudy autumnal weather, she could make out their grey shapes only a few miles ahead. A mass of rock ascending from a forest floor, the summits shrouded in cloud.

She noted too, a dark cloud forming in the sky ahead of them, lightning forked and a clap of thunder echoed down the valley. 'Thank you, lord. I won't let you down.' More thunder rumbled in the distance. 'Seems that rain is approaching, we have a lot of men strung back, they will have no shelter before it gets dark'.

Thornheart glanced behind him, then shrugged his immense shoulders. 'I can afford to lose a few. But, nevertheless, I will send someone to move them along,' he shifted in his saddle to face her. 'Thank you, Nyla. You've been a tower of strength. The rewards promised will soon be ours.'

Nyla bobbed her head in acknowledgment, then turned, riding back down the line where she ordered Kartis to gather the men she needed, for once happy that Thornheart had relented. It seemed his mood had lifted, maybe she had been wrong to doubt him? Perhaps he just wanted her counsel for as long as possible on the road? When he remained sober, and he listened, he could be a good commander.

CHAPTER 27
TOWERS OF DUST

F or two days they had ridden hard, the horses were starting to struggle, their flanks white with sweat and mouths frothing at the bits.
But Brennand and Arthek urged them onwards all the same, only breaking for the odd rest before forcing the group hastily onwards. Thornheart's scouting party still followed behind. Never getting too close, but
always within sight.

There were ten of them now, every so often a couple of the chasing
horsemen would break off and disappear before returning hours later.
Gordar had said they were relaying messages back to Thornheart, he
would know their every move.

Jaydon was completely fatigued—the euphoria he had felt only a
few days ago had completely vanished. He felt delirious, images of his
family and Ridley flashed in front of him. In his mind he could hear
Jenna's voice calling to him. He knew it wasn't real, it couldn't be. Exhaustion pushed his body to its limits.

Conversation within the group had been low and the provisions
provided by Ally were almost gone. At least they were able to refill water
as they crossed streams and brooks, allowing the horses to drink before

pushing on once more. They had arrived at the foot of a small hill, now travelling due north as they kicked the flanks of their steeds one more time, urging them up the grassy slopes.

Mid-afternoon approached, the skies above were dark and heavy with rain that would no doubt pour down on them before they reached their goal. Jaydon heard a distant rumble of thunder and he moaned aloud. The fatigue was enough, but a heavy rainfall would demoralise him further.

Raven must have heard him groan as she rode alongside him. 'Don't despair, Jaydon. We are almost there. Keep the faith. Mieses is behind us, pushing us forwards.'

'I feel like the gods are forcing us backwards, not forwards, Raven. Never have I known such a journey. Every bone aches. Every part of my body is screaming at me to stop and lie down. I'm not sure I can continue. And now a storm comes.'

Raven scanned the sky ahead. 'That storm is not for us, Jaydon. See it heads eastwards. It has been summoned by the gods. Anyone venturing toward the Temple from that direction will certainly feel its wrath.'

Jaydon studied the skies again, and sure enough the heavy clouds appeared to be moving in an easterly direction. But how? Were these more magical clouds like the ones outside the arena at The Wyke? 'Is this your doing, Raven? More magic?'

'I told you Jaydon, the gods are willing us along.'

Magic. Raven continued to be a mystery to him. Jaydon had never met anyone like her. He wondered why his father had never talked of magic. Battles, yes, but never magic, or the stones, nor the gods for that matter – not really. It did prick at him a little. There remained so much he did not understand. He felt completely unprepared.

Ahead, Gordar gave an excited cry, he had halted at the brow of the hill, the others caught up with him to see what had caused the commotion. As he reached the summit Jaydon held his breath at the sight before him. Below spread a valley of lush green fields, dotted with farmsteads surrounding a tiny hamlet. Through the valley wound a river, as grey as the clouds above, and beyond that a small mountain range grew out from the valley floor. A forest of green at the base of the range before the landscape changed to the black rocky peaks. The tips of the ranges were lost in low clouds. Clouds that appeared to shimmer despite the overcast day. Again, Jaydon doubted what he saw, his tired mind surely playing tricks with his vision.

'There,' Gordar called. 'The Resas Mountains. The Temple lies near the summit on the southern side.'

The news gave Jaydon some hope, they were almost there. Above he heard the screech of a circling falcon—a sign from the gods or a warning? Would all be well after all, surely the end was in sight? The melancholy seemed to lift, as though somebody had whipped away a shroud of darkness. 'We're nearly there? What a sight to behold.'

'We aren't there yet,' Brennand cut in. 'How do we reach the temple, Raven?'

'There is a path that winds its way up.' She pointed to the base of the forest, even from this distance a small gap could be seen. Her finger traced toward a thin silvery line that snaked upwards and into the cloud. 'It's the only way to the Temple. The High Priestess knows we're coming.'

'How does she know?' asked Jaydon.

Raven gazed upwards, her fingers again clutching the pendant at her throat. 'The falcon has told her.'

Jaydon, turned toward her, bewildered. She spoke of magical things with ease, as though they were the most natural thing. Yet to Jaydon it was otherworldly.

'C'mon, let's get going then,' Arthek called. Then glancing behind at the enemy scouting party still following. 'We can't afford to stay here idly chatting.'

The group cantered down the hill toward the valley, Brennand had them keep a wide berth from the hamlet and farmsteads. They arrived at the shallow river where the horses could cross easily. The thin forest below the Resas Mountains lay just under two-miles away.

They made good progress, with their goal in sight it seemed to revitalise them all. A feeling that appeared to have been transferred to their horses too, as though they understood the end of their journey was within reach.

Jaydon patted Frugo on the side of her neck, calling into her ear. 'Go, girl, you've done me proud. There'll be plenty of hay, maybe even a barrel full of apples for you at the end of this. See, Frugo. Just a short way now.' His horse snorted as though she understood his every word.

A sudden call from Gordar made them all pull on their reins, bringing the horses to a halt again.

'What's up, Gordar.' Bren called out, pivoting in his saddle.

Gordar stared eastwards. Jaydon spun Frugo around and observed in the same direction, and his heart sank.

In the near distance, less than a couple of miles to the east, plumes of dust rose into the sky, like great towers. Thornheart's forces were catching up with them after all, and judging from the dust clouds, they would head them off in the valley ahead.

CHAPTER 28

A STORM FROM THE GODS

---•••◆•••---

Nyla had gathered a small group to ride ahead of the main army. 'Right, men. We ride hard,' she called out. 'We ride fast. If we are quick enough, we will head the enemy off in the valley at foot of the mountains. Loosen your weapons in your sheaths. I want this to be over swiftly. But remember, keep the boy alive.'

The men roared, blood lust rising.

'Nyla, over there, in the valley.' Kartis, whose eyesight was sharpened, pointed into the distance valley across from the foot of the Resas mountains.

Nyla squinted, but she could make out the recognisable shapes of three men and two smaller figures on horseback galloping down a hill.

'With me,' she screamed, sword held aloft.

A crack of thunder suddenly bellowed above their heads, the loudest Nyla had ever heard, shaking the earth beneath them. Nyla's horse reared and shrieked in fright. It took all her skill to get it under control. Chaos erupted around her as again thunder boomed, rattling the very bones of her body. Lightning exploded at their feet. Horses panicked. To her right a couple had thrown their riders and were bolting across the open fields.

Grappling with the reins, Nyla fought with her horse again, eventually she managed to turn in the saddle, as she did a colossal bolt of lightning forked and struck the ground to her right with a loud crack. Brightness momentarily erupted around them. Then came the rain, it teemed down, heavy sheets cascading from the black clouds above. Day had turned to night, only the flashes of lightning provided any visibility, albeit for just a brief moment, but blinding when it did.

Horses began squealing, an eerie high-pitch whinnying that echoed out between the claps of thunder. Men cowered and dropped to their knees. More had been thrown from their mounts. It became madness as beasts and men ran every which way. Within mere moments the ground beneath their feet turned into a quagmire of mud, heavy with thick puddles.

What in the heavens? Nyla had never seen rain like this, it streamed like a waterfall, constant and frenetic. With enormous effort she spurred her horse, the whites of its eyes bulging as another enormous flash and deafening crash of thunder rang out. Looking behind, she could just make out Thornheart in the pandemonium who was still with the rest of the army to her rear. He remained on horseback, but was fighting to keep his stallion under control.

She struggled to gain control of her horse too, but eventually managed to steer it back towards Thornheart through the mud and puddles that only moments earlier had been dry earth.

'Lord…Lord,' she called out, her voice hardly carrying through the din of the downpour and relentless thunder. 'What in the gods is this?' Drenched to the bone, with rain gushing down her face, Nyla tried wiping the water away with wet hands, it made little difference. 'What shall we do?'

Thornheart's face screwed, as more lightning flashed around them. He struggled to hear her. 'We need to keep the men together the best we can.' He bawled. 'Come, Nyla. We must rally them. Quickly.'

The pair of them rode up and down the lines as best they could, screaming and shouting at their forces, trying to keep them calm in all the confusion. Their horses slipped and slid in the mud beneath them. The rain never relented; Nyla had never experienced anything like this. Roar after roar of thunder boomed down from the skies. Lightning zipped in every direction.

Still, Nyla and Thornheart tried all they could to encourage their men. Nyla screamed words of reassurance, showing them there was nothing to fear; even though she felt nothing but terror. But they had to let them the men seem them both atop their mounts. It seemed to work. Others too took up the calls and they started to gather in small groups, huddling together into a sodden mass, very few of them remained on horseback. The storm continued for what seemed an age with a ruthless energy. Then, almost as soon as it came, it started to wane.

Nyla reached down and struggled to retrieve her cloak from a saddlebag, still battling with the reins to control her skittish mare. Eventually she manged to free it, throwing the cloak over her head...not that it made any difference, she was saturated, skin deep. Peering out from beneath its hood she noted the rain had turned to a gentle drizzle, the storm clouds above had all but vanished. Very little daylight remained, the gloomy air still heavy with the smell of the storm.

Everything she wore, even her muscles felt heavy from the rain. She took in the sights around her, men, hardened warriors cowering together, trembling from both the storm and their cold damp bodies. From the shadows she caught sight of Thornheart, wading toward her through the mud, dragging his horse behind him by the reins.

'Lord, are you okay?' She asked. His face, grim, like a slab of old granite, beads of rain water dripped from his thick beard.

Thornheart shook his head vigorously. Water scattered in all directions as he did so. 'This was their doing,' he said pointing toward the Resas Mountains, his voice a low growl. 'Gather the men, Nyla. We ride on tonight.'

Nyla nodded; she knew that tone. His mood had darkened once more. She knew better than to do anything other than what he asked. She cursed, knowing the chance of catching the boy and the stone before they reached the Temple had been lost.

Thornheart mounted his stallion, turned, then called over his shoulder. 'I will see you at the foot of the mountains, you take the men. I wish to be alone.'

Slowly, she regrouped what men she could, night was almost upon them when they finally set off again slowly through the drenched road. Less than half of the horses had been found, most still skittish from the storm. Nyla had no idea how many men remained with them, but she thought it was just a shadow of what they had before the storm hit.

Ahead, Nyla looked at the dark silhouette of the Resas mountains, she spat in anger, cursing the gods for leading them to this forsaken place. Further along the road she watched the lonely figure of Thornheart on horseback, disappearing ahead of them. She cursed him too.

CHAPTER 29
SOULS OF THE SERVANTS

————◆————

They had reached the outer edges of the forest, the cart-track had well-worn wheel marks that led inside, disappearing into the darkness. Jaydon took one last look over his shoulder before entering. The scouting party behind them had crossed the river, but halted in the fields.

Jaydon glanced to the east, the storm clouds hung heavy over the trade road. The boom of the thunder rumbled constantly, as great bolts of lightning flashed; great forks striking one after the other. Never relenting. Relief swept over Jaydon, glad that they were not caught beneath such a storm. Even from here he could see great sheets of rain pouring from the colossal clouds above.

'See, Jaydon.' Raven had pulled her horse alongside him. 'Mieses has done her work. We are safe from evil, for now.'

Jaydon nodded silently.

'Come, let's not delay further,' Brennand called across to them. Then turning his head around, he nodded back to the direction of the scouts. 'Let's not forget those bastards behind us.'

Three of the scouts had dismounted, whilst a further two were heading east. Riding at a faster pace, toward the storm clouds. Jaydon could only hope that Thornheart's army had been caught underneath the vicious clouds.

'It appears like they've stopped,' Jaydon replied.

Arthek nodded. 'Aye, lad. They know where we're headed. They'll watch the path's entrance and the forest until Thornheart arrives. Assuming he makes it through that storm.'

'Then what?' Jaydon asked.

'Good question, Jaydon. Good question.' Arthek shrugged. 'He has a hundred men. He'll wait us out. I know I would. Let's worry 'bout that when we need to. For now, let's get to safety and the Temple.'

They entered the forest, the already dull evening turned dark and foreboding, yet their spirits rose as they spurred their horses on with renewed vigour. Jaydon felt the excitement pulsating through his body, the delirium of earlier, and the panic as they raced down the valley, now vanquished.

His thoughts turned to the High Priestess, wondering what she would be like? What would she tell him? Raven had said she would reveal all he needed to know...the secrets of his family, the guardianship, why the stone came to his father? Perhaps, she would take the Stone of Radnor from him, then he would be released from his burden. With a pang of sadness, Jaydon again questioned why his father had never told him of the stone.

But the sadness outweighed hope. It charged through him as he thought that maybe his troubles would soon be at an end.

'What's the High Priestess like, Raven?' Jaydon asked as they followed the winding track upwards through the dark forest. The air within had an eery stillness, not even bird song could be heard from the canopy above their heads. Little light seeped onto the forest floor, and oddly, thought Jaydon, despite it being autumn the leaves remained a dark green, none had fallen to the ground below.

'She's magnificent, Jaydon. The most beautiful woman of this earth, with the wisdom of a millennia. She is the most godly, pious, kindly person I have ever met. And she is excited to meet you.'

'What will she tell me? Will she let me know of my family, and why we have the stone?'

'She will reveal all Jaydon, but of what I can't say. My task was to bring you to her. And for now, that's all I know.' She observed him earnestly, her pale face seemed radiant in the dim light. 'You're a special person, Jaydon, more special than you can ever know…especially to me.'

Jaydon felt his heart would burst; a flush of blood ran to his cheeks. 'And you to me, Raven,' he mumbled back.

A short way ahead the forest broke, and the riders emerged into a clearing. The day now colourless as dusk approached. Ahead, to one side of the track, lay a shelter, a wooden stable, well maintained. Within were four troughs, all topped with fresh water. Mounds of crisp hay lay waiting there too, as though they were expected.

'Are these for us?' asked Brennand. 'Do they expect us to stay here for the night?'

Raven shook her head. 'No Bren, just the horses. The path ahead gets steeper and more treacherous. It's not safe for them. We leave them here now. They will be looked after.'

'By whom?'

'By the carers. Folk who serve the High Priestess.'

Brennand frowned. 'I am not leaving him here. How will I know he's safe? He's been with me for many years, a good horse is hard to come by. Besides, I told you already, Gordar and I won't be staying long.'

'And I told you already, Bren. We are well protected now. No one here will allow any harm to come to us, or the horses. They will be well fed and watered. They will be cared for and rested when you leave. Thornheart's men won't, indeed they can't, enter the forest.'

Brennand grunted and gazed at Gordar who just shrugged. 'Very well then, but if anything happens to them, I will want compensation. D'you understand?'

Raven nodded. 'Come then, we need to reach the summit before nightfall. And ensure the stable doors are closed when we leave.'

Raven was not wrong, the path soon disappeared and became just a thin trail that twisted its way upwards through the rocky terrain. Gradually it got steeper, to the point where they were now having to climb, using hands and feet, hauling themselves ever upwards. Sweat poured down Jaydon's face, neck and back. He breathed hard with the exertion, but he understood why Raven thought they were safe.

There was no way on the gods' earth an army the size of Thornheart's could make a full assault up here, despite any mystical powers that might protect them. The climb became harsher and more severe, they had to be ever mindful of loose stones and rocks. Jaydon had slipped once already, sending a small avalanche of gravel spiralling below him towards Brennand, who cursed and swore as a couple of tiny pebbles struck him on his head and arms.

Yet, as Jaydon looked up, Raven seemed to have no trouble with the climb. She didn't even seem to be out of breath. She floated up the mountain path, as though some unseen force pulled her upwards. She led the way, this was one path that Gordar did not know.

Every now and again she paused, allowing the men below to catch up, permitting a short rest before continuing onwards.

'Hurry now, all of you. We need to be at the Temple before nightfall. It isn't too far, but we can't be out in the dark.' Raven urged.

They had reached a narrow shelf. The outline of a pale moon became visible behind the darkening clouds. The sun hung above distant peaks of the Scarlet Mountains, the sky a deep orange silhouetting their jagged ridges. Jaydon looked again to where Thornheart's army were. From this vantage point he could just make out dark trails in the dusk light, a hoard of men straggling through the valley below them.

'What's so important that we're there before nightfall?' Brennand asked Raven, draining the last droplets of water from the skin that hung around his neck.

'Aside from it being dark, and the path ahead being perilous? This is a magical place, Bren. And at night? Well, there are strange creatures you would not want to come across when darkness falls.'

'What creatures?' Jaydon asked. 'What do you mean? You never said there were strange creatures up here? Do you mean bears or wolves?' He asked anxiously. There were things in the world his father had never explained to him. Stuck in their village at Hardstone Woods most of his life, he had never seen magic, or strange beasts, nor heard of them. They were just stories told to small children at bedtimes. But he never imagined they were real.

'What claptrap,' Brennand replied. 'Pay no attention, Jaydon. Creatures indeed…I wager it's just wild boar or deer.'

'Actually, Bren,' Arthek interrupted. 'I have heard this too. Night Beasts, they protect these mountains.'

'What are Night Beasts?' Jaydon asked with alarm.

Raven replied, 'They are creatures of the night, no bigger than a cat, sprites, created by Mieses and put on this mountain to safeguard the Temple. They run wild in the dark hours, feasting on the wildlife…any life that they find and come across is devoured. No one travels out here after nightfall. Sometimes you can hear their strange chatter, a sound like grinding teeth or a hundred croaking frogs.'

Jaydon stared up again at the pale moon, the skies seemed to darken with every passing second. The hairs stood on the back of his neck—a creeping sensation crawled over his skin like hundreds of tiny spiders. Unconsciously he scratched his arms and head. 'Let's keep moving then. How far now, Raven?'

'Not long now. If we hurry, we'll be there before the sun fully sets for the night.'

The group made haste, every noise or strange sound gave Jaydon a chill. He kept any fear inwards though, focussing instead on getting to the summit in one piece. He ached from the exertions, forearms bulging with the effort. The blisters on the soles of his feet renewed, they felt like tiny heated pin pricks every time he put his foot on the ground to propel himself forward. Yet he kept going, whether the Night Beasts were true or not, he didn't wish to be caught on the mountainside when darkness fully arrived.

Before long they reached a plateau, Jaydon hauled himself up with the remaining strength he had and joined Raven at the top, panting heavily. They were now in thick and clogging clouds, yet oddly the air did not feel cold, but warm, almost humid. Within the clouds, Jaydon noticed strange specks of silver that seemed to swirl and dance like tiny stars. The silver lights appeared to leave a purple trail behind them.

He blinked several times, rubbing his eyes, yet the lights remained. Was he seeing things? Maybe it was tiredness from all the stress and the physical exertions he had been through? Yet they did not vanish. He shook his head again, Jaydon had never seen anything like them, all thoughts of Night Beasts were erased as he watched the tiny sparkles in the air swoosh through the air, like tiny fireflies. He reached out an arm and tried to grab them, however they swiftly evaded his grasp, darting out of reach as his clutched at thin air. Raven giggled as she watched him.

'Am I seeing things? Are these stars floating in the cloud? Is it real?' Jaydon blurted out the questions.

'Yes, Jaydon. They are as real as you and I. They are the tiny souls of those who have served our goddess. They linger still to safeguard the entrance to the Temple. One day, I will be one of these lights, still serving Mieses. In this place we are as close to her in mortal life as we ever can be. I can feel her warmth now and it fills me with joy.'

Jaydon had never seen anything like it, and could not comprehend Raven's words. Were these really the tiny souls of dead people? Suddenly his head started to feel featherlike, and a warm sensation began to seep into his body, easing any pain that he felt.

Could he too be feeling Mieses like Raven? The air appeared to be charged with an energy that he could not explain, but he sensed it with every fibre of his being. It's truly a magical place, he thought to himself.

The others joined them on the plateau, they all stood in awed silence, even Brennand, who stood aghast, slack jawed at the dancing lights in the cloud. Raven turned to them, and outstretched her arms.

'You are all fortunate, very few men get to step foot on these mountains, and even fewer inside the Temple. The gods favour you all,' she said, then glanced across at Brennand. 'Regardless of whether you believe or not. None of you need be frightened by what you see, or hear. We are safer here than anywhere on this earth.' Then she turned her back to them all, lifting her outstretched arms above her head, so that her splayed fingers pointed skywards and repeatedly chanted in a strange tongue, quietly at first, then rising to a crescendo. '*Iommesk ságosnár áðuc rákannann Mieses mráuskár, kanskár ull vuresknár frugos ir vrámas.*' Then, suddenly Raven fell silent, letting her arms fall back down to her sides. Ahead of them the swirling clouds appeared to quicken, then parted, to reveal a path that led to the entrance of a cave.

Jaydon could see a dim gleam of orange flickering within the darkness beyond. Slowly, as his eyes adjusted, he could make out markings on the outer walls around the cave's entrance. Strange runes and symbols carved into the rock, their meaning to him unknown. And in the centre, directly above the middle of the entrance, the shape of a chalice. The symbol of Mieses—the goddess who the High Priestess and Raven served.

'Welcome to the Temple of Resas. Please, follow me,' Raven said, as she stepped forwards and walked toward the cave through the parting cloud. Jaydon hesitated only a moment before he and the rest of the group followed, except Brennand who remained rooted to the spot where he stood, still gawping at the lights within the clouds. A chattering sound behind him broke the silence, it startled him into action and he moved forward quickly to catch the others as they entered the cave and into the Temple of Resas.

PART THREE

CHAPTER 30
THE TEMPLE OF RESAS

————◆————

Raven led the way through a dark corridor lit with torches that flickered, casting dancing shadows on the surrounding walls, their footfalls echoed before them. Jaydon was astounded, the Temple had been carved into the mountain itself, how could men dig such a thing? It must have taken a thousand years.

Onward they went, Jaydon losing all sense of direction as the corridor twisted and turned, rising up before dipping back downward once more as they descended deeper into the core of the rocky peaks.

After a short while he saw movement, ahead two figures approached, both carried torches that cast shadows across their faces. Two girls, no taller than himself. As they neared, he saw that they both had bright yellow hair, almost golden, and wore dark robes, with frayed hems that trailed down to their ankles. Raven stopped just a few yards from them. The girls also came to a halt, then both dipped their heads. Raven acknowledged them, bowing herself.

'Greetings Carwen, Greetings Alaysha, I have returned with the Guardian of the Stone of Radnor. We have travelled a great distance, fraught with distress and much sadness. Please, let the High Priestess know we have arrived.'

Carwen replied first. 'Welcome home, Raven. The Priestess knows you're here.' She smiled. Then her eyes turned to Jaydon. 'She is glad the Guardian is safe and well. But first, you will need to clean, hot baths have been prepared for you all. We have laid fresh clothes within your chambers.'

'You will all feast this evening in the great hall,' Alaysha added. 'The High Priestess will see you in good time. She's in prayer at the moment. Please, follow us.'

The girls led them further into the mountain, until suddenly, the corridor opened into a wide cavern. They were hit with an unexpected brightness, Jaydon had to squint as his eyes adjusted from the darkness of the corridor.

Only a few torches lit the great hall, the main light seemed to emanate from an unseen source. Jaydon had no idea from where. He gazed upwards to the ceiling, yet all he could see were walls that rose endlessly until he could make out no more, just a blackness above.

The room itself was a vast hall, the most enormous he had ever seen in his life. In the middle stood three wooden tables, benches sat at each of their sides—each table appeared large enough that fifty people could fit along each side of them. At one end of the centre table stood a chair, more imposing and grander than the others, the back carved with elaborate runes and symbols, similar to those at the entrance to the Temple. A carved painted golden chalice sat at the top of the head rest, which glowed in the unnatural light.

Jaydon sensed Raven at his side, her arm brushed his, making his hairs tingle and stand on end. 'It's beautiful, Jaydon. Don't you think?'

It mesmerised Jaydon, the sheer scale of everything around him made him speechless. All the men stood in awe, even Brennand, who for so long had derided the gods and Raven's devout belief. Yet, only the gods could have created such a place, nothing here felt natural or of this earth. Raven stole a sideways glance at Jaydon as she walked by his side, gently enclosing her hand in his and squeezing it reassuringly.

'Come now,' Alaysha called to them. 'Allow us to show you to your chambers. You can bathe, cleanse yourselves and dress for tonight's feast. Come,' she beckoned them forwards, leading them down another corridor at the end of the hall.

•••◆•••

Jaydon had never had a bath like it. Steam rose from the brass tub as the hot water soaked into every pore and deep into every aching muscle. The water had been scented with some strange herbs and spices that relaxed not only his body, but his mind too. The dirt and grime just seemed to drift away, then dissipate as it reached the surface.

As a child Jaydon hated baths. He recalled the many times his mother had dragged him, kicking and screaming, to the wooden barrel they all used, usually still full of dirty water from Jenna who had bathed before him. But this? He felt as though he was floating in the heavens— like nothing he had ever experienced in his short life. The other men all sat in similar tubs. He glanced over at them, Brennand had untwined his beard, running a comb through his tangled whiskers. Arthek sat whistling a tune as he scrubbed at his skin.

Gordar just lay, as though asleep, with his blond hair hanging over the back of the tub, a pool of water beneath where it dripped onto the floor below.

Taking a huge breath, Jaydon ducked his head under the water, immersing himself fully, letting the heat seep into him. He could feel the dull aching of his nose, though still broken, slowly ebb away. He held his breath as long as he could, his lungs burning before he shot himself back up to the surface. Water sloshed over the side of the tub, drenching the floor with puddles.

'Oh, my,' he spluttered, coughing up some of the bathwater from the back of his throat.

Arthek bellowed with laughter. 'Enjoying yerself, lad?'

Jaydon rubbed water from his eyes with his forefinger and thumb. 'Ha—oh, Arthek, this is heaven. We never had baths like this back in my village. I never want to get out of this tub. Shoot me full of arrows if I try.'

'I know what you mean, Jaydon. I ain't had a bath like this for many a year. I think it was with yer father…after the final battle at Winter's Harbour. Some local girls in town looked after us well enough then.' Arthek winked at Jaydon before erupting into another side-splitting roar. An infectious laugh that soon had Jaydon and Gordar joining in, eventually followed by Brennand.

They wallowed in their baths a while longer, Arthek regaled with another tale of Jaydon's father, then broke into a song of the heroes of old, Brennand and Gordar joined in. The joy of laughter, of comrade-ship filled the room, echoing off the stone walls around them. Watching them sing together Jaydon too felt a kinship and understood why men bonded when they fought side by side. He knew now he had forgiven Brennand for taking him captive on the grasslands. It may only have been a few weeks ago, but already Jaydon felt years had gone by. He considered Arthek once more, with forearms thickly muscled from years of hammering hot metal on an iron anvil, acting like a little child. He felt content, his woes and burdens cast aside.

After a short while they were interrupted by three girls who entered the bathing room, carrying robes for the men to dry themselves with. Once they were covered, the girls ushered them to their bed-chambers where clean clothes waited.

As he started to pull up his breeches, excitement rose within Jaydon, perhaps he would be feasting with the High Priestess this evening. She would tell him all he needed to know. Why he had been brought here, why he had become the guardian, and more of his father's past. He couldn't wait, and hastily buttoned up his undershirt and made his way to the great hall.

••◆••

The tables were set, roasted hogs and game sitting on wide silver platters. Bowls of fruit of all colours were scattered amongst them. Jaydon tucked into an apple, it crunched as he bit into it, the sweet juices exploding on his tongue.

After days of stale bread and hard cheese it felt as though his taste buds would burst. Raven sat opposite him, Arthek to his right. They were seated at the centre table, Jaydon given the honour of being placed next to the grand chair at the end. The High Priestess had not yet arrived, but for now Jaydon did not care, as he took another chunk out of the apple.

They were joined at the table by other servants of the High Priestess, all young women, all robed in dark clothing. Conversation remained carefree. Other girls served more food and poured wine into silver jugs.

Jaydon took a cup full, the only wine he had tasted before was at the armoury with Rodrick, the morning of his fight at The Wyke. That tasted like urine, but this wine had a sweetness as it ran down the back of his throat like a river of velvet.

'Oh, my,' Jaydon said again. 'This is delicious.' He quickly poured himself another cup. Arthek erupted into laughter again as he clapped Jaydon on the back.

Spirits were high, even with Brennand who, since leaving Everwood, had let his thoughts known on his lack of belief in the gods, especially to Raven. He raised his own cup of wine; glistening meat juices dripped down his freshly cleaned beard. 'A toast,' he cried. 'To those we lost. To Korban, to Morgen and to young Ridley. All who gave their lives for us to be here this night.'

Everyone round the table raised their own cups of wine and toasted the departed, Brennand continued. 'To Raven, thank you for guiding us here safely this evening. I doubted you. But this is truly a magical place.'

Then a voice, as gentle as the wind, with an undertone that commanded respect, responded from behind them. 'Magical? Did I hear that correctly, Brennand Derowen? I thought you did not believe in gods or magic? What was the word you used? Codswallop…was that it?'

Raven and all the girls rose from their seats and bowed their heads. Jaydon turned, then he too rose as did the other men. Standing behind them, as if appearing from nowhere, the High Priestess. Tall and slender, she wore plain white robes that trailed onto the floor as she glided to the chair at the end of the table.

Around her neck, a silver chalice pendant, the same as Raven's, that sparkled in the hall's unnatural light. She stood elegantly over them, standing upright as she rested her left hand on the back of the chair.

One by one her eyes explored each of her guests, she carried a serene smile on closed lips and acknowledged each of them in turn with a slight nod of her head, ultimately stopping at Jaydon. She held his gaze for a moment or two, her features captivated him, unable to tear his eyes away from her. She had a plain, yet beautiful face, her brown skin youthful, showing no lines of age. Her eyes were blue and as bright as a cloudless sky on a summer's day.

Jaydon had never seen anyone with skin so brown before, he had heard stories from the travellers in his village. Men who claimed to have sailed across the Golden Sea to lands south of the Isle of Thulia. Men who told stories of people with painted skin, as dark as oak tables. He had never believed until now. He stood as though spellbound before she eventually spoke.

'Welcome, Jaydon Riler, son of Stefan Riler, Guardian of the Stone of Radnor. Welcome to the Temple of Resas.'

CHAPTER 31
THE FOREST EDGE

————⋆ ⋆ ⋆◆⋆ ⋆ ⋆————

The remains of the army was cold, tired and hungry. Their clothes were still drenched as they marched slowly with drooping heads and weary bodies. Thornheart's decimated troops finally arrived in the valley, joining the scouting party, who were already settled.

Slowly, the men made camp, fires dotted across the landscape. Less than half of the army that had left Everwood remained, most had disappeared after the freak storm. Some had been killed, trampled by horses, or dragged into the wild grasses. Nyla suspected others had deserted as they rode onwards toward the Resas Mountains. She could not blame them, Thornheart had promised riches and an abundance of rewards. Instead, they had only been inflicted with suffering and failure. Mirenians were mercenaries who only stayed loyal for silver and gold—they had been shown nothing so far but empty promises.

Nyla dismounted and sought out Thornheart; in his anger he had ridden on ahead alone after the storm, whilst she helped to gather the remaining army. One of the scouts pointed her in the direction of a nearby hovel that he had commandeered for himself. Two mutilated bodies were slumped by the gate—no doubt Thornheart had used force, and taken his anger out on whoever lived here. She hesitated at the entrance before knocking. Light seeped from the gap beneath the wooden door. A shadow moved across it, to and fro. Nyla held her breath and rapped on it three times, the shadow stopped.

'Who is it?' Thornheart growled from within.

'Lord, it's Nyla. May I come in?'

'Aye, and close the door behind you.'

The main room had few furnishings, a battered table sat in the centre with two rickety chairs either side. Against one wall a fireplace, burning with a few bright embers. Two cot beds stood end to end against each other. Copper pots and pans hung above the fire from iron hooks. Nothing suggested this had been a home, it was perhaps a place to stay for a couple of shepherds rather than a farmer. Thornheart stood in the centre as she entered. She noted the wooden casket on the table, then stared at his face. The eagle tattoo on his forehead creased.

'Lord, the men are setting camp now. I have instructed some to set out in the morning to seek food. But...' she faltered.

'Go on, Nyla. Tell me.'

She took a deep breath. 'We are down to less than fifty men. Some deserted after the storm, others...well I guess they were lost when it hit us.'

Thornheart stared into the embers of the fire as though searching for inspiration. He nodded. 'Very well. Can't say I'm surprised. You had warned me before, Nyla, that the men were getting restless. I should have listened to you. Perhaps we've been too hasty. Maybe we should have raided a village or two on the way for plunder, kept the men happy with treasure in their pockets?'

Nyla stood waiting for him to go on, sensing he had more to say, yet he remained silent. She glanced again at the casket on the table. Knowing what it contained. That little green stone that had started this whole series of events off. Then she felt it, slowly at first, but a gnawing at the back of her mind. Itching, clawing for attention? She tried to draw her eyes away from the casket, but she couldn't, it felt as though it sang a soundless tune just for her. Calling her name.

Thornheart noticed her staring and stepped across, blocking her view. Immediately she came to her senses.

'Lord? Ah…yes, I agree. We need to regain the men's trust,' she said, recovering quickly. 'The scouts told me there is a hamlet further down the valley, perhaps that will sate the men's bloodlust and greed? Tell them that they can keep any spoils for themselves.'

Thornheart nodded and gauged her through the narrow slits of his eyes. He scratched at the scar on his cheek, as he always did when deep in thought. 'Perhaps... no, not yet. I want us to send groups into the forest and around the mountains at dawn. Scout things out, I want to know if anything moves in there. I can't afford for the boy to escape again. We block the track too, set up check-points along it—with whatever men we can spare. No doubt the locals support and feed the Temple. We cut off their supplies.'

'I agree. It buys us time to regroup and plan our next steps.' Nyla replied.

'It does, I don't want to leave anything to chance. The north face of the mountain is a sheer drop. Impossible to climb. The track at the forest edge is the only safe route—so we patrol it regularly. The men can do shifts.' Thornheart turned and reached to his waist belt, he withdrew a leather purse and threw it toward Nyla, who caught it in her left hand. 'There you go. There should be enough silver in the purse for those that are left. Now, leave me Nyla. We can talk in the morning. Elokar demands an audience. Have one of the men fetch me some ale.'

•••◆•••

Nyla walked back to the remains of Thornheart's army. Most of the men were settling down for the night, dark shapes huddled around sporadic campfires. She found Kartis, he had started organising the night's watch with a group of them. All were withdrawn and fatigued. She reached into the purse that Thornheart had given her and handed each one of them a silver coin.

'For your troubles this evening, men. You can rest tomorrow...we'll keep the fires burning for you. I'll ensure the cooks feed you all a good breakfast in the morning. Double helpings. You've done well...all of you.'

The men gave their thanks, pocketing the coins. It wasn't much, but enough to keep them happy...for now. Nyla turned to Kartis, his face grim.

'How bad is it?' she asked. 'I counted less than fifty when we arrived.'

'Including the scouts? Fifty-six. We've lost most of the horses also. Two we had to cull as they'd gone lame. I've ordered the cooks to butcher them for meat. That storm, Nyla...I ain't ever seen one like it. That wasn't natural.'

Nyla nodded in the darkness, she stood and stared at the dark forest ahead of them, then up at the shadow of the looming mountain range. They were not great in height compared to other mountain ranges in the north of Calaria, but they were steep and Nyla wondered how they could ever launch an attack on such a place.

She handed the purse to Kartis. 'Thank you, Kartis...share this amongst the rest of the men, equally. Tell them Nyla thanks them for their trouble. There will be more soon enough.'

Kartis weighed the purse in his palm and raised an eyebrow questioningly, but said nothing. Nyla had been surprised that Thornheart had been so willing to hand it over, he usually ensured that he was seen to be the one rewarding the men. But the shock of losing so many of them in one night must have forced his hand.

'Oh—and have someone take some ale to Thornheart.'

Nyla waited alone for a while, deep in thought. Then strode to the track at the edge of the forest, looking into the darkness beyond, not even the moonlight could breach down to the forest floor. She stood at the opening and listened. Not a sound could be heard within. A sensation of unease washed over her, raising the hairs on her arms.

She had never known a forest so still, even in the dead of night. She scanned the outer edges, her eyes straining to see inside, for movement, for life. But nothing. Her thoughts started to wander, she could only ever remember serving Thornheart, one way or another, either as slave or a warrior. What would her life have been like if she had not been enslaved as a child? Where had she come from? These questions constantly nagged at her these days, why?

Nyla unconsciously reached a hand up to rub the back of her neck, the tingling sensation she had felt earlier with Thornheart when she caught sight of the casket returned. Her head clouded with confusion. Just the thought of Elokar sent fear running through her veins, yet in that moment in the cottage she felt drawn to the stone.

In an almost trance-like state she stepped forward, creeping into the forest. Just a few paces. Her thoughts were suddenly broken with a strange sound from within the dark world in front of her.

What was that? Could there be some life in there after all? She listened, turning her head slightly, mouth open to help amplify any sound. Yes, there it was again, ever so faint, but a clicking sound.

No, she thought, a chattering. There it was once more, only this time louder, closer. She shivered as a chill ran down her spine, her blood turned to ice. She caught a movement to her right, just a flicker of something in the corner of her vision. Then a crashing of branches, twigs snapping.

Panicking, Nyla turned and swiftly ran back to the main camp. Breathless, and unsure of what she had just heard, not a sound of any normal forest creature, that much she knew for sure.

CHAPTER 32

THORNHEART GAINS HOPE

Thornheart glared at the door for some time after Nyla had closed it behind her. Something chewed at him about the way she gawked at the casket. But the stone within could be a devious tool. Perhaps he was reading too much into things, his mind had certainly been playing tricks on him recently.

He took the casket into his hands, tracing his thumb over the carvings on the box, the symbols of the gods. He dragged one of the chairs by the fire and removed his bearskin cloak, hanging it on one of the metal hooks to dry. His body ached, he was damp, tired and incensed. He thought again about the storm, how it had come from nowhere. He had never experienced a storm like it—I bet that witch brought on that storm, he thought, that witch in the Temple. I could wager she's been behind everything all along. Well, when I have all four stones in my hands, she will regret crossing me. I will hang her from the tallest towers and peel her skin away from her body, strip by strip. Her and that boy, Riler's son…I will take his head and mount it on a spike. I will have it carried around like a banner for all to see.

He rubbed his forehead with the forefinger and thumb of his free hand and closed his eyes. Another rap at the door. Thornheart rolled his eyes. What now? Was he not entitled to any peace? Then he remembered asking Nyla to have someone fetch some ale – he missed Petari.

'Yes?' he called out, impatiently.

A voice, muffled behind the door, answered. 'Lord, I was asked to bring you ale.'

'Come in then.'

A man with a grizzled appearance entered, his face tired and haggard, wet clothes still clung to his body. He had dark rings around tired eyes. In his arms he carried a couple of skins, his weapon still slung at his waist.

'Ah, thank you. Place them on the table. What's your name?'

'Malfin, Lord.'

'Malfin, thank you. Tell me…why are you still with me? Why haven't you deserted with some of the others? Be honest Malfin, I would like to know?'

'Lord? I…I've fought for you loyally for nearly twenty years. We've suffered in the past. But you've always rewarded us in the end. Why should I doubt you now?'

'So, you trust me then, Malfin? Trust me even though you know not our purpose? Do not know why I am chasing this boy?'

'I trust you with my life, lord. I fought with you at Winter's Harbour. I lost my brother that day. But, despite the defeat, you compensated us…every last man left with silver in their pockets. I have no family, Lord. Your army is all I have known and you always come out on top… in the end.'

Thornheart took in these words, maybe Malfin had a point? He did always win through, eventually. Winter's Harbour had been the lowest point, he was deeply wounded, both physically and mentally. But that was when the stone came into his hands. He had been let down by the Voranians, who failed to deliver the armies and men he needed.

Their Prince had felt Thornheart's wrath after that and he had taken the stone as payment, took it from his headless body. Elokar had spoken with Thornheart that very day for the first time. Giving Thornheart renewed strength, renewed belief, so that he had come back stronger. Stronger than he had been before, and he would grow stronger still— once he had the Stone of Radnor in his possession.

He glanced down at the casket clutched in his hand, the heat of the stone pulsating in his grip.

'Thank you Malfin. For the ale, your loyalty and your belief. Rewards are ahead of us, I guarantee it.'

Malfin left. With a deep sigh Thornheart opened the casket, the stone seemed to shimmer stronger than ever, a bright green hue. The red markings flickered and danced within. Time to speak with Elokar once more. Normally he dreaded— no, feared speaking with him. But the words from Malfin, just a lowly solider in his army, seemed to have raised his spirits. The belief that he would get through this grew.

He took the stone, curled it tightly in his heavy fist and whispered. The room dimmed, the fire blazed more brightly and Elokar's voice came to him, hissing like a snake inside his skull. This time Thornheart felt stronger.

Thornheart, what news do you bring? Elokar's voice, just a whisper. *Have you found the boy and the stone?*

Thornheart hesitated a moment, the flames from within the fire grew, a hooded figure appeared within them. That familiar stench of decay filled his nostrils, as it always did when he spoke with the fallen god. 'Great Elokar, we have located him. He is with the High Priestess at the Temple of Resas. We have blocked the routes in and out. He cannot escape. My men are patrolling the surrounding forests. It is only a matter of time now.'

Be wary, Thornheart. The Priestess is a witch, she is full of deceit and trickery. All is not as it seems. Never assume…haven't I made that clear with you before?

'You have. My men will prevent all supplies to the temple too. We have them trapped.'

There is another way, Thornheart. You have a woman with you. Do you trust her? Does she know what you are searching for, and why?

'Nyla? Yes, she is my lieutenant. I trust her…she knows about the stone and the boy. She has been by my side for many a year and has never let me down?' A flicker of doubt crossed him. Why had Nyla been staring at the casket on the table? Did she want it for herself? 'Do I have a reason to mistrust her?'

No, you need her, Thornheart. She is a key spoke in the wheel. There is more than one path into the Temple. There is another way, a secret way, only known to those with the sight. You must travel by daylight; the path can only be revealed at dusk. Take Nyla, no one else. Travel to the west side of the mountains and follow a trail northward. I will show you.

A vision appeared. He could see the outer edges of the forest, then a force guided him until a break appeared in the treeline, hidden by a fallen tree. Some of the tree's roots were burrowed deep beneath the earth. Others were now long branches that had grown into tall narrow trees of their own, sprouting up to the heavens. At this tree the vision shifted and entered into the dark forests, steering Thornheart upwards, following a barely visible animal trail. Up it twisted and climbed, out of the forests and still upwards into the rocky terrain. After a short while, the vision came to a stop on a small square of flat ground. Rocks and boulders surrounded the opening, in one corner, by the largest of the boulders, sat a single walnut tree.

Follow this trail, wait in the plateau that I showed you. At dusk, the path to the Temple will reveal itself. Only take Nyla with you, she has a part to play. No-one else must know of this path. Kill the boy, get the stone…and Thornheart? Do not fail me.

The flames in the fire withdrew back to a few smouldering embers. Thornheart placed the stone back into the casket, and held the box tight within his fist. He considered the skins of ale and decided he did not need them tonight. He needed a sober mind instead.

Tomorrow, he and Nyla would seek out this path then wait. He felt a wave of hope and renewed optimism. For now, he craved sleep. He threw another log on the fire and lay down on one of the beds, that creaked under his weight, the casket still clutched in his hand as, for once, he drifted into a deep sleep.

CHAPTER 33
THE STONE OF RADNOR

———————◆———————

The banquet at the High Priestess' Hall was drawing to a close. Flagons of wine were emptied, platters were full of crumbs and left-over joints of meats, carcasses picked to the bones. Jaydon had never had a feast like it. His stomach bloated, his head dizzy from the wine.

The High Priestess turned to face Jaydon, her face passive but her voice held a graveness that could not be ignored. 'Jaydon, we must talk. I've been made aware that Thornheart has men camped in the valley. As much as we would welcome you all, you cannot delay here any longer than necessary.' She shifted in her seat. 'Raven, can you take Jaydon to the chapel? I need to speak with each of the men first. I will join you shortly.'

'Yes, High Priestess,' Raven dipped her head and stood, pushing her chair backwards. 'Come, Jaydon, this way, follow me.'

Jaydon took another quick sip of his wine, and despite the light-head-iness he stood and followed Raven down a narrow corridor, catching up to her so they could walk side by side.

Nerves began to take hold; he had been wondering about this moment ever since leaving Everwood. 'What will she say to me, Raven? I have been wanting to speak with her about my family…but now all I feel is apprehension. What if I don't like what she has to say?'

Raven took his hand as she guided him into a room lit with torches. At the far end sat an altar, carved from stone, a fabric, patterned with purple swirling shapes and strange symbols, lay across its surface. On the centre stood a golden cup, a chalice, and next to that a flagon of dulled silver.

An enormous tapestry hung on the wall above the altar, its edges embroidered with more runes and symbols. In the middle a picture of a woman, dressed in a plain white robe, her arms outstretched, behind her yellow rays of sunshine emanated like spokes of a wheel—Mieses.

Raven turned Jaydon to face her, she stroked his upper arm and smiled at him, he did not know if she gave him a sweet smile, or a sad one? Jaydon could not determine which. 'Only you can decide whether you like what she says, Jaydon. She has many things to tell you, not all of it will be easy for you to hear…but if you are to be the guardian, you will need to understand everything.'

'That doesn't help me. My father told me nothing of the stone, his sword and the guardianship. And now that I'm here, I'm not sure I want to know.' An uncontrollable shudder ran through his body. 'Do I have to accept this charge? Can I say no to the guardianship?'

'Your path is already laid out, Jaydon, but you always have a choice. No one can force you to take this on. Every path has a junction, a crossroads to decide your direction of travel, you are at yours now.'

Behind them the High Priestess swept silently into the room. Her voice interrupting them both. 'You need not fear, Jaydon Riler. The gods guide us—I know you will make the right decision.' Then to Raven. 'Thank you, Raven. We shall speak in the morning.'

Raven bowed once more and left Jaydon alone with the High Priestess for the first time. His mouth had become parched, his tongue felt like old leather, dry and withered. He could feel the blood rushing through his ears, thumping loudly inside his head. The Priestess looked upon him in a kindly manner. She stood tall, at least a head above him.

'This way,' she guided him toward the altar. 'It is time, Jaydon. Time for you to know who you are, why you are here and for you to decide what you must do. But…before you do, are you sure you want to know it all—the full story?'

Nervous tension wreaked havoc through his body, although scared he had to know. He had come this far in such a short space of time. He needed the truth, no matter what choices they said he would have, he knew he had to have that. The truth of his story, of his family and why he has the Stone of Radnor. 'Yes…I'm ready, High Priestess.'

'Very well. And I'm sorry you did not learn all from your father. Events changed quickly, more quickly than I anticipated.' With that she turned to the altar, took the silver flagon, pouring water into the chalice.

The water glistened as it fell into the cup, as though stars shone within the cool liquid. Then taking a vial from within her robes she emptied a few drops of a blueish substance into the chalice.

Jaydon watched silently, as she lifted it high above the altar, raising it to the tapestry of Mieses, and uttered words, using the same tongue that Raven had earlier, when they entered the Temple. '*Rákan Mieses, oðriskár ann uc gráuthornár tá jáennaskimár. Tár bruc vuresk kannornann jarðaðár.*'

She turned and held the chalice toward Jaydon with outstretched arms. 'Take this cup and drink form the chalice of our goddess, Mieses. Drink and all will be revealed.'

Tentatively, Jaydon took the cup in trembling hands; the chalice of Mieses. An odd thought came to him, the plainness of the chalice, a holy relic. No symbols, no runes, no jewelled stones decorated it. Just a plain, unpolished golden cup, close up he could see scratches and dents on its surface. Only something so dull could be so full of power. He hesitated, glanced up at the High Priestess, then took a draft of the liquid. It had no taste. It felt neither cool nor warm. Just a smooth liquid that ran down his throat. He handed it back to the High Priestess, who too took a sip herself before placing it back upon the altar.

'Now, Jaydon. Your mind will be open, the goddess will show you what you desire.'

A warm feeling began to worm its way up from the pit of Jaydon's stomach, gradually working, in a circular motion, around his body. Through limbs, to his hands, to his feet and his head.

The world around him dimmed, his eyes began to lose focus. A floating sensation overcame him, a weightlessness as everything around him shifted, changed. The world swirled until he no longer stood in the chapel of the Temple, but in a small, well-furnished room.

Many shields hung from the walls, each emblazoned with a variety of colourful emblems—a golden eagle on a green field, a black wolf's head howling at a half-moon, leaping stags, along with other icons and shapes. In the centre, between them all, a larger shield. The heart of the shield decorated with a red sword.

Jaydon stood dazed, mystified. The High Priestess no longer with him as he remained alone. Where had she gone? What magic was this?

He swivelled on his heels, trying to get his bearings. Behind him came a voice. Jaydon turned to the source. Two men strode into the room, neither paid any attention to him, one closed the wooden doors behind them. Both men wore clothes and robes made from the finest material, patterned with reds and golds. The one who spoke wore a thin golden crown atop a head of flowing brown hair – a king?

The king looked familiar, but Jaydon could not put his finger upon exactly why? Then he recalled the coin given to him by Arthek. The same nose, the same flowing hair…could this be King Ethon?

'Darrok, you can tell the Lord of West Scar that I will play no part in his scheming.' The king said with a commanding voice. 'If the Voranians want to meet with us, then King Taelaris can tell me himself. Sovereign to sovereign. Why are you acting as his envoy anyway? Who gave you and Lord Stanner authority to have these discussions?'

'Sire, I only wish to keep the peace between our great nations, as does Lord Stanner. He agreed to speak with King Taelaris, and thought that I, as your cousin and advisor, would be able to assist. To smooth talks.' The second man's voice was nasally, his tone patronising. He had a sour face, weaselly face, with eyes that were too close together.

'Do you, Darrock? Peace? It seems whatever we do, whatever we say Taelaris is seeking war regardless. And Stanner is always in the middle of such discussions. No, I should speak with Taelaris directly. Face to face. You can ride to West Scar and arrange that for me.'

'Lord, King…I can assure you, Taelaris seeks peace. But you should not meet with him, that I do advise.'

King Ethon shook his head, the whites of his eyes were rheumy and tired, dark rings circled his green pupils. 'If he seeks peace, then why does his army invade our lands in the east?'

'Stanner and I have your and Calaria's interest at heart. But you are our king and must remain here, in Winter's Harbour, for our people. I will act as your messenger.'

King Ethon sat silently, his chin ridged, jaws clenched. 'No, it's ploy, That's what it is.' He said through gritted teeth. 'Taelaris has had his spies in Calaria and in my court for a while now. But never did I suspect you cousin? I never trusted Stanner. But you? Do you conspire with our enemies?'

'Sire, cousin...have I not always given good counsel? King Taelaris merely wishes to speak, to parley. He is waiting with Lord Stanner at West Scar castle. Waiting for my word.'

King Ethon sat at a table, his head in his hands. Jaydon watched on, enthralled, wondering where this vision had come from. Had the draught form the chalice been drugged? Or could this be a dream? What had all this to do with his family, or the stone?

Eventually, the king spoke. 'I can't trust you, cousin. There will be no talks. Tell Taelaris to leave Calaria. Leave or feel my wrath.'

Darrock shifted stealthily behind the king, moving like a cat hunting its prey, as the king continued. 'And you, leave me. Fetch my brother then leave this court. Go to Vorania for all I care. You are finished, Darrok. Whether you are my cousin or not.'

A grimace spread across Darrock's face. Silently he unsheathed a blade, hidden from within the folds of his robes, but when he spoke his tone remained calm. Jaydon tried to scream out a warning, yet it was futile, neither of the men could see or hear him.

'I'm afraid I can't do that, Your Majesty. The wheels are already turning.' He lurched forward, grabbed the king's hair, yanking back his head, and cut a bloody line across his throat. The crown tumbled to the floor with a heavy thud and rolled beneath the table.

The room started to swim again, colours shifted, Jaydon felt a rush of wind batter his body as he started to spin around and around before coming to a halt once more. This time another room. Two more men stood over the body of the now dead king, where he peacefully lay to rest on a table in regal clothing. He wore his crown again, carefully placed upon his head.

In the dead king's hands, he held his broadsword. Jaydon gave a start, decorating the pommel a red-stone...*Devil's Bane?*

One of the men now spoke, his eyes red with tears. He had the look of King Ethon. 'Where is my cousin, Danlar? Where is the traitor, the coward who murdered my brother?'

'Lord, we believe he has fled to West Scar, hiding behind Stanner's walls. But I bring other news.' The second man wavered before continuing. 'The armies of Vorania have invaded. Stanner has declared with them too. Your cousin is claiming to be the new Lord of Calaria, and is supported by Taelaris and his armies. We will be outnumbered. Calaria could fall if we do not act fast.'

The king's brother cursed, 'Damn them all. We must make haste. Rally the army, order the burghs to arms. We will leave here to fight on. In the name of the king, we must avenge him and push them back from our lands. Do we have the forces to take West Scar?'

'We do, lord, but this palace is not safe.'

'Then go, Danlar, I will join you at West Scar with my men once I have buried our king.'

Once Danlar had left, the king's brother stayed awhile longer, speaking to him through tears and grief. 'Forgive me, brother, I was not there to protect you. But I will avenge you…even if it takes a lifetime. I will summon the power of Onir and Radnor to take back what was lost. But I need something from you first, brother. I need your help also. Please forgive me,' Carefully, he pried the dead king's hands away from the hilt of the sword that lay upon his chest.

As he picked up the sword, the stone reflected brightly from the beams of sun light that cascaded in from an arched window, and he held it aloft, hollering these words, 'I swear to the gods, and pray to Radnor that I will seek revenge for this evil. Vorania will pay, our enemies will be crushed.'

Again, the world around Jaydon shifted, he had the sensation of flying, of rushing once more until everything came back into focus. He found himself back inside the chapel at the Temple; the High Priestess stood before him. A wave of dizziness spun through him and his legs quivered as he struggled to stay upright. The High Priestess ushered him to a seat where he gratefully sat. Gathering himself, heaving in breaths.

His mind a whirlwind, Jaydon eventually spoke. 'What did I just see?' he asked. 'What were these visions?'

'You saw your ancestors, Jaydon. Five hundred years ago King Ethon ruled Calaria. He was a good king. But the power of Elokar was already at work. He had corrupted the mind of the Voranian King, Taelaris. Elokar manipulating Taelaris to take Calaria and bring all the god-stones together. Taelaris promised King Ethon's cousin, Darrock Rane, the Lordship of Calaria as his thrall if he helped rid the land of Ethon. But he had been betrayed, Taelaris had lied to him, and to the Lord of West Scar, a weak-minded man named Barden Stanner.

'Ethon's brother, Jaron Rane, rallied his armies. He struck back with his sword. With *Devil's Bane* and the Stone of Radnor. He took West Scar for himself, repelling the invading Voranian forces.'

Jaydon sat, wide eyed, not wanting to believe what he had heard, nor what he had seen in the visions. His thoughts were in disarray, like an old puzzle he and Jenna used to play with broken tiles, all jumbled up and from which they had to make a picture. But here he had no clue what the picture was.

'What are you saying?'

'I am saying, Jaydon Riler, that you are a descendent of Jaron Rane, brother of King Ethon. And the true born guardian of the Stone of Radnor.'

'Wha...h...how? I don't understand?'

The High Priestess crouched down in front of Jaydon, taking his hands in hers. He peered into her eyes, eyes that shone like the brightest sapphires. She observed him back kindly. 'The death of King Ethon was the trigger for the beginning of the the old wars. Wars that raged through Calaria for centuries. Not coming to an end until your father finally defeated Thornheart and the Voranian forces at Winter's Harbour. But, before that, Jaron had formed a council. It was clear Elokar had started to play his hand. Preying on the greed of men. Myself, Jaron and another—I will come to that other in a moment. We knew Elokar sought all the god-stones. We had to protect the remaining three the best we could. They were scattered to all corners of Calaria, protected under the guardianship of those with good hearts and strong minds.'

The High Priestess paused for a short while, allowing Jaydon a moment to absorb everything. His head reeled, overloaded with emotion. She squeezed his hands before continuing. 'The Stone of Radnor stayed with Jaron, he vowed to keep it safe with his family for generations to come. A vow that remains still to this day. The Stone of Mieses is my burden, it's what has allowed me the longevity of life, yet keeps me locked in this temple. But it has remained safe under my guardianship for five hundred years.'

The High Priestess, releasing Jaydon's hands, stood, taking a few steps to the altar, then turned to face him once more. 'That leaves the Stone of Onir—the father of our gods. The most powerful stone of them all. I said there was another in this council of the stones. One who, in his day, was an eminent warlock. He took the Stone of Onir to safety in the far northern islands of Calaria. And to this day, he hides there still, alive and as old as the lands we live in. Isolated from the world we know. He endures, as does the stone.'

'So, where do you want me to take the Stone of Radnor?' Jaydon asked, dreading the answer.

'With you, Jaydon. *Devil's Bane* is your heirloom, your birth-right. The Stone of Radnor and your sword are as one. Radnor is the God of war, and his god-stone can only wield power with such a weapon—a weapon forged with spells and the magic of the gods.

'But what I ask of you is not as simple as keeping the stone safe. Thornheart is being led by Elokar. He has twisted his already corrupted mind. The Stone of Elokar has been passed through the Voranian kings and princes, each weak minded enough to allow Elokar to force his will. To prey on their flaws and frailties. What Elokar seeks is to unite all four-stones. For over five hundred years he has sought them. First, he tried with Taelaris, now with Thornheart. But Elokar grows stronger, and we cannot delay our only course of action…'

The High Priestess paused for a moment. Jaydon felt the hairs on his arms and neck raise, he shivered as though a chilly breeze had blown across him, yet the air remained still.

'…our only course of action is to unite the stones ourselves. Bring them here, to the Temple. The godliest place on this earth. With the three we can destroy the one, the Stone of Elokar. Rid the fallen god of his powers on earth for good. But for that, Jaydon. You must bring all of the stones here. To this place…this is what I ask of you.'

Jaydon sat, deflated, in his heart he knew this would be his task. But how could he, a boy, no warrior, take this on? An impossible task. 'Y… You can't ask this of me Priestess. I am not worthy of a thing of such importance. We would be doomed to failure.'

'It can only be you, Jaydon. I am so sorry this has come to you, but time is against us. Thornheart seeks a way into the Temple as we speak. Tomorrow, you must leave and seek out the Stone of Onir. You must travel across the Crystal Ocean and seek out Gunlak the Hermit, the old warlock, and take the stone from him. Bring it back to Resas.'

'How?'

'You have already proven your worth. But you won't be alone. Your travelling companions all have their parts to play. Now, it is late Jaydon. You need to rest. We shall speak more in the morning; you have one final challenge before you leave. You will need to make a decision tomorrow. I trust you to choose the right one, Jaydon Riler. Sleep well.'

CHAPTER 34
CHOICES AND PATHS

———— •••◆••• ————

Jaydon struggled with sleep throughout the night, his thoughts scrambled and confused. When sleep did come his dreams were littered with magic stones, gods, kings and strange creatures that roamed in the night. He woke, fretting about what he had to do next, the burden of the Stone of Radnor weighing heavy on him.

He felt pangs of anger towards his father for never explaining any of this to him. Why had he been silent? All this time his father had known of his birth-right, his family history and the true nature of the stone and *Devil's Bane*…yet he had not said a word. Not even in one of his many stories about the old wars and his battles. Yet he missed him, and more than ever he yearned for his father's counsel.

At breakfast Jaydon sat silent, he could feel Raven's eyes on him as he ploughed through a bowl of porridge and hunks of barley bread. But she left him to his own thoughts, as did the men. He finished his meal, made his excuses and returned to his bed-chamber. He lay on his mattress, deep in thought as fatigue started to washed over him. A short time later a gentle knocking at his door woke him.

'Yes? Who is it?' he called out.

From behind the door a muffled female voice called back. 'Jaydon, the High Priestess has asked me to bring you to her once more.'

Jaydon rubbed his face with the palm of his hand, to waken himself fully and opened the door. Alaysha, one of the twin girls who had welcomed them into the Temple the night before stood waiting for him. She beckoned him down the stone corridor that led back to the chapel where the High Priestess waited by the altar, the cup of Mieses still sat on the on its surface. She turned to face him; her hands clasped in front of her chest and nodded her thanks to Alaysha who turned to leave them both alone.

'Jaydon, I trust you slept well last night?'

'Not really, High Priestess. My head was reeling from what you revealed and those visions. I can't believe my father never explained any of this to me.' Jaydon surprised himself at the bitter way he spat out the words.

The High Priestess smiled warmly. 'I know there has been lot for you to take in and understand. But, please, do not blame your father. You were to learn all at your coming of age, when you turned fifteen. Elokar played his hand unexpectedly soon, we were all taken by surprise. Time is against us. Thornheart is close and you cannot delay any longer, you must all leave the Temple today.' She waited a moment, her fingers fiddling with the pendant at her throat, just as Raven always did, then continued. 'Last night we spoke of a further challenge for you. One more decision for you to make. To see if you truly are worthy of the guardianship. Come, this way.'

The High Priestess led Jaydon to a dark corner of the chapel, within the gloom sat a nondescript wooden table. On top of the table, hidden beneath a black cloth, sat an object, about the size of Jaydon's fist. Jaydon could feel an unnatural energy around him, an invisible throbbing that seemed to emanate from whatever was beneath cloth, beating in time with his own heart. Jaydon glanced down to his hip to *Devil's Bane*, where the Stone of Radnor gleamed brightly, an iridescence swimming within the deep crimson.

Carefully, the High Priestess removed the cloth to reveal a bright orb, as white as the late winter snowdrops that scattered the fields in his village. The white stone didn't glow but appeared to swirl and shift, like clouds trapped inside a crystal ball. The pulsating around him increased, it felt like low rumbling thunder that constantly shook the air around him.

Jaydon stared, slack jawed, his hand instinctively went to *Devil's Bane*, to the Stone of Radnor that he grasped tightly. The warmth of the stone ebbed through his body.

'Is...is this the Stone of Mieses?' he asked, his voice just a whisper.

The High Priestess nodded. 'Yes, Jaydon. Our mother stone. A stone that gives us life on this earth. That allows the trees to grow, the rivers to run and the birds to sing. The stone that provides us crops so we can eat, and gives mortals hope of eternity through the creation of life.'

Jaydon still clutched at the Stone of Radnor, but it seemed to have a life of its own. Pulsating within his palm.

The High Priestess continued, 'This is the first time the two stones have been together for five hundred years, Jaydon. Can you feel the power, the strength in the room as they sense each other's presence?'

Transfixed, Jaydon could scarcely breath, nor move. His lips quivered as he spoke. 'I feel it. I feel it in my veins. It...it surges within me.' He released the Stone of Radnor from his grip, yet the power within him still burned, not with pain, but with vitality. He felt a confidence rush through his body, a raw energy that he had never experienced in his life, a feeling of invincibility.

'Only few can feel such forces within the presence of the stones. Only those of good heart, of strength of mind can control their power...and now, Jaydon. Now you must decide. A test.'

Jaydon gazed upon her, at the deep raw beauty of her dark age-defying skin. The wisdom within her sapphire-coloured eyes. 'A test? What test?'

'Together, the stones can give life. They can give back life to where it no longer resides. To one who has fallen—this is one reason Elokar seeks the stones. He wants to bring his physical presence to the earth. To walk amongst us and rule, bringing darkness to our world.' The High Priestess paused, allowing Jaydon a moment to understand the gravity of the choice he would have to make. 'A true guardian knows how to unlock that power, to release and control it. A true guardian knows the true path, is enlightened and will choose that path no matter the consequences.' The High Priestess' features seemed to shift, her eyes became brighter, but her face grave. 'You have a choice, Jaydon Riler. Take the Stone of Mieses. Take it from this place. I cannot stop you. You are the Guardian of the Stone of Radnor. You could cut me down with *Devil's Bane* now, if you would choose to do so. Take both the stones with you and become the most powerful person on this earth. Just as Elokar seeks the stones to bring back his life and rule over us all, you too could use both the stones to give you the power. The power to bring a loved one back from the dead. Pluck them from the heavens to live a mortal life again. Who do you love that you could give life to once more, Jaydon?'

Jaydon's head whirled as images of his father flashed before him. Could he bring his father back to life? Give him back *Devil's Bane* and the Stone of Radnor until Jaydon was ready. Have his father seek out and unite the stones and not him. The images shifted and changed, the face of his sister, Jenna, now appeared to float in front of him. Her green eyes, full of tears of joy. White teeth like stars as her laughter seemed to echo around the room. He reached out a trembling hand to touch her cheek, to wipe away a tear.

'Jenna,' he whispered. 'Jenna...could I give her life? Could I have her return to me? Truly?'

'Yes, Jaydon. You could live the rest of your days together. Grow old together. See each other married, have nieces and nephews. You could have all of that…but a warning. If you choose to use the power of the stones to bring a loved one back from the dead. You cannot unite all of the god-stones. You must relinquish the guardianship. You cannot take on the quest before you. Either you bring back your sister, giving up your birth-right, or seek out the other stones and bring light to the world and protect it from a darker power. What will you decide?'

He recalled Jenna running through the fields around their village, her hair strewn behind her like a golden trail. He could remember every minute detail of her face, like he and his father, green eyes that shone brightly, her wrinkled brow when she was angry or frustrated.

The way she stuck her tongue out of the corner of her mouth as she concentrated on a difficult task, or tried to remember her words. The tiny scar on her left eyebrow, where she had cut herself on a branch when she had fallen from a tree.

What would Jaydon give to have her innocent beauty in the world once more? He always thought he would gladly have given his own life for that. And now he faced that very question.

•••◆•••

Jaydon sat in the chapel alone, the High Priestess had left him to his thoughts. Candles lit the room around him, shadows flickering along the walls. He stared at the tapestry of Mieses hanging above the altar. His emotions swung and swayed, anger at his father still resided deep in his gut, and resignation as he knew the truth of what he had to do. No matter how he would love to see Jenna's face one last time he knew he could not.

The stone had not been passed down through his family for generations for it to fail at the last hurdle, at the final reckoning. He sighed inwardly knowing his fate, the High Priestess had given him until midday to come to a decision, no matter which way he chose, they would leave the Temple today, and Thornheart still waited beyond its safety.

He unsheathed *Devil's Bane*, the sound of the steel sang out loudly in the silence of the room as he held it upwards. Runes ran along the blade either side of the fuller. He had never known what they meant, he had seen them all his life, yet had never thought to ask his father what words were etched into the steel.

Maybe if he had he would have understood, maybe that would have forced his father to reveal just some of his fate, his birth-right. The Stone of Radnor still shone brightly in the dimness of the chapel.

Behind him he heard a knocking. Arthek stood in the doorway, his face held a friendly smile, one that recognised the weight of the decision Jaydon had to make.

'It's a fine sword, Jaydon. May I come in and join you? Or do you wish to be left a while longer?'

'Please, come in, Arthek. Sit with me a while,' Jaydon shifted along the wooden bench, allowing room for Arthek. 'Do you know what these words are, here on the blade? Did my father ever mention these to you?'

Arthek beheld *Devil's Bane* for a while, Jaydon took in the man's features, a man who had known his father far longer than Jaydon ever had.

'I think yer father told me once, lad. But not sure I can remember. Something to do with power and protection. But that symbol there—' Arthek pointed at an intricate rune carved into the centre of the blade, just beneath the handguard. 'That means Radnor, it is the Old Calarian word for the god of war.'

'What about these other runes?' Jaydon asked.

From behind them, another voice responded. 'I can answer that, Jaydon.'

Raven entered the chapel. Her eyes scanned the inscriptions on the blade.

'*Ámraeth ác berak varukáskár, purnask rákannasknann, yhsask skáel-lornánn*'. She said, before continuing. 'Arthek is right, the runes are *Calar Ahunn* – Old Calarian. The inscription can be translated to mean: *I hereby summon my sword, Devil's Bane, protector of gods, destroyer of evil.* The stone and the sword are as one. One tool of power. Old Calarian, is a language only spoken now by those that serve the gods. For prayers, spells and incantations. The language long lost, known by just a few – we study it here when we join the service of the High Priestess.'

They sat a while longer, side by side, in silence. Jaydon ran his fingers along the runes, tracing their shapes along the blade. Trying to understand the power he held within his hands. Eventually Arthek broke the silence once more. 'Have you decided? For we must leave soon before it's too late. Before it gets dark.'

Jaydon sighed, the words escaped from his lips before he had even realised. 'Yes. We travel north, to find the old warlock, this hermit and seek out the Stone of Onir. I said my goodbyes to my family back in Hardstone Woods.' Slowly he sheathed *Devil's Bane*, then stood. 'Come on. I guess we get ready to leave.'

'How are we to make our way down the mountains?' Arthek asked. 'You say Thornheart's men are patrolling through the forests, yet there is only one way out. That I know of, that is.'

They stood in the great hall, Jaydon, the men, Raven and the High Priestess. The High Priestess responded. 'Thornheart's army is

258 | THE STONE OF RADNOR | PAUL R SOMERVILLE

depleted. Many have deserted, but many remain loyal still. However, there is another way. A secret way. It leads out to a plateau. From there you have two paths; south back to the valley and Thornheart's men. Or north, but it's a dangerously steep cliff, you can only climb down…that is the way you must take. Once at the bottom of the cliff face you will reach a stream, across the stream you will find that your horses will be waiting for you, by an ancient lone oak. They are safe and well rested and have been loaded with provisions for your journey.'

'You don't make it easy for us do you, High Priestess?' Brennand asked. 'And I suppose we have to be down before dark? Before the Night Beasts are out. And where's Gordar?'

Jaydon glanced around; he had been so lost in his own thoughts that he had not realised that Gordar was not with them.

'Yes, Brennand…you have to be down by nightfall and Gordar has left already. I gave him instructions, he is with our carers. The gods are protecting him and he has taken the horses north of the mountains. He will meet you all at the ancient oak. But come now, let's not delay any further…nightfall comes early to the mountains.'

The High Priestess led them down more corridors that twisted downwards within the mountain. The group walked in silence, one behind the other. Jaydon felt invigorated, the confidence that flowed through his veins in the chapel had remained. Yet he knew a long road waited ahead for them, and that Thornheart and his army still had to be contended with. Eventually the corridor came to an abrupt dead end.

'Where now?' Jaydon asked, confused.

The High Priestess did not respond, but held aloft the flaming torch that she carried, above her, carved into the rock Jaydon saw more runes. The High Priestess started to repeatedly chant more words in the strange tongue – Old Calarian. '*Rákam Mieses ur, er naskarnasknár uc jáennaðár.*

Mjar vuresk frugosknann tár mrunnaðá' As she did, from within the rock came a low rumbling sound, stone grating on stone, the ground beneath their feet trembled as slowly, a chink of light weaved and arced its way upwards, growing wider and wider until the brightness of the outside world shafted into the dark corridor revealing a doorway out into a narrow pass.

'Now—' The High Priestess turned to face them all. 'I bid you farewell. You cannot linger here any longer. You have a long perilous journey to undertake. Your fates are entwined, as is the fate of our world. We cannot allow Elokar to win, so you must not fail.' Then facing Jaydon, she added. 'You truly are the Guardian of the Stone, Jaydon. You have proved your worth tenfold. I know the burden being asked of you is immense. But the gods have put their faith in you, and you too must put your faith in them.'

Jaydon thanked her.

'Remember this, Jaydon,' the High Priestess continued. 'Above all, the only thing that matters are the stones. Not Thornheart. Not revenge. Go with a pure heart and you will prevail.'

The High Priestess reached into her robes and withdrew a silver pendant, shaped like a chalice, which she handed to Raven. Raven took the pendant, then faced Jaydon and placed it around his neck, fastening it at the back, her fingers lingered at his throat as she straightened the silver chalice.

'Mieses is with you too now, Jaydon,' she said her dark eyes shining in the daylight. 'Guardian of the Stone of Radnor.'

Jaydon could feel an inner strength, like shafts of golden sunlight, snake its way through every sinew of his body. He bowed his head and spoke. 'I will not fail,' then scanning the faces of those around him, Arthek, Brennand and Raven...his friends, he continued, his voice stronger. 'We will not fail. We go with the gods at our backs and in our hearts. We seek out the Stone of Onir and will vanquish Elokar for good…once and for all.'

Gripping the hilt of *Devil's Bane,* he strode forwards and out into the pass, not glancing back as the rest of the group followed, leaving the High Priestess within the mountainous temple as the secret door slowly closed behind them.

CHAPTER 35
THE FINAL STAND

———————◆———————

They walked slowly down the narrow track that led from the secret doorway, flanked by steep rocky boulders that towered high above their heads. A hazy veil of cloud shone iridescently with the same specks of light that they had seen at the Temples entrance the day before, swirling above them, shrouding any remaining daylight, rendering it impossible to gauge the time of day. It was late afternoon and Jaydon knew they had to be away from the mountain before nightfall came and the Night Beasts swarmed the land.

They spoke very little, but Brennand especially had hardly spoken a word since leaving the Temple. Instead, he walked behind, head bowed. Jaydon held back, allowing Raven and Arthek to pass until Brennand caught up with him.

'Bren, you seem quiet. Is everything okay? Are you worried about Gordar?'

Brennand patted Jaydon on his back as they walked. 'I don't fear for Gordar, he can take care of himself and I know the High Priestess wouldn't have allowed him to leave alone if it weren't safe to do so. I'm just deep in my own thoughts.' Brennand exhaled noisily. 'You know, I have doubted the gods and religion for so long. To come here, to these mountains and see what I have seen. To speak with the High Priestess… well, it has left me with a lot to think about.'

'Are you a godly man now, Brennand Derowen?' Raven called back, a hint of a smirk on her face.

'Godly? Raven, I don't know about that. But I believe now. When I spoke with the High Priestess yesterday evening, she explained to me the designs of the gods. My purpose on this earth and the part I have to play.' He shook his head. 'I have not lived a worthy life, yet the gods see fit to have me help Jaydon on this task. I have lied, stolen and killed; all for silver. Jaydon, I am truly sorry for taking you that day on the grasslands. I regret my actions, yet the High Priestess made it clear to me, that you had to go through those trials. It was a greater design. You had to prove you were the guardian. But again, I hope you find a way to forgive me before the end comes.'

Jaydon nodded, he felt Brennand's sincerity and had long forgiven him. Perhaps the High Priestess' words had helped Brennand come to terms with his past deeds. Jaydon though, was glad to have him with them, both he and Gordar. He pondered over some of his words, what did Brennand mean by *when the end comes*? 'There is nothing to forgive, Bren. You served my father and we fight together now.'

'Thank you, Jaydon. Now, come, we must be off this place before the darkness arrives.'

The group descended the secret path – it became steep, though not difficult to traverse down. Jaydon had a sense of comfort, like a blanket warmed on a hearth—he had come through a lot these past few weeks. But, for the first time he felt glad to be on the road, to be travelling with a purpose, the burden of the stone no longer felt like a heavy millstone on his shoulders, but gave him renewed resolve.

Ahead, they walked around a bend in the path, and as they rounded it, they were confronted by a shimmering haze. The group came to a halt.

'Is this the end of the path, Raven?' Jaydon asked. 'Do we just go through?'

'There should be a small opening, a plateau, beyond. We must not linger though as I fear the day is long now already.'

Just as Jaydon stepped forward to pass through, Arthek yanked him backwards by the crook of his elbow. 'Wait. We don't know what's on the other side, lad. Let Bren and I go first…just to be sure.'

'I agree,' said Brennand. 'I'll go first. I'll call you if all is safe.' Then without waiting he stepped through the hazy cloud as though walking through a cascading waterfall. Arthek followed quickly behind. Jaydon and Raven waited, then the shouting started.

•••◆•••

Nyla sat on a cold grey rock, covered in pale green lichen. The climb had been as Thornheart predicted, but they had made good progress through the forest and up the steep slopes. Thornheart himself sat nearby, drinking water from a skin.

They had reached the opening with the rocks a short while earlier and sat to rest while they waited. A lone walnut tree stood opposite where they sat. Nyla mused that it was a strange place for such a tree. Thornheart had said they were to wait until dusk for a secret passage to reveal itself. Nyla peered up to the skies; the sun hid behind heavy clouds, making it difficult to determine the time of day, and how long they must wait. Probably less than an hour now, she speculated.

A crow flew down from the walnut tree, in its beak it carried a fruit that it had plucked from a branch. Nyla watched as the bird started to throw down the thick shelled fruit over and over again until the outer layer cracked, leaving the brown nut within it exposed. The crow gave a triumphant caw as it picked out the nut and flew off over the boulders that surrounded them on the plateau and away into the distance.

Realising her own hunger, Nyla reached into her cloak and pulled out some dried beef. She tore off a strip with her teeth and offered the rest to Thornheart.

'Thank you, Nyla,' he said as he reached across and took the beef from her. 'The path will be revealed soon enough. Not long to wait now.'

'What then?'

'We follow it. It should lead us into the Temple. We find our way in, and kill all who stand in our way. The stone is in there…and so is the boy. I want him dead.' He said grimly.

Nyla nodded, speaking of the stone made her think of that gnawing sensation she felt the night before, when she saw the casket containing the Stone of Elokar. She just could not shake it off, it had played on her all night, pecking at her like the crow did with the walnut fruit.

Suddenly she caught movement in front of her, out of nowhere Brennand appeared, then beside him Arthek Mulliner. Instinctively, she stood, unslung her bow and reached for an arrow from the quiver, guiding it into the bow with one fluid, well-practised motion. Thornheart stood too, gasping in surprise as he drew his broadsword.

Brennand issued a warning, as he and Mulliner withdrew their own weapons. 'Jaydon, Raven—stay where you are.' He called, but too late as they both crashed through the invisible doorway; one moment there was just a narrow gap in the boulders, the next the four of them stood before them, surprise on their faces. Nyla felt shocked too. Were these tricks being played on her? More magic or an apparition? No, the prey they sought stood opposite them, they had to seize the opportunity and swiftly.

Unable to fully hear what Brennand had shouted, Jaydon and Raven had dived through the secret doorway. It felt cool as they entered the shimmering cloud, a chill washed over him as they emerged onto the plateau.

But what waited for them on the other side brought on an even icier chill. Thornheart stood there, facing off to Brennand and Arthek. Next to him stood a woman, who reached for her bow. How could this be? Had they walked into a trap? He reeled with confusion. Only moments earlier he had felt euphoric. But that evaporated, replaced with the shock of the sudden twist of fortunes that awaited them.

Without a seconds thought Jaydon withdrew *Devil's Bane* from his sheath, protectively shoving Raven to his rear with his other arm.

'Lay down your weapons!' the woman shouted, aiming her bow toward Arthek and Brennand.

The two men both stepped forward, swords aloft and crouched into a defensive stance, ready for the fight. 'Arthek,' Brennand called out, his voice calm and clear. 'You go, take the kids with you. Go now.'

'No, Bren. We stand together.'

Brennand commanded this time, steel in his voice, not once taking his eyes from the foes standing before them. 'Arthek, you *must* go,' he said through gritted teeth. 'The High Priestess has already told me my fate. My journey is to end here today. But not yours. Take Jaydon and Raven. Protect them, or it will all be in vain.'

'No, Bren. Arthek is right,' Jaydon narrowed his eyes, never taking them from Thornheart. Hating every fibre of the man. 'We all stand here now. Together, as one.' Then, raising *Devil's Bane*, Jaydon pointed it directly at Thornheart. A challenge. 'You killed my father. But it is you who will die here today.'

Jaydon's mind cleared. Just weeks earlier he had left his village and had vowed to kill Thornheart. Now the man stood here before him, he could stand with Brennand and Arthek, surely the three of them could take him down, his vengeance would be complete.

Thornheart bellowed and raised his own sword back at them all. His face breaking into a sneer, revealing yellowed teeth within the heavy bristles of his beard.

'No, Jaydon,' Raven placed her hand on his shoulder. 'Remember the words from the High Priestess. You have a bigger part to play. If you die here, today, on this spot. The world we know is lost.'

Images of his family flashed before him. The death of his father. His mother, with Jenna cradled in her arms. The burnt ruins of his village. Ober, his eyes wide, the spear lodged between his shoulder blades. His nostrils flared as he breathed heavily. He had to fight every instinct that impelled him to rush across the opening and bury *Devil's Bane* into Thornheart's guts.

Then he felt Raven squeeze his shoulder once more. He understood. He knew what he must do. Guilt stung his conscious. Today would not be the day he took that revenge, bigger things were now at stake. Then realisation as in truth he recognised Brennand's fate all too well.

'Bren's right, Arthek,' he said, his voice quavering. 'We must go. Bren...' but he trailed off, unable to finish his sentence.

'It's alright, lad. Now, be off with you.'

Jaydon took one last look at Brennand. Everything around him slowed, but he re-focussed. Grasping Raven's hand Jaydon suddenly flung himself into the treeline to his right, hoping this was the way the High Priestess had spoken of. Behind him he heard Brennand pleading with Arthek to go one more time as he crashed through branches that raked his arms and legs. Still dragging Raven with him.

Thornheart growled aloud and stepped forward, in doing so he moved across Nyla's line of sight. She saw Mulliner spring to his right and follow the boy, she released the bowstring, the arrow flashed forward ahead in his direction, but it struck off a boulder as he too disappeared into the forest beyond the plateau. Cursing, she drew another one quickly and held it in front of her, her sights now trained on Brennand. But Thornheart strode forward, blocking him from her view.

'Stand aside Bren, we will leave you unharmed. We just want Riler's son. Step aside, or die.'

Brennand laughed and shook his head, his sword held defensively in front of him. 'I no longer fear you. We have the gods with us. You will have to kill me, but I had better warn you. I am not an easy man to kill. Many have tried and failed.'

'Very well then…you fool. I warned you in The Wyke what I would do to you if you had lied to me. I've been contemplating this moment.' Thornheart sprang forward, bringing his weapon down with all his strength.

Steel on steel rang out, a piercing noise that echoed around the plateau. A couple of woodpigeons suddenly took flight from a nearby tree, their wings clapping loudly as they hurriedly escaped in panic. Thornheart swung again as Brennand thwarted the blow once more, grunting as the physical strength and power of Thornheart forced him backwards. Nyla kept her arrow trained ahead, waiting, should she fire? Something held her back as she waited?

Thornheart swung over and over again, battering Brennand backwards, he could only defend and parry each blow. Thornheart's strength and power started to subdue him, pinning him against one of the stone boulders. The light above started to fade as Thornheart brought his weapon down once more. The force knocked Brennand's sword clean out of his hands. The sound of metal rang out as it crashed against the boulder and dropped to the ground.

Thornheart planted his left boot on the blade of the fallen sword, then brought his own upwards. Nyla could hear the ear-splitting scream from Brennand, as Thornheart slowly thrust his weapon into Brennand's guts. Then, as he wrenched it out, blood splashed around their feet. Brenannd's body slid down the boulder and sank to the ground. Thornheart stepped backwards and roared in triumph.

The hairs on Nyla's neck pricked, a sensation of tiny spiders creeping across her skin, then without thinking, she let fly the arrow. It thumped into Thornheart's right shoulder. He grunted and jerked, then turned on her in surprise as again she quickly nocked another from the quiver and drew back the string with steady hands. Thornheart's mouth dropped open, his eyes staring in disbelief. She struck once more as he tried to speak, his mouth forming a shape. The arrow took him in the chest, taking the word away before it even left his lips.

Thornheart looked dumbfounded, as he stared at the shaft. He dropped his sword as Nyla struck a third time with pin-point accuracy. Again, she hit his chest, the shaft buried deep as Thornheart collapsed onto his knees. A droplet of blood trickled down the corner of his mouth and into his beard, he gasped for air, struggling to take in deep breaths before he fell and slumped backwards onto the ground.

Nyla felt as though an unseen force had guided her, she strode forward until she stood over Thornheart. The blood foaming at his lips now a pinkish colour. With a clarity of thought, she took another arrow, then at point blank range she fired again into Thornheart's chest—the quivers of the three arrows protruded from his rib cage. He jerked and let out a gasp, spitting blood upwards in an arc, droplets spattered his face and hair. His eyes white and wild, rolled in their sockets.

Nyla felt little emotion as she peered impassively down at him.

Darkness had started to descend onto the plateau. Slinging her bow back over her shoulder she knelt on one knee and reached a hand into Thornheart's cloak and withdrew the wooden casket. She could hear his breath wheezing and gurgling, death would approach him soon. She knew what a punctured lung sounded like. Relief overcame her, after so many years she was really free. He tried to speak, his mouth flapping open like a fish gasping for air.

Nyla leant closer. 'What's that?' she asked calmly, as a whisper.

'W…why?' The only word that left his lips, just a murmur. Thornheart's breath rasped. He tried to lift himself, but no longer had the strength to do so, his head thumped back to the ground.

Nyla stood, gazing down at the fallen giant. The wooden casket clutched tightly in her fist, she could feel the heat emanate from the stone within as it pulsated within her grip. The prickling sensation still crawled over her skin.

'You are a weak-minded fool, Thornheart,' she hissed. 'You have cost us many men, good men. You are not fit to carry such a weapon.' She held up the casket, then it tucked it away within her own cloak. 'I despise you. I have feigned loyalty to you for far too long. As you lie here, dying, your men…no, my men, are gathering in the valley, waiting for me.' She laughed at the irony. 'That purse of silver you gave me last night…I told the men I was the one rewarding them. Mercenaries are only loyal to who paid them last…you taught me that.'

Thornheart spat more frothy blood, then his eyes fluttered, rolling upwards revealing their whites. Nyla strode around the two bodies, to the narrow gap where the boy and the others had disappeared. She scanned the treeline ahead, but all remained still and dark. She cursed loudly, then she heard it. The same chattering sound she had heard at the forest edge the night before. Nyla shuddered as a chill rippled down her spine.

A loud crack came from the forest, branches snapping, the chattering sound grew louder, closer, as something in there began to run at speed toward her. Without a second's hesitation, Nyla turned and fled back to the path she had taken earlier. Not once glancing back, her senses alert but dread clung to her heart like ice.

CHAPTER 36
THE JOURNEY BEGINS

———◆———

Darkness enclosed them as Jaydon and Raven sped through the forest. Branches whipped at their faces and legs as they raced ever onwards, not stopping, not daring to turn back. Arthek caught up with them as they sped headlong into the dark woods.

Then, dim light in front of them as they emerged from the treeline, the sun had begun to set, just the last vestiges of daylight remained. Ahead, the ground in front of them disappeared, a vast drop that loomed rapidly. Quickly realising he didn't have much time to react, Jaydon dug his heels into the loose earth, attempting to grind himself to an abrupt halt. He threw himself to the floor, grabbed an exposed tree root with his free hand. Then, without any warning, the ground beneath him crumbled and gave way.

Jaydon felt his whole body plunge downwards. He clung desperately to the tree root, jarring the tendons in his shoulder. The roots were the only thing preventing him from crashing to the depths below. Soil and pebbles tumbled downwards as he hung in mid-air, legs flailing over the edge of the cliff.

'Help!' He screamed in desperation. He looked down into the never-ending darkness below. 'Help me!'

'Here, lad. Grab my hand.' Arthek's face peered over the cliff edge, his arm outstretched down towards Jaydon.

Jaydon still held *Devil's Bane* in his free hand. 'Take the sword.' He screamed.

'No, fling it up, Jaydon. No time to waste. Hurry.'

With as much strength as he could muster, Jaydon swung his arm and released the sword, it flew upwards, then over the rocky edge, landing in the ground above. Jaydon felt his hold on the tree root slip, the muscles in his forearm bulged, as his finger slipped.

He yelped, but as he did Arthek thrust his own hand downwards and grabbed the wrist of Jaydon's free hand, just as he thought he would plunge to his death. He swung in the air, peering up into Arthek's face where a bead of sweat hung from his nose. Arthek reached down with his other arm and grunting heavily he slowly hauled Jaydon back up onto the safety of the earth,

Jaydon fell forwards onto his hands and knees, gasping in huge breaths. Raven came to his side, safe. Finally, he allowed himself to glance back into the forest, praying to the gods that Brennand would soon be following on behind them. Then he shuddered as he recalled the piercing shriek that echoed through the forest as they ran and knew Brennand was gone.

'We must continue,' Raven said, panting. Her face bleeding from the scratches caused by the branches and twigs. 'Nightfall is coming. We need to move. Quickly follow me.' She headed along the cliff edge, to a rectangular boulder. 'Down here. Come on.' she urged, before disappearing as she began to scale down the cliff face.

The silence behind them broke, a chill crawled across Jaydon's skin, raising the hairs on his arms and neck as the chattering of the Night

Beasts started. He headed for the boulder. Arthek joined him, panic etched across his face.

'You go first, Jaydon. No time to hang around now, lad.'

Jaydon's heart pounded, he sheathed *Devil's Bane*, and glanced behind Arthek one more time. He could see movement in the darkness beyond the forest line. Several creatures were bounding on all fours over rocks and branches…heading directly toward them. Their bodies were covered in coarse hair, brown and black. Their wide feral eyes shone yellow in the darkness, above teeth, like needles, that gnashed as they closed in on their prey. Jaydon needed no further prompting as he flung himself over the verge and started to scramble down the cliff face.

Arthek followed as the first of the creatures reached the edge, spindly arms with long claws swooped down, gripping Arthek's hair. Arthek yelled, but managed to tear himself free, a lock of silver hair still grasped in the claws of the Night Beast, as he shinnied behind Jaydon. The chattering and screeching from the Night Beasts echoed over the cliff and to the valley below as the group made their escape.

Jaydon looked downwards, in the gloom of the night he could just make out the shape of Raven below him, already halfway down the cliff face, making it seem as easy as when they climbed the path up to the Temple the day before.

Scaling down the cliff seemed to take forever in the darkness, making Jaydon disorientated. He shimmied down, searching out hand and foot holds, causing loose rocks and stones to tumble below. Luckily, he missed Raven, who was now almost to safety at the foot of the cliff. Arthek provided further encouragement from above as Jaydon eased himself downwards.

His hands were torn to shreds; bloody blisters burned as he clung onto fissures in the rock. His knees scraped, sharp edges slicing through his trousers, cuts and bruises exposed to the rocky surface. But he kept moving, the muscles in his arms burning, every fibre of his body ached.

Eventually he made it, his feet found solid ground. He let himself drop and collapsed onto damp grass, gasping for breath. Raven pulled him back to his feet as Arthek leaped the final couple of feet from the surface, landing to their right.

Jaydon studied the surface of the cliff face above them where it disappeared into the darkness. He felt sure he could still hear the terrible chatter of the Night Beasts. Reaching out he grabbed Raven, pulling her into his body, hugging her tightly into him. The scent of her sweat filled his nostrils as he took in deep breaths, filling his lungs with her. They stood like that for a while, bodies entwined before Jaydon took a step backwards, placing his palms on her face, wiping away some of the blood from her cheeks.

'Are you alright?' he asked her, his eyes searching her face.

'I'm okay, Jaydon.' Then she tilted her head towards his and kissed him firmly. The muscles in Jaydon's legs turned to liquid as he embraced her once more, their lips locked. He had never tasted anything so sweet.

Eventually they broke, Jaydon felt breathless. He knew he should say something, but words would not come, instead he stared into her dark eyes and beamed.

Arthek broke their silence. 'Come now, you two. We must move on. Where to, Raven? The High Priestess mentioned a lone oak tree.'

Raven stepped away from the embrace, scrutinising the landscape around them; gathering her bearings. 'Ah, yes. This way,' she said pointing ahead into the night.

They trudged on, walking side by side through damp grasses. Ahead they heard the tinkling of running water, and soon they came across the stream, its surface barely visible with the moon hidden behind clouds, for which Jaydon was thankful. He worried they would be seen as they crossed the open land. None of them spoke of Brennand. Jaydon hoped that Thornheart had killed him quickly, he had only heard the one scream. More so, he prayed the Night Beasts had caught Thornheart. But he had no way of knowing either way.

After a short while the shape of a wide tree loomed out of the dull night, then the sound of a horse, nickering. They stumbled toward the sound where Gordar sat beneath the oak. He stood to greet them as they approached, grasping each of them in his strong arms. Then he examined out into the night behind them, eyes searching into the darkness.

'Bren?' he asked.

Arthek just shook his head. Gordar nodded and inhaled deeply. 'I should have known. He said something to me last night about the end coming and knowing his true purpose. It was after he spoke with the High Priestess.' Gordar bowed his head, strands of hair fell, obscuring his face. When he looked up his eyes glistened. 'He's with the gods now.'

Arthek patted him on his shoulder. 'He died to save Jaydon. For a greater good. Whatever he did in life, he's made amends now and he will be in the heavens. Bending the ear of Onir no doubt.'

'Aye, no doubt at all.' Gordar chuckled.

They travelled further into the darkness, leaving the dark shape of the Resas mountains behind them. Finally Gordar brought them to a halt, leading them into a coppice of trees. 'We rest here,' he said, tethering his horse to a stout branch. 'Just until dawn then we must move on again.' Gordar sat under a tree, resting his back against the gnarled trunk. The rest of them followed and sat with him as Arthek regaled a story of a similar dark night on the northern shores of Calaria. It was way past midnight when they agreed to sleep. Jaydon pulled a fur around himself, to keep out the chill of the night air, a gentle breeze wafted across his face.

Raven lay next to him under her own furs, she had already drifted off, her breathing shallow. Jaydon watched her chest rise and fall for a while before he too succumbed to fatigue.

The next morning, they breakfasted on the bread and honey that had been packed into the horses' saddlebags. Jaydon sat a while, his thoughts drifting. He stole a glance at Raven, who smiled back at him. Jaydon thought back fondly to the kiss they had shared the previous night and his heart swelled.

The sun had started to rise, in the distance the peaks of the Scarlet Mountains, that rose like stone giants, glowed a dim orange.

'Where to?' Gordar asked as he climbed atop his horse.

As one the group turned to Jaydon, somehow, he seemed to be in command, their leader. He brought himself back to his feet, placing his hand on the hilt of *Devil's Bane*. Jaydon paused for a moment, closing his eyes. Images of this family flashed before him. He imagined his mother, hugging him, wishing him well as she straightened his dishevelled hair with slender fingers. Or Jenna, teasing him, demanding that she come along with him too. Finally, his father looking down at him now, proud of all he had achieved, and the young man he was becoming.

The wind ruffled his cloak, curling itself around his legs before unfurling again.

'We make for Winter's Harbour. We need to find a ship to take us across the Crystal Ocean,' he said. 'Then our journey begins.'

THE
END

ACKNOWLEDGEMENTS

The Stone of Radnor would never have been published, or even have been written without the help of so many people whom I must thank.

First and foremost I am indebted to Melanie Whipman, who has been a source of encouragement and has been there from the very beginning of Jaydon's journey. Mel has given me incredible confidence, guidance, input, advice and belief that this story had a place in the world to be told. If it was not for her it would not have seen the light of day.

I would also like to thank Yvonne Barlow at Hookline Books for providing me the opportunity and for believing in the story enough to initially agree to publish, but more importantly for the assisting with the editing process. Her guidance and professionalism in getting Radnor into a position where it was ready for a wider audience cannot be understated; any errors within the story are mine and mine alone.

Various people have given me input throughout the development of Radnor. In no particular order I would like to thank the following for advice, editing, reading and again providing me the confidence to bring this story to life: Mark LoGalbo, Belle Manual, Klio Nicolaidou, Chris and Sam Hatchley, Mick and Erin Tennent, Jayne Bonner, Karl Di Mascio and Dorothy Grace Franklin. In addition, thank you to everyone from Melanie Whipman's Thursday evening creative writing workshops, who have had to endure chapter by chapter reads, providing amazing comments and critique's – particularly Irina Mukhina, Rebecca Burton, Julie Donald, Elizabeth Smith, Katarina Oravcova, Sarah Chappell and Sarah Cafora. My apologies if I have missed any of you.

Before I started writing the Stone of Radnor, there were a few people who gave me the encouragement to step out of my comfort zone and join that creative writing course. If I had not been pushed this novel would never have been written; so thank you to Elaine Innes, Steve Smith, Sarah Francis and Susie Somerville.

To help me to bring the world of Calaria to life I would like to thank both Angel Perez for the incredible maps, they were perfect, and Xayden Djan for the superb language and the detail you went to – it blew my mind. In addition thanks to Nazia for the amazing book cover – wow!

A special mention to Jayne Bonner, who came into my life unexpectedly but at the perfect moment. You have given me enormous encouragement and belief. You are an amazing person and I am lucky to have you by my side.

Finally, I would like to express my enormous gratitude to my family. To my parents who have supported me throughout my life and have always been there for me during tough times. Also to my sister, Nicola Savory, you have been a grateful shoulder for me to lean on in recent years – more than you know. Last and not least a big shout out to the two most important people in my life to whom this book is dedicated; to both my children Fraser and Isla – not only are you both sources of inspiration, but I am incredibly proud of the young adults that you are both growing up to become. I love you both more than you would ever know.

Paul R. Somerville

Alton, Hampshire, United Kingdom – November 2022

ABOUT THE AUTHOR

———•••◆•••———

Born in Burnley, Lancashire, Paul joined the British Army at the age of just 16 and served until 1999, having travelled widely (Norway, USA, Canada, Alaska, Germany, Belgium, Italy, Turkey, Portugal, Denmark, Croatia, Bosnia, Gibraltar) and completing three operational tours in the Former Yugoslavia during the Balkan conflict.

Since leaving the army Paul has worked in a variety of roles and organisations – but moved into Cyber Security, and is now a Principal Consultant for a UK based consultancy. Paul has lived in Malvern, Rugby, Farnham and now resides in Alton, Hampshire, with his two children, a mad-cat, two gerbils and several fish.

Outside of writing and work Paul is an avid supporter of Burnley FC and enjoys walking in the Hampshire and Surrey countryside and taking mini-adventures in his twenty-five year old campervan.

The Stone of Radnor is Paul's debut novel…watch out for book two.

Printed in Great Britain
by Amazon

11986348R00160